D1714739

He Don't Deserve You 2

A.J. Write & Veronica Malone

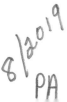

8/2019
PA

He Don't Deserve You 2

Copyright © 2017 by A.J. Write & Veronica Malone

Published By: Lucinda John Presents

Dedication
Author Veronica Malone

Wow! Let me first start this off by thanking the many readers that went out and purchased part one to this title. I had no idea it would be as popular as it is, and I am completely humbled at the feedback. To Author A. J. Write (Ayana Bennett). I could not have done this without you. The twists and turns this novel took were an absolute jo, and your pen matched with mine made for a genius storyline. I want to extend a dedication to my publisher Lucinda John for allowing us to collaborate on this project. Last, but not least, I want to thank every supporter and every single person who is looking at this second installment right now. I hope that I have gained a new fan for life. To read more of my work, check out my titles listed below:

Life Goes On
A Love Worth Dying For 1, 2, &3
Love Licks 1 & 2
Until The Streets Do Us Apart 1 &2
Say You'll Ride For Me: Until Death Do Us Apart
He Doesn't Deserve You 1

Author AJ Write

Here we are back at it with the finally. Just like the first book, I truly enjoyed writing it. The feedback that Veronica and I received and still are receiving on the first book has been nothing short of a humbling experience. I hope we've, not only given you a story to enjoy but to empower women to love themselves before anybody else. I have to thank Veronica for giving this project a chance with me. It's been nothing but fun, and I've honestly added this series to one of my favorites that I've written. I can't end this without thanking our supporters. Without you, we wouldn't go as hard as we do. I thank you for the kind words and encouragement to keep showcasing my gift. I hope that this series helped Veronica and I gain even more fans. I and Veronica hope you enjoy part 2. If you would like to read more work by myself, check out the titles below:

A B-more Love 1-3

Me and A Boss 1-2

Three Kings Cartel 1-3

Three Kings Cartel: A Royale Family Affair

Love From A Thug

Captured By His Love

He Don't Deserve You

Table of Contents

Chapter 1

Nina

This was all my fault. Drake was dead, and it was all because of me. I couldn't stop shaking, as I cried in the car.

"Nina, stop all of that fucking noise. When we get in this airport, fix your fucking face, or I'll off you next. I still can't believe you let him knock you up. I'm about to give your ass some act right," Reno said.

I sniffled, as I tried to contain myself. When I heard the gunshot, I just knew that Drake didn't survive it after seeing Reno beat him, too. I would never forgive myself for the damage I've caused. If I wasn't carrying his baby, I would give up right now. Why was my life such a living hell? I couldn't win even if I tried.

"Wow, that was fast. You weren't playing when you said you would be right back," an airport attendant said, licking her lips at Reno.

"I never play. I had to come get something that belonged to me," Reno said, smacking my ass really hard.

I winced in pain and shame, as people looked at us in disgust. I hated Reno right now. The lady handed us our tickets and mean mugged me as we walked off.

"Jace, tell Lena and Tena we got her and we out," Reno said.

My mouth dropped. Never in a million years did I think the twins would have set me up. Reno caught onto my expression and laughed.

"What? You thought they were like you? You thought they didn't know the rules of loyalty? Nah, those are my sisters, and Jace is my brother, remember that shit," Reno said shoving me.

I officially felt trapped. No one seemed to be on my side. As we sat and waited for the plane, Reno went to the bathroom.

"Nina, it's not that bad. You know how my brother is. I thought you loved him," Jace said to me.

"Your brother cheats on me and abuses me," I snapped.

"Don't go off on me, shit. I didn't do a damn thing to you. You stayed after you found out he was Bipolar and had anger problems, so I guess you wanted it," Jace had the nerve to say.

"Shut the fuck up," I hissed at him.

Jace just shrugged, sat back, and got on his phone.

"What's up, sis! Yeah, we got her? What you mean? Of course, she missed Reno! Nah, they over here kissing and shit; you can see her at the house," Jace said lying through his teeth.

The plane ride was horrible. I had a horrible sickness, and Reno got mad every time I got up to throw up. I knew it reminded him of the baby I was carrying. Once we got back to Little Rock, I allowed my tired body to go to sleep on the drive to wherever he was taking me. I woke up to Reno carrying me into the house, but I didn't feel like a princess at all.

"Aw, hell no! What the fuck is she doing back? Reno, what is this?" Xena asked mugging me.

Reno put me down on the couch and slapped Xena. She wanted my position so bad, and now that she has it, she knew how Reno was. As bad as I felt, I laughed at the sight. That is, until RJ ran downstairs.

"Mama?" he cried.

Then, his eyes zoomed in on me.

"Nina!" he yelled, running towards me.

I put on a fake smile and tried to hug him but my wrist was still broken.

"What happened to your wrist?" he asked.

"Boy, shut up, and help your mama," Xena yelled.

"Get this place cleaned up. I'm going to go take Nina to get her wrist looked at," Reno said.

The ride to the ER was silent ,and Reno's phone kept going off with calls from the twins. He finally turned to me, with sad eyes, once he parked.

"Was I that bad to you?" he asked me.

I put my head down afraid to answer.

"Nina, look, if you don't love me anymore, just say it, and I'll stop. I know it was probably Drake who filled your head up with thoughts to leave me," Reno said.

As bad as I wanted to say that wasn't true, the tear that ran from his eye made my heart crumble. I wasn't in love with Reno, anymore, but I did care for him. With the thought of Drake being dead, I was left on my own. I had no choice but to stay where I was. This was now about survival. He reached his hand out for mine, and I took a deep breath, swallowed my thoughts, and placed my hand in his. I finally realized that there was no escaping Reno.

We walked inside of the hospital, and I felt like all eyes were on me. The last time I was there, I knew that every nurse and doctor was judging me, and I feel like this again since I'm back because of Reno. It felt like we were in and out. My wrist was wrapped up, and I put my arm in a sling to make sure I didn't put any pressure on it.

The whole time all I could think about was Drake and how I got him killed. I shed a few tears knowing that the last time I spoke to him I hung up on him. I wish I told him I loved him instead. Another thing I thought about was the first time the twins snitched on me to Reno.

****

I was sitting on the bed doing homework when Reno burst in the room looking angry as hell.

"Hey, is everything ok?" I asked looking concerned.

I knew how his moods went, so I knew I had to tread lightly with him. I was still learning how to deal with him and his mood transitions.

"Why the fuck was you in the nigga Jericho's face? You not happy with me or something?" he asked standing in front of me.

"What are you talking about Reno? Jericho is in my class and the teacher paired us up. We were discussing our project," I said, innocently.

"I don't give a fuck what the teacher did. Don't talk to no niggas, period. I don't need niggas thinking they can just approach you like you not with me or something. I don't like feeling disrespected. You're going to respect me," he said with his chest poked out.

"Didn't nobody disrespect you. You know how I am about my education. Nobody or nothing can get in between that. I asked for another partner, because I wasn't cool with the partner situation, but there wasn't shit I could do about it. If you have such a problem with it, then go talk to the damn teacher your damn self," I exclaimed, pushing past him to leave out the room.

"Where the fuck do you think you're going? I'm not done talking to you," he said, grabbing my arm.

"Reno, let me go. Who the hell told you about me talking to Jericho, anyway?" I asked, curiously.

"Don't fucking worry about it. Just know I have eyes and ears everywhere," he said, pushing me away. "Don't let that shit happen again," he said walking away.

"Fuck you, Reno. I can talk to whoever the hell I want," I said, turning to walk away myself.

Next thing I remember was my hair being pulled and being slapped across my face.

"Watch who the fuck you're talking to. You will do what the fuck I say or it's going to be consequences. I run this shit, and what I say goes. Now, go clean yourself up," he said, walking away for good this time.

I stood there holding my face for a few minutes, stuck on the fact that he'd just struck me before walking into the room and sitting on the bed, letting the tears fall. I stayed in that spot for hours before my door opened and in walked the twins.

"Hey, Nina. Girl, are you ok?" Lena asked.

I looked up and her, and I could tell by the look on her face that she could tell what happened.

"I told you not to say anything," Tena said, shaking her head and sitting down beside me.

"Damn, I didn't know what was going on. Had I known he was going to do this, I wouldn't have. I'm sorry, Nina," Lena said.

"You said something? Why? That doesn't make any sense to me. I wasn't even touching dude, and he wasn't touching me. Mind your business the next time," I said, getting up and walking into the bathroom, slamming the door.

****

That wasn't the last time they opened their big mouths. I understand that's their brother, but I felt they should've had some loyalty to me as well. When we got back to the house, the first car I saw was one of the twins, and I did not want to see them. I got mad all over again.

"Oh, my God, Nina. We missed you," Tena said, running to me with open arms.

I walked right past her ass.

"Damn! She big mad or little mad?" Jace said.

His ass was still sitting in the same spot from when we left.

"What's your problem?" Tena asked catching up to me.

"Are you serious right now? You fucking opened up your mouth once again. If I fucking wanted to be here, then I would've been here. I fucking told you what the deal was," I said going off.

"But Reno's my brother. I'll always have his back no matter what," she said, crossing her arms.

"Yet, you're in my face smiling like everything is good. Please leave me alone," I said, walking away.

"If you had a brother, you would understand," she said.

I stopped in my tracks and turned around.

"If I knew my brother was beating on his girl, I would try to fucking stop it. If she left, I would be happy she got away. No one deserves to be abused unless their ass is in jail for some fucked up shit. I would mind my business," I said, walking away again.

I felt obligated to get back in routine, since there wasn't shit else I could do. I went through the cabinets grabbing everything I needed to cook. I got lost in cooking sometimes. It was reality away from reality, because no one disturbed me while I was cooking.

"Damn, I missed your cooking. Xena's ass can't do shit. She don't cook, clean, and can't fuck for shit," Reno said, coming up behind me.

I tried walking away, but he held onto me.

"You're back at home. Ain't no leaving again. Try leaving, and I'm going to put a bullet in your head," he said, kissing my cheek before walking away.

I was officially scared again.

Chapter 2

Leo

"Lena, why the fuck you tell on Nina? That shit ain't none of your business. I don't like messy bitches," I told her while lying in bed.

I was feeling some kind of way about the situation. My fam is in a tight spot on this situation, but it's not my business to be all in the mix.

"First off, don't call me no bitch. Secondly, that's my brother. He hasn't been the same since she left him," Lena said.

"You sound stupid as hell right now. I understand that's your brother, but we all know that nigga is crazy. I'm sure he was abusing that girl. If she wanted to leave, that was by choice and not by force. Who the fuck are you to open your mouth? Man,watch out," I said, pushing her off of me and getting up.

That shit had me a little hot, and I was feeling like a female by talking about it. I hadn't heard from Drake since parting ways from the meeting, so I called him, but he didn't answer. I grabbed my keys and headed to his spot when a fire truck sped past me going in the same direction. When I got into his neighborhood, his street was blocked off.

I parked as close as I could, hopped out, and ran around the back of niggas' houses until I got to Drake's. I peeked around his house to see that the fire truck was right in front of Drake's trying to put a fire out on his truck.

"What the fuck is going on? Where the fuck is this nigga at?" I asked myself.

I went to the other side of the back of the house, pulled my key out, and opened the storm door. When I moved there, he gave me a key in the event something went the fuck down. I'm glad I took the damn key.

I went searching for this nigga but didn't see him anywhere. I headed to the front of the house making sure nobody saw me as I moved about. I came across some blood in the foyer and it was a lot. I was confused. *Was he dead or did he survive and got the fuck up out of there?* This shit was crazy.

I left out being careful that no one saw me. I made my way back to my car and took off. I called Drake's phone again and still no answer. I wasn't sure what to do. I don't fuck with the pigs, so there was no way I was going to find out if he was dead or not. I got back to the apartment, and Lena was in the kitchen bent over wearing some booty shorts. My dick got hard immediately.

I forgot about everything from earlier and what I had just witnessed. I walked up to here and grabbed her hips thrusting my pelvis against her. She stood up putting an arch in her back on the way up and looked at me. She rolled her eyes and tried to pull away, but I held onto her.

"Where you going?" I asked in her ear.

"Fuck you, Leo. Where the fuck did you just go?" she asked with her arms folded and lip poking out.

I turned her around to face me and bit her lip then sucked on it to lessen the stinging feeling.

"Don't question me, Lena. I'm a grown ass man. Just know that you can trust me," I told her moving her curly hair out of the way and kissing her neck.

She loosened up some against my body. Her arms slowly fell to her side, before she put them around my neck. I grabbed her ass and lifted her up, putting her on the counter. She spread her legs and I stood between them all the while still kissing on her neck. She was moaning, which was turning me on even more.

I pulled at her shorts, and she lifted up so that I could pull them down. I loved looking at her pussy before diving in and tasting it, but my dick was too hard. It couldn't wait any longer to feel her wetness. I dropped my shorts and slid right in without warning. She moaned when my teeth sank into her neck.

"Ugh," she moaned out, as soon as I hit the bottom of her shit.

She held onto me tightly, as I lifted her up and walked over to the table and laid her on it while holding her legs in the air. I watched as I slid in and out of her as she got wetter and wetter with each stroke. She was damn near a virgin when I met her, talking about she didn't like dick, just head only, but I changed that shit real quick. I dug in as deep as I could and kissed her.

"Oh, Leo, I love you so much," Lena cried.

"How much?" I asked, sliding all the way out and sliding back in as slow as I could.

"Oh, Leoooo, yes!" she cried.

Lena was the only girl I've made love to. You better believe, every time I was in her, I put that pussy on a pedestal. I need a loyal rider by my side, and although she was a little childish, I knew I could take her and get her right.

"Stop holding back; let that shit out," I whispered in her ear. She arched her back and started shaking. "There goes one," I laughed.

I let her ride the high of her orgasm before I flipped her on her stomach and dug into her from the back.

"Baby, wait! Wait!" she moaned, trying to run.

I never knew why she tried to run, because I would never let her. I grabbed a fistful of her hair and made her arch that back just right.

"You belong to me, you hear me?" I asked her.

"Yes, baby, I'm yours, I'm yours."

Once I put her to sleep, I called multiple hospitals making sure Drake wasn't admitted. Just as I suspected, he wasn't in any of them. *Where the fuck could this nigga be?* I called his phone one more time for the hell of it and he answered, sounding sad as fuck.

"Yeah?" he said.

"Fam, what's up? You good?" I asked happy he finally answered but anxious to find out what the fuck was going on.

"Fuck no. Man, they took Nina! Reno came and took her and my baby and tried to off me. I almost died tonight," Drake said.

"Fuck Reno! We're going to get your girl back and put some hot lead in his ass," I said mad as fuck.

Lena rolled over and looked at me with big eyes. I reached out to touch her, but she backed away like I was a monster and not the person who had just fucked her.

"I slept on his ass, and that was the wrong thing to do," Drake said.

"Well, the good news is that he woke your ass up. How the fuck you survive? I saw blood all in your crib?" I asked.

"I still had the bulletproof vest on from the meeting," Drake said.

"You better thank God or some damn body, but hey, I'll get up with you in a minute. I got some shit to address over here," I said, watching Lena throw clothes into her bags.

"Bet," Drake said.

Once I hung up, I walked up on her and swooped her up.

"No, put me down, Leo," she said, kicking and screaming.

I put her on the bed and pinned her arms down so that she couldn't move.

"Your brother tried to kill my fam and kidnapped Nina. If I was the bad guy, I could kidnap your ass and play the game he's playing," I told her.

I saw her eyes get wide with fear, and I shook my head.

"So what, you don't trust me now?" I asked her.

"You're trying to hurt my brother. I didn't know he would kidnap Nina or hurt Drake; I was just trying to help," she cried.

"Lena, let this be the last time I have to tell you to stay out of grown men's business. Women, y'all just don't think shit out. Now, I have to fix some shit that could've been avoided," I said, letting her go and getting up.

I walked to the shower, and once I got out, Lena was packed and looking sad sitting on the edge of the bed. I tried to ignore her, but she knew I was weak for those puppy dog eyes of hers.

"What Lena?" I asked.

"You're mad at me," she said poking her lip out.

I sighed before answering. I wasn't going to pretend that I wasn't mad, but at the same time, she didn't make Reno do the shit he did.

"Baby girl, look at me. I know you know what type of shit your brother is involved in. This game is real as fuck, and you just got your first wake-up call. Now, I can vouch for you this time, but next time, I might not be able to or want to. Now, tell me, are you on my side or your brother's?" I asked her.

Tears flowed from her eyes, and I knew right then I wouldn't like the answer. I hated to put her in this position, but fuck it, she and her sister brought it upon themselves.

"Leo, this is not fair," she cried.

"Life isn't fair, baby girl. Take care," I said, kissing her forehead and opening the hotel door.

She cried, as she walked out, and I made a mental note to change hotels. You could never be too careful. Just look at my cousin Drake.

Chapter 3

Reno

"Where the fuck is Lena?" I asked Tena walking into her room.

"Uh, she stayed with her friend," Tena said looking away from me..

"Call her ass right now," I demanded.

Lena kept sending me to voicemail, and I had just noticed that she wasn't there. Lena and Tena never did anything without the other. She called Lena, and she answered immediately. I hit speakerphone.

"He broke up with me, Tena. He knows what we did and he's mad Drake got hurt!" she cried.

I sat up and looked at Tena for answers. Who the fuck was Lena fucking with that knew Drake?

"Lena, bring your ass home now!" I yelled at her.

"Really, Tena?" Lena cried before hanging up.

Tena snatched her phone from me. "Why the fuck would you do that?" she asked.

"Fuck all that. Talk," I demanded.

"I'm not telling you shit until you calm the fuck down," Tena said.

"I'm as calm as I'm going to be. so talk before I snap your fucking neck," I said.

"That's not calm, and you don't scare me, Reno," Tena said with her arms crossed.

I stood there looking at her with my head tilted. Tena was always one tough cookie. She and Lena were the same but opposites. Lena was boy crazy, and Tena was gay as fuck. She dressed like a female but carried herself like a nigga. She has never been scared of me, and that shit has always pissed me off. Her ass will go toe to toe with me, and she's small as fuck. I was always able to get Lena to do what the fuck I wanted her to do, because she was scared of me but Tena never budged.

"So, calm your ass down, and then, I'll tell you what the hell is going on," she said.

"I'm good," I said, calmly.

"You know how Lena is about you. Nina hit us up a while back, and Lena thought we should've told you. She would've told you sooner, but I told her to leave it alone. If you wanted to find her, you would on your own. You know how Lena is always telling on somebody instead of minding her damn business. I told her to do what the fuck she wanted, and that's when she went to you," Tena said.

"So you wasn't going to tell me?" I asked.

"Fuck no. I love Nina like a sister, and I hate what the fuck you be doing to her. I would be selfish as fuck to want her back only for you to continue to do her the same. You're not going to change until the right female comes along. You need to meet your match. Nina is good for you, but she's not the one for you, bro. She's fucking scared of you. Let her be, man. Don't do her like this. She don't deserve it, and you know it. I know you love her, but let her go," Tena said walking off.

"Fuck that. She's been mine. She's always going to be mine," I said behind her.

Tena shook her head as she walked out.

"What the fuck is wrong with these motherfuckers? She's been my bitch. I don't give a fuck if she's happy or not," I said to myself.

I walked out and headed to the living room to smoke a blunt. These motherfuckers got me heated, and I needed to calm myself down. Tena walked right past my ass.

"I hope you're going to pick your big headed ass sister up. Tell her I'mma fuck her up when I see her," I said to Tena's back.

She just threw up the deuces and walked out the house. I got to the living room to see Xena sitting on the couch.

14

"I swear to fucking God, if you put a dent in my fucking couch, I'm going to beat the fucking brakes off your ass. Do you go anywhere else in this fucking house?" I asked, sitting in my spot.

"What the fuck can I do, Reno?" she asked.

"Get the fuck out is what you can do. Go get a fucking job and stop mooching off of me. The only time your ass leaves is to get your ugly ass hair and nails done. You don't even pick up RJ no more. You're a weak ass excuse for a mother. I don't know why I ever nutted in your ass," I said, lighting my blunt.

"Because you love this pussy," she said, sexily.

"No, because I was too damn dumb to fuck over Nina with your hoe ass. Your pussy ain't shit. It wasn't all that back then, and it damn sure ain't shit now. The only thing you're good for is sucking my dick. Now, get over here and suck my dick," I told.

And like the good bitch she was, she came over and got on her knees. I pulled my dick out and put it right down her throat. I didn't even care if Nina walked in on us or not.

Chapter 4

Lena

All I ever wanted to do was make my family proud. Growing up, my father and brother always talked about loyalty to your family and the people you really trust. Tena and I always argued about what loyalty meant. She always called me a snitch, but I didn't agree. I called it always looking out. Every time I did, Reno would always thank me and give me money. Call me what you want, but I love money.

When I met Leo, I just knew he was going to be mine. We played around for a long time before he actually started making some serious moves with me. The more time we spent together, the more I fell for him. I didn't know that he was related to Drake until I heard his phone conversation, nor did I know that Reno was going to try and kill Drake. I had no idea that Leo even knew hidden details, while I was gossiping about what we did.

When Leo opened that door and had me walk out, I knew it was over for us. I cried the entire flight home. I never expected for us to end like that. When I walked in and saw Nina, I was happy and ran to her, but she swerved the fuck out of me.

"Lena, bring your ass here," I heard Reno say, but I kept it moving behind Nina.

I wanted to see what her problem was, but she swerved my ass again. I got mad and went to see what the hell Reno wanted.

"What?" I asked when I got back in the living room.

"Where the fuck have you been?" he asked.

"I was with an old friend," I said, as a tear escaped my eye.

"The fuck you crying for?" he asked.

"Nina's not talking to me," I said. This nigga had the nerve to laugh. "What's funny, Reno?" I asked annoyed.

"What the fuck did you think was going to happen? You been snitching on her ass since we got together. I wouldn't be talking to your ass, either," he said, still laughing.

"How could you say that? I've been doing that shit for you," I said.

"You did that shit on your own. I appreciate it, but shit, you made that decision yourself. Hell, I didn't even ask, y'all came to me," he said.

"What about all that shit you and daddy talked about when it came to loyalty?" I asked.

"Yo, you acting dumb as fuck. I see why Tena stay cussing your ass out. You of all people don't understand what the fuck loyalty means, and I'm going to need your ass to figure it the fuck out," he said, getting up.

I stood there feeling dumb as hell and used. I grabbed my shit, went to the guest bedroom and sat on the bed and cried.

"Man the fuck up. We fucked up. Get over it," Tena said, coming in and being insensitive.

"Leave me alone," I said.

"You know I could care less about them damn tears. Shit don't mean nothing to me. So, dry them the fuck up. You lost your Leo? Why?" she said, sitting at the edge of the bed.

"He's Drake's cousin," I said, looking at her with big eyes.

"Oh, shit. So, let me guess, he felt torn and had you choose, huh?" she asked.

"You know I'm going to always ride for my family, but that was my man," I told her.

"And that's where you fucked up. If you felt like forever with Leo, you should've chose him. Reno will always be your brother. You'll never have a husband if you keep picking motherfuckers that'll always be there for you anyway," she said. "Now, get the fuck over yourself, and let's go out to eat," she said, rubbing her stomach.

"Hell no; Nina cooked, and you know I love her cooking," I said wiping my face.

"You better hope she don't spit in our plates," she said.

"Why would she do that? Nina knows I love her," I said.

"Damn sure could've fooled me. How you love somebody you snitched on? If you loved her, you would've minded your fucking business. I don't know why I let you talk me into this shit. That's why I was always fighting niggas and bitches for you. You stayed in somebody else's shit and could never stay in your own. I've been telling you this shit for years. It's finally blowing up in your face, but you'll be ok," she said, hitting my leg before walking out.

Tena could be so blunt, but I loved my twin. I followed behind her. I could smell Nina's cooking from the hallway. We got to the table, and everybody sat down while Nina served us all.

"Nina, this looks amazing," I said.

She didn't even acknowledge me. She kept it moving and sat down when she was done. Damn, I really fucked up.

Chapter 5

Drake

If you really thought I was dead, then you really don't know who the hell I am. I may have been Reno's right hand, but I'm still motherfucking Drake. I'm not stupid by a long shot. I was happy as hell I still had my vest on, but Reno got me good when he pistol whipped my ass. I waited until they were gone before getting my ass up. I looked out the window to see my shit was on fire.

I always drove one vehicle, but I wasn't stupid, like I said. I called my doctor up and told him I was coming through. I could tell I needed stitches. Fuck a hospital; I wasn't about to leave a meeting and go lay around in doctors' and police officers' faces. My new plug would think I was a fucking fool. I couldn't risk any fuck-ups, and well, this shit is a part of the game. The real Gs have nine lives. I went into my garage, grabbed the keys to my other car, and peeled out of there. I wanted to get my girl back, but I needed to come up with a plan to do so. On the way to the doctor, I called the police, disguising my voice, saying there was a car vandalism while the family was out of town. I couldn't risk them going in my shit, even though they probably would.

I got to the doctor and was out of there in no time. He was the shit, and he knew it. I saw when Leo was calling me, but I couldn't answer. It was still too hot, and I knew he might've been with Lena. Nah, I had to come up with a plan first. When he called that last time, I knew his ass was worried for real. I had to let him know that I was alive and fucking kicking. I'm going to get my girl and baby back, you can believe that shit, but first, I needed to rest up. Reno may not be a joke to fuck with, but he better be ready for this war. He was not raising another one of my seeds, fuck that! I'm coming back and coming back hard.

I stood in the airport as my mother and my aunt, Leo's mother, walked in off the plane. I had to get them out of harm's way. Yeah, I may have gotten hit at my place, but I'm 100% sure Nina opened the door. I had alarm systems set and a technician coming ASAP to set up cameras.

"Mama, I'm going to warn you now, there was a fight at my place, and it's blood on the floor, but don't trip, your son is alive and kicking," I whispered to her.

Her eyes got big as she took in what I said. My mother was no dummy; she knew what I did out here. The difference between me and a lot of these other hustlers is I got my mother's blessing before jumping in this shit. Call it a southern thing, but it just seemed like life was a lot easier when you had mama praying for you.

"Drake, where is Nina?" she asked.

I never lied to her, never.

"Reno took her back home, but I'm going to get her back," I said assuring her.

"Drake, listen, I know I don't fool with with my ex-husband, your father's other family, but use them for help. Don't go in there blind, because Reno has his whole family with him," she warned.

"I got you, OG," I laughed.

"Shut up with that," she said.

Don't sleep on her now. My father may have died young, but when he was with us, I watched her in action. Every time SWAT came to the door, she would go stall the police while my dad hid in the attic. We never kept shit in the house, and they never once arrested my dad, either. Mama had the game on lock. She was the true definition of a ride or die.

"Where is my Leo?" my Aunt Lorene asked.

"He's checking out of his hotel now; he'll be at the house when we pull up. Make yourselves at home when we get there," I told them.

It was actually a plus having them there. Now I didn't have to wonder who would run in my house when I was gone. I sat with them for an hour at the house, so it wouldn't cause too much alarm, and then, I left out with Leo right behind me. I had another car outside of the truck but I was going to leave that here and we took Leo's car instead. Instead of booking a flight, we took the drive from Georgia to Arkansas. I needed the time to think shit out.

"So check it, we're going to lay low at this bitch I used to fuck with place," I told Leo.

"Bet. You sure she game for it?" Leo asked.

"Shit, she has no choice. I kept her bills paid when I was fucking her," I said.

I hit Candy up and she texted me saying she missed me and was glad I thought of her. Candy never stayed in the streets, so I knew she probably hasn't heard that I was with Nina now. Another thing I liked about Candy was that she wasn't extra clingy. Sad to say, she was one of those females you can cut off at any time and hit back up years later and she would still let you fuck. Her condo only had two bedrooms, so I was going to have to sleep in her bedroom. *Fuck*!

"Take this left; my girl stay out in the mountains and shit," I told Leo.

"Damn, you calling her your girl now?" Leo asked.

"That's what I'm making her believe while we're here. She know I'm hustling; she don't sweat me leaving as long as I come back," I schooled Leo.

I wasn't married yet, but that's how I survived. I always kept a bitch tucked away for a rainy day. It was in the handbook. Most people fuck up when they get a bitch that's highly known. Candy was so low-key, I barely noticed her when we met.

****

"Your total is $167.90 ma'am," the cashier said to the lady in front of me.

I was in line at Whole Foods looking at all the healthy shit. My current freak of the week was into this shit so I decided to surprise her, so she could surprise me later. The lady in front of me was dressed in workout gear with a Polo hat on her head. I glanced at her out of boredom before looking back at my watch. By the time I looked back up, shorty was walking off chatting on her phone while the cashier was calling her for a bag she left. I set my food down and decided to take the bag to her.

"Excuse me, Miss Lady," I called behind her.

She turned around, and I took in her light complexion and pretty eyes. She wasn't wearing an ounce of makeup, and I could tell she'd just left the gym. She was still gorgeous as hell.

"Yes?" she asked, looking me up and down like I did her.

"You left your bag," I told her.

"Oh, my goodness, thank you! Hey Mona, let me call you back; you have me leaving things," she said, pulling her phone away from her ear.

"Thank you," she said again.

"It's cool. I know this may be forward, but can I take you out sometime?" I asked her.

"I don't know; you look a little young," she said.

"Young?" I asked, "Sweetheart I'm 24."

"And I'm 32," she smirked.

"Damn," I said, shaking my head.

She looked better than bitches that were 22. I had to get her now.

"Does my age scare you?" I asked her, trying to get in her head.

"Scare me? Not at all," she laughed.

"So if you're not scared, you will exchange numbers with me and let me take you out," I told her.

"I can do you one better," she smirked.

Just like that, I was following her to her place and canceling my current plans while she started kissing my neck the moment we walked through the door. She was the only woman I met who almost had a higher sex drive than me and didn't play all the games to let me fuck. From that day forward, I fucked with her, until Nina finally came to me.

****

"Hey, baby," Candy greeted me when I walked in with Leo. "OH, my god, are you ok? Your face looks beaten!"

"It's part of the game, baby. This is my cousin Leo; he's going to stay with me for a while," I explained.

"That's cool. I can go ahead and start cooking," she said, kissing my cheek before walking off.

Leo was rubbing his hands at the sound of food.

"Nah, fam, her cooking don't got shit on Nina's," I said.

Chapter 6

Jace

"Damn, who the fuck is she?" I asked Reno, as he slid a picture of a pretty, brown chick with curly hair.

"That's Drake's little sister. He has her hidden out in the country some damn where," Reno told me.

"Sister? Damn, he secretive as fuck," I said, still looking at the picture.

"The plan is simple. She works behind the desk of the local gym, and she talks to Drake all the time. I need you to take a few trips down there, look around, and get close to her. Once you get a bitch's trust, she'll open up to you. I need to know if Drake is still alive, and if he is still in Georgia," Reno said.

"Shit, this job easy as hell. Nobody can resist my handsome self," I joked, playing with my goatee.

I felt like the luckiest motherfucker right now as Reno ran down the specifics of the plan. I kept eyeing that picture. It was something about her eyes that drew me in. She looked sweet as hell and not fast like the rest of these bitches who chased me down. Right now, I was in my senior year of high school, but I was basically done with school. My mama stayed on my ass about grades, and I only had three classes, Algebra 1, English, and U.S. History. Three days a week, I would be out of school at twelve, and two days, I would be out that bitch at ten-thirty. Plus, it didn't hurt that I paid Tena and Lena to do my work sometimes. I had women as old as 30 chasing my young ass down. Right now, I was driving a 2011 Dodge Charger that was white like Reno's. It was my dad's old car that he gave to me since I kept my grades up.

"So when can I start?" I asked, cutting Reno off.

"Tomorrow, and don't fuck this up trying to get ya dick wet. If you can fuck her, cool, but if she not going, don't push her. You gotta work her slow to get in her head," Reno said.

"I know how to finesse a bitch," I laughed, getting up.

****

"Damn, why the fuck we come two hours to hoop?" my partner Dylan asked.

"Man, I been hearing these country niggas claim they can out hoop us, so I'm about to find out," I lied.

"Fuck that," Dylan exclaimed like I knew he would.

Dylan was supposed to be a star athlete, but he got kicked out of school after being caught with weed. As soon as we pulled up and got out, niggas were mugging us and shit. That shit never scared me. I discreetly raised my shirt so that they could see I was packing two guns and they eased up a bit.

"What's good, young blood? Where you from?" an old head asked me.

"I'm from the city," I said.

"What? You came all the way down here to play ball?" he asked.

"Hell, yeah; we the coldest players up there, so we trying to find competition," I said.

"Nigga, you gone find it today?" a guy around my age said.

"So, what's up? Two on two?" I challenged.

"Bet," he said.

We walked in the gym, and I saw her. Her head was down in a book as everyone signed in. I wanted to look in her face, so I lingered while everyone went to stretch.

"Excuse me, Miss," I said.

She looked up, and I knew I had her. Once they saw my dreads and hazel eyes, they all froze up.

"Yes?" she sweetly asked.

"I'm new here, so how does this work?" I asked, smiling at her.

"They didn't tell you? I swear, it's like y'all dumb asses only can run your mouths and sling dick but can't do what they're supposed to do. Look, you sign in and keep it moving," she said, rolling her neck while looking me straight in the eyes.

I stood there with my mouth open. I don't know what I was expecting, but that damn sure wasn't it. Baby girl looked so innocent.

"Ummm, ok. You're too beautiful to have that much attitude," I said trying to calm her down.

"So, I've heard. Now, keep it moving," she said, burying her head back in whatever book she was reading.

I glanced at the book to see that she was reading one of them damn sex books that these females like to read. I looked to the side of her to see a whole damn stack of books.

"So you like reading?" I asked trying spark some conversation.

She sighed and rolled her eyes before looking at me.

"Did you come to talk to me or play basketball? Judging by your boys in the gym, they're waiting on you," she said, looking around me.

"What if I came to do both?" I asked licking my lips.

"Then, your timing is off. Figure it out first, then come holler at me," she said, smiling.

I nodded then winked at her before jogging off.

"It took you long enough. We came to ball, not get bitches," Dylan said.

"Aye, man, leave her alone. She don't fuck with nobody, and her mouth is reckless as hell," one of them niggas said.

We all looked in her direction. She wasn't paying us no attention. She may not fuck with them niggas, but she ain't met a nigga like me yet. I turned back to them, and we got the game going. Just like I thought, Dylan and I dusted them niggas. They were big mad and talking mad shit, but I didn't give a fuck. I was coming back to, not only to dust everyone that played there, but to see that beautiful face each time I came. She had me intrigued now.

"I'll see you later," I told her, knocking her book out her hand and walking away.

"That was uncalled for," she called out.

I didn't respond. I just kept it moving towards the car and got in.

"Aye, nigga. You know I know you. What's the real deal?" Dylan said as soon as he got in.

I didn't want to tell him, but I knew he would keep asking so I lied.

"I'm here to scope out some niggas that's supposedly trying to slide in and take over some of Reno's turf," I said.

"You should've said that shit in the beginning. You know I'm down for whatever," Dylan said cracking his knuckles.

"And that's why I didn't say anything at first. I needed your ass to act normal and not like you was ready to bounce some heads off the bleachers. You're a fucking hot head," I said, seriously.

"I feel you," Dylan replied nodding.

I knew he was in his feelings. I get on his ass all the time about that shit, but he don't listen. The ride home was quiet which was exactly what I needed. I needed to come up with a new approach for Drake's sister. That girl is going to fall for me whether she likes it or not.

Chapter 7

Nina

Being in this house has been hell. Lena is still trying to talk to me, and I keep ignoring her ass. I don't see how she doesn't get it. I wished she would go back to her parents' home already. I tried sleeping in one of the other rooms, but Reno wasn't having that. He's even tried having sex with me, but each time, I had to remind him that I was pregnant with Drake's baby. I could tell he wanted to hit me, but he wouldn't. He would just leave out the room. I was happy about it, because I would sleep peacefully by myself.

I don't know if he was trying to make me jealous or what, but I could and would hear him and Xena fucking until I would fall asleep. It didn't bother me any. As long as he wasn't trying to rape me, then I was good. Every second of the day, I was thinking of Drake. I don't know if we were truly meant to be together, but I just feel like he isn't dead.

My spirit won't allow me to feel it. I would catch myself smiling and then crying every time I thought about it. I called my old doctor and I have a doctor's appointment coming up, and I told Reno. He basically cussed me out, but I didn't care. I asked Tena if she could go with me, and she gladly accepted. I was beyond bored in this house and couldn't wait until my appointment. I told Reno that Tena was going with me since I knew that he wasn't letting me go by myself, and he for sure wasn't going since it wasn't his baby. I was actually happy he wasn't going to be up my ass. The funny thing is, Reno hasn't really been up my ass or at home. I don't know what's going on, but I think he found another woman. Good for him, so I hope when Drake comes and gets me, he will let me go peacefully. I just know my Drake isn't dead.

"Can I talk to you, please? This is ridiculous. We've never gone this long without talking," Lena said, coming into my study room.

"Then, let's set a damn record," I said, not even bothering to look up at her.

I was on the floor like I usually was, creating my business profile. Since I had both of my degrees, I decided I needed a web page to make myself appear professional. My depression had faded, and I was back to pursuing my goals.

"Come on, Nina. We're better than that," she said, sadly.

"I thought we were, but you've proven otherwise. Just please leave me alone," I said.

I could tell she was hurt and defeated, but I couldn't care less. She should've minded her own fucking business. I went back to doing my work since I really didn't have anything else to do. A few hours later, I was in the kitchen cooking as usual.

"Man, will you talk to Lena so she can stop bugging me, please?" Tena came out of nowhere and asked.

"No, we always baby her and give her her way. I'm sick of letting shit slide. You know I'm not with that shit she's been doing, and this time tops the cake. I'm through with her ass, and yours too for the matter," I said, not bothering to turn around.

"Look, I'm going to need y'all two to fix it, because this shit ain't cool, and if you were so mad, you would still be ignoring me. I see through you," she said.

"Then, it's not cool. I've been getting ran over all my life. I'm done. It's time I stick up for myself. I have a damn baby on the way, and if I don't start now, they'll see that I'm weak. And that's something I never want to be seen as again, so if you don't understand that, then I'm sorry," I said.

"I feel you, but for the sake of my sanity, please talk to her. Shit, I'll do whatever you want. She is more annoying now than ever. You know she dick crazy, and since her dude left her and you're not talking to her, she's bugging the fuck out of me," she damn near whined.

"I'll think about it," I said.

"Think quick and hard, because I'm about to hang myself," she said.

"Do it after my visit," I said seriously.

"That's cold, Nina. Real cold," she said before walking away.

"Dinner is hot and ready," I called out behind her.

I really didn't want to eat, but I knew I had to. Everybody came in and we all sat down like we were one big ass happy family. I couldn't wait to check on my baby. I only asked Tena to come, because I knew deep down the plan to snitch was Lena's.

Chapter 8

Reno

I thought having Nina back would make things go back to the way they were, but that was far from the truth. As bad as I wanted to fuck her, I couldn't. It was a constant reminder that she let that nigga Drake fuck. I could smack the hell out of her, but I couldn't do that either, so I took my frustrations out on Xena, sexually and physically. Since Nina was back, I thought Xena would want to leave, but hell, she didn't have a damn place to go.

RJ was loving having Nina back, and even though Nina wasn't liking the situation, she was putting on a brave face for him. Xena knew not to say one damn word to Nina, and Nina walked around like Xena didn't even exist. I had Jace going to go check out that nigga Drake's sister Amber to see what information he could get. He hasn't reported back anything, yet, but I'm sure he's going to bring me some good information.

I haven't been home lately, and for the first time, I'm cool with it. A nigga is still handling his business, but I've been going up to my doctor's office to see Serenity. I've been taking her out to lunch, and I actually have been enjoying her company. Out of all the females I've been with, including Nina, she has been the most fun to be around. Today, I was going to meet up with her for lunch.

"Where are you going?" Xena asked when I got out the bed.

"To mind my fucking business. Something you need to look into," I told her still walking.

"So you can fuck me then leave to go fuck another bitch?" she asked getting up and trying to run up on me.

"First off, back the fuck up. I can do whatever the fuck I want to do. I pay the bills around here and yours too, so don't get to trying to act all territorial and shit. Fuck out my face," I said pushing her.

Her dramatic ass fell into the closet knocking over shit. I stood there and shook my head. She hopped up and swung on me. Wrong damn move. I picked her ass up and threw her the fuck back in the closet.

"You done lost all your fucking mind," I told her walking up to her with my fists balled up.

"Wait, baby. I didn't mean it. I'm sorry," she said with her hands up in front of her face.

"Naw, Fuck that," I said.

I drew my fist back when my phone went off. The ringtone caught me off guard. I looked at Xena one last time.

"You're not even worth it anymore," I said before walking off.

I grabbed my phone off the nightstand.

"What's up?" I answered.

"I know it's going to take you some time, but please don't answer the phone like that when I call," Serenity said.

She's been real demanding, and I can't help but play by her rules. She has yet to give me some pussy or let me up in her place. I'm going to get in them draws. I've never been turned down, and I'm not starting today. I didn't even reply to her, because I was trying to keep myself calm.

"I was just calling to see if we were still on for today," she said, sweetly.

"Yea. We are. I was getting ready," I told her.

"Ok. Good. Just wanted to make sure. I know you're a busy man," she said. "I'll see you in a few," she said before hanging up.

I finished getting dressed and headed out. Serenity liked flowers and shit like that so I stopped and picked some up for her. As usual, she came to my car looking good as a motherfucker. Today, she had on black leather leggings, a white sweater that almost covered that big ass, and heels. Her hair was in a bun on top of her head, and she painted her sexy lips red. My dick was hard as hell looking at her.

"For me?" she smiled, taking the flowers from me.

"Always for you," I told her.

"You're so sweet! Ok, so this restaurant is called Cajuns Warf, and it's on the riverfront," she said.

"I've been there before," I lied.

I didn't know what the fuck a Cajuns Warf was, but I didn't want her to think a nigga was too hood. I ended up letting her drive after I got lost, and I sat in the passenger's seat watching her. She was so in control and sexy as fuck. *Damn, why haven't I at least tasted her yet?* That's how bad she had me feigning for her.

"You know, sometimes staring is rude," Serenity spoke at a red light.

"You say that like you can read my mind," I said.

"I can," she smirked.

"So what am I thinking?" I asked her.

"You're wondering why we haven't had sex yet," she smiled at me.

"No, I'm wondering why you're acting like you don't want me to give you what you've been needing," I told her.

"You're not ready yet," she laughed.

"Shit, you have no fucking idea," I said.

"No, you don't," she shot back, biting her lip.

It was little shit that she did that had me damn near ready to take the pussy. If I was still cool with Drake, I would've asked his soft ass for advice on her. Speaking of Drake, I got word that he wasn't dead and his moms was MIA. I paid attention to shit like that, because I knew he was plotting something.

"Where the hell do you have me at?" I asked, looking at the building.

"Relax, I promise it's better looking on the inside," she laughed.

I got out and opened her door, and before she could get away, I pushed her against the side of the car and kissed her. I didn't know how she would respond, but she didn't push me off. I grabbed her around the waist, and I felt her shaking.

"Damn," she whispered, finally pulling back.

I placed my hands on both sides of her, so she was trapped and looked into her eyes.

"Stop playing with me, Serenity. You wet right now, aren't you?" I asked, whispering in her ear.

For once, Miss Confident wasn't so confident. She reached up and wiped the lipstick off my lips, but her hands were still shaking. I had that ass weak.

"Reno," she whispered.

"What?" I replied.

"I'm not ready for this," she whispered with her eyes closed.

"For what? What am I doing wrong?" I asked her, seriously.

"It's not what you're doing wrong, it's what you're doing right," she said.

"Oh, yeah? So, why won't you let a nigga keep going," I smirked.

"Because, it's not the right timing yet," she replied, moving from my space, "but when it is, I promise it'll be worth it."

I walked behind her and watched her ass switch in that leather. I give her ass less than a month before she lets me hit that. The food was good as hell, and the band was pretty straight. I had to give Serenity props; she picked a good place. Once we finished eating, I slid into the booth beside her and got all in her space again. Hell, she never invited me to her place so I had to try her when I could. I decided to fuck with her head a little bit since she was the therapist's daughter and all.

"So, I know you know why I go to see your moms and shit, so why aren't you afraid of me?" I asked her.

"Who says I looked in your file?" she said.

"You're a woman, y'all are bossy and nosey as shit," I said.

We both laughed, and she looked at me seriously before she answered.

"I don't judge you. You're like you are for a reason. I can feed off your energy, and I haven't gotten a bad vibe from you yet. As far as your problem, well my mother and I spoke on it, and I'll let you in on a secret. We think your bad habits, are because you're searching for something fulfilling in life, and you have yet to find it," she said.

The shit kind of blew me for a second, because she was right. Don't get me wrong, I love Nina and her sex is good, her cooking is great, her body is amazing, all of that shit, but I still fucked around on her. It was like Nina settled with me, because initially, she didn't want to fuck with me until I rescued her. That shit always got to me, because I felt like she was with me out of loyalty, not love.

"Did I go too deep for you?" she asked me.

"Nah, you might have hit the nail on the head," I admitted.

"I'm good at what I do," she smiled.

"That you are," I said, leaning in to kiss her again.

She got weak for me, again, and it made me feel something I never felt before. I felt like I was enough for her, shit probably more than enough. I didn't have to admit shit to her because she met me knowing the worst about me already and here we are tonguing each other down in the middle of the restaurant. I could admit that my feelings for Serenity were heavy, and my mind was telling me to just let Nina go, but I didn't want that fuck nigga Drake to think he won. He still took my bitch before I was done with her, so now I was keeping her until I fucking said so.

Chapter 9

Drake

"Your old man talking mad shit right now, huh?" I asked Oscar.

"Nah, I didn't tell him what happened. I told him you had a death of someone close to you and needed a few months to bounce back. He was on some, 'Black people mourn forever' shit," Oscar said.

"Aye, good looking out, and tell him to chill on the Black jokes," I laughed.

"Anytime; remember, this is my ass on the line, too. If you think you can't handle it, tell me; don't get knee deep and fuck us all over," Oscar warned.

"Hey, I'm no rookie; I got this," I told him.

I hung up the phone and leaned back to think. Something about Nina being kidnapped didn't sit right with me. I always told her not to talk to the twins, but she still did anyway. Nothing about Reno's entry looked forced. I knew how stupid women could be when they were in love, and I wondered if maybe she was secretly reconnecting with Reno behind my back. *Nah, my baby wouldn't do me like that, would she?* Hell, she did it to Reno.

"Do you love her?" Candy asked me.

She was still salty over my dick going soft in her this morning. I couldn't help it; I only craved Nina these days.

"What you talking about, woman?" I asked her, pulling her into my lap.

"I know I'm a sexy woman. I have men chasing me down, and I know men. The only time they won't fuck a willing pussy is when they want another one," she said.

"It doesn't matter if I love her anymore; she's gone," I sighed.

I wanted to believe this would be like the movies and I could rescue Nina and we would live happily ever after, but right now, I couldn't trust her. She went behind my back, and I didn't know what her motives were. Maybe this was my karma for disrespecting the game and taking my partner's bitch. I couldn't help but think like that, but then again, Nina didn't know if I was dead or not. I had to try and find a way to get to her without anybody knowing.

"So what about me, Drake?" she asked.

"Look, you know what it is, but just give me a few, and I'll be out of your hair," I told her, getting up and walking to the door.

"So you don't care if I do me then?" she asked.

I stopped walking and looked at her.

"Listen, I'll always have love for you, but somebody else has my heart. I'm not trying to string you along. If you want to do you, that's fine by me, but out of respect for me and that nigga, I'm sure you need to keep that shit outside of this house until I'm gone," I told her.

"Are you serious?" she damn near yelled.

"Have I ever lied to you?" I asked.

"No, but damn. I didn't think you would just give up like that," she said, sadly, putting her head down.

I walked over to her and lifted her chin, but she wouldn't look at me.

"Look at me," I told her.

She slowly lifted her eyes to look at me, then I leaned in and kissed her. There was nothing... no spark or anything.

"Don't make it complicated. We always kept it 100 with each other. If you have feelings for me, then I'm sorry that I don't have them for you. I've been in love for a long time, and when I finally had my happily ever after, it got snatched away from me. I'll do whatever I can to get my family back," I told her keeping it real.

"As mad as I want to be right now, I can't. You've always been honest with me. I know, and I understand what it is you mean. I wanted us to work out, but I would be wrong to even try when my heart belongs to another as well," she said.

"So why have you been trying so hard to get with me?" I had to ask.

"Because I want to get over him," she said.

"Why?" I asked.

"Because his heart belongs to another," she said even sadder.

"Who is it?" I asked.

"Don't ask questions you don't want to know the answer to," she said trying to walk away.

I grabbed her arm making her stop.

"Who is it, Candy?" I asked.

"Reno," she said pulling away.

I watched her walk away. I stood there wondering when in the hell did they even hook up. For some reason, I just can't get away from this nigga. This nigga done fucked every damn body in the city. I know Little Rock was small, but damn. I've had her around this nigga, and he never even flinched. I shook my head and walked back into the office to sit down. I called Leo up. It was time to come up with a plan.

"Yoooo," he answered.

"Yo, meet me at my mom's," I told him.

"Bet, fam," he said hanging up.

I didn't know where Candy went, and at this point, I didn't care. I didn't hear her as I left the house. I headed over to my mom's house. Leo was pulling up at the same time I was. We both got out and headed towards the house. The closer I got, this feeling in my stomach got stronger that something wasn't right. The front door was open. Leo and I looked at each other and pulled our guns. The shit I was looking at had me wanting to kill somebody.

Chapter 10

Leo

Ever since Lena left, it's been hard to act like I wasn't missing her ass. I haven't tried calling her and she hasn't tried calling me. She's been heavy on my mind, but she made her choice. I knew shorty was a little naive to bullshit, but I didn't think it was that bad. It is what is. A nigga still got to keep it moving.

Lately, I've been hanging with my niggas at the gym out in the country where I grew up. I was related to Drake by his sister, which didn't make us blood cousins, but we always claimed the shit. Anyways, anybody who knows Reno knows his family. I've seen his brother hanging out at the gym asking questions and shit. Amber is my little cousin, and I know how she gets down. I had to find out what the fuck was going on.

"Aye, Am. What's good?" I said walking up to her.

"I'm tired as hell, and everybody is getting on my last damn nerve," she said rolling her eyes.

"Like you don't get on our nerves with that damn attitude. What's up with that new nigga that's been coming around lately?" I said getting straight to the point.

"I don't fucking know, but he's getting on my nerves too. I think something is up with his ass. How the fuck do you just come out of nowhere like that?" she said.

I knew her ass had to be up on game. Drake taught her well. I didn't want to use her, but it seems as if that nigga wants her. She doesn't know that that's Reno's brother, and I want to keep it that way.

"Look, I need you to find out what the fuck he wants and what he's doing here," I told her.

"What?" she asked, looking at me like I lost my damn mind.

"You heard me," I told her.

She put her hand out and looked at me like I knew what was up.

"Bring me some information, and I got you," I told her smacking her hand.

"Leo, don't fucking play me. You know how this works," she said seriously as hell.

"Man, you tripping," I said, digging in my pocket and giving her some money. "I'll give you more once I get what the fuck I want," I told her.

I stood there and watched her thumb through the bills like the money hungry ass she's been her whole life.

"I hope you find a nigga that makes your ass realize that you can't go through life worried about money all the time," I said.

"Money makes the world go round. How are you able to do whatever the fuck you want?" she said.

"Because I worked for it instead of having my hand out or scamming niggas. At least I know that I'll always have money coming in and not have to plan to get some. I plan to make more," I said.

"Whatever," she said walking away.

I watched her walk away and got in my car to head back to the city. I was rounding the corner, and as I circled through a few blocks, I saw Lena talking to some nigga. I got pissed and slowed down ready to get the fuck out and yoke her little ass up, but then I remembered that she made her choice, and I wasn't it. I sat there and watched her talk to this nigga, but by the way she was reacting to him, she wasn't looking interested.

"That's my girl," I said, aloud, even though she couldn't hear me.

She looked in my direction, but she couldn't see me, because I wasn't driving my normal car and my windows were tinted. She was looking good as hell standing there with her arms crossed and weight shifted on one leg. I couldn't help but lick my lips. I had to get her out of my system, so I kept it moving to the house. I went in and took a shower. As soon as I got out, Drake was calling me to meet him at my aunt's house. He said he wanted to he low-key, but he was out here making risky moves. When we pulled up, something wasn't looking right, but I knew I didn't need to say anything. It was written all over Drake's face that he felt the same. When we saw that the door was open, I knew it wasn't going to be good.

Opening the door up, we saw blood all over the place. I knew one damn thing. If something happened to another one of my peoples, there was going to be some more bloodshed going around this bitch. We heard movement, so we stopped and listened. The closer we got to the noise, the weirder it sounded. It was coming from my aunt's room. I was confused as fuck since we had them hiding out in Georgia.

"Who the fuck could that be?" I whispered.

Drake shrugged, and we both continued to the bedroom. When we opened the door, I got really fucking confused.

"What the fuck!" Drake exclaimed, with big eyes.

"Drake, this Reno's baby mama, right?" I asked.

Drake didn't answer as he walked up on her.

"Who the fuck else in here with you?" he asked her.

She shook her head I guess signaling nobody. Shorty was beat the fuck up. Both her eyes were black and swollen shut, and she looked like she had been tied to that chair for a week. I could tell she pissed and shitted on herself. I covered my mouth and nose and walked into the room looking for anyone else while Drake took the gag out of her mouth.

"Who did this? Why are you tied the fuck up in my mama shit?" Drake asked.

"Reno," she managed.

Damn, she was even missing a few teeth. I knew Reno was crazy, but damn, I didn't think he would do this to his own baby moms. I didn't understand why Drake wouldn't put him out his misery already.

"Xena, look at me, what the hell happened to you?" Drake asked, freeing her body from the chair.

Xena was still very out of it so I went to get a cup of water for her. By the time I came back, Drake told me Xena was in the shower, and we both had bleached and cleaned the room. Drake was silent, and I was confused as fuck. What kind of shit was going on here?

"Nigga, you mind telling me what the hell is going on? All of this over you taking his girl?" I asked him.

"I got a feeling this is deeper than Nina," Drake sighed.

Xena walked back in the room in a big T-shirt and stood awkwardly against the wall. The times I remember seeing her, she was a cocky ass female, but now she looked broken down and lost.

"He knows. About RJ," she whispered.

Drake sighed and ran his hand down his face. I looked between the two of them still trying to put two and two together.

"So he knows RJ is mine?" Drake said.

Xena nodded and burst into tears again. Damn, my cousin really was fucked up in the game. No wonder Reno was acting crazy as fuck right now.

"It slipped when we were arguing and he beat me until I confessed. I'm sorry, Drake; I just got tired of him disrespecting me for Nina," Xena said.

"Where the nigga at? And Nina, where is she?" Drake asked.

"At the house. The twins are there, too, and even Jace spends the night sometimes," Xena said.

I thought about Jace pushing up on Amber but decided that this wasn't a good time. Too much shit was going on right now.

"He put me out and took RJ from me," Xena said.

"Xena, I'm going to put you up in a hotel, but understand this, if you go back and tell Reno shit about me, I'll murder you my damn self. The only reason you're not dead now is because I need you on my side now," Drake.

"Drake, please don't kill Reno; I still love him," this silly bitch said.

I shook my head wondering just what the fuck that nigga was doing to these women out here.

"D, man, she's a weak link; I say we off her ass right now. Look at her sitting here beat the fuck up and hollering she still love that nigga," I jumped in.

I could see Drake debating what I said, but I needed fam to boss the fuck up. I don't know where this soft shit was coming from, because right now, Reno was strong arming him like a bitch. Suddenly, Drake pointed his gun at Xena and she scared as fuck.

"Bitch, what did you just say? You love who?" Drake asked.

"No, no, I'm sorry," she cried.

"You are sorry, bitch. That nigga never loved you and never will. And how the fuck this conversation on RJ being mine come up anyway? You trying to add fuel to the fire?" Drake yelled.

"No! Please, it's just, I was tired of him hurting me so I wanted to hurt him back," Xena explained.

"Nah, you wanted him to off me, bitch; I know your ways," Drake said.

"Please don't kill me; I'll help you get Nina back, I swear," she begged.

"Get to talking, and this shit better be good," Drake said.

Chapter 11

Jace

"Why do you come here so much?"

I damn near choked on the water bottle I was drinking when I turned around. We had just finished two games, and I was shooting around the gym. I looked down at the petite Amber in awe. Damn, she was barely 5 feet and she had a nice, slim body with thick, athletic thighs. I wondered what sport she played.

"Hello?" she said, smiling slightly.

"You're gorgeous, ma," I said, ignoring her question.

I went back to shooting while I stalled for an answer to her original question. Shit, I wasn't going to say, "to set up your brother", but I needed something slick. She was definitely a smart one.

"I told you on the first day," I finally answered her after making three shots, nothing but net.

She ran after my rebound and kept the ball. I looked at her as she walked up on me. She was getting lost in my eyes, and hell, I was dreaming about getting lost between those thighs.

"You're not from around here. Damn near this whole town is my family, and they don't know you and have never seen you before. What, you just randomly googled us one day?" Amber asked me.

I bit the inside of my cheek and laughed a little. Damn, if this wasn't part of a plot to get at Drake, I would consider cuffing her. She was a little street smart diva.

"Maybe, I wanted to meet *Theexoticlocal*," I smirked, calling out her Instagram name.

Her mouth dropped a little bit but she recovered fast. My sister Lena was hell on a computer, and even better on researching people. I remember when she and her friends would lurk for hours online and find years of dirt on niggas they met at school.

"So you follow me on Instagram and decided to come find me? That's stalkerish don't you think?" she asked with attitude but was holding back a smile.

Shorty was feeling me tough with her mean ass.

"Nah, I don't follow females on social media," I said, cracking her smile, "I'm not even on there. I saw you on my sister's phone and was like damn who is that, I need her," I gamed, walking up on her, "Just so happens you left your location on one of your work pictures."

I was toe to toe with her looking down at her and she broke. She looked down, but I reached down and lifted her chin up to look at me.

"Does that make me a stalker or someone who goes after what he wants?" I asked, looking at her get weaker and weaker.

"I have to go back to the desk," she said, slowly back away.

She dropped the ball and damn near ran from me. I had that ass hypnotized, and she thought running would stop it. She didn't understand, once she looked into my eyes, she would be stuck dreaming about me.

"Nigga, who you supposed to be? Prince Charming or some shit? I heard that bullshit you was talking," Dylan asked, walking from the bleachers.

"Fuck you," I laughed, shooting the ball. "You know how the game goes. Tell these bitches what they need to hear to get what you want."

"You sound like that bitch off *Player's Club*," Dylan laughed.

"You wild man," I laughed at him.

I started stretching since it was game over, when I got a weird ass feeling that made me check for my pistols. As always, they were on my side. I shook it off and walked with Dylan out the gym. I looked towards the desk for Amber, but she wasn't there. Hell, nobody was inside for that matter, not even the old head who guarded the door.

"Man, what's going on with that big ass crowd?" Dylan pointed outside.

I looked where he pointed and saw niggas crowded around a fight. Typical shit, nothing new with that. It wasn't until I saw Amber looking hysterical and crying while a guy held her back that I jumped into action. I took off to the crowd and Dylan was behind me.

"Please, leave my cousin alone," Amber cried.

I walked up to the guy holding Amber and gave him a look that made him release her. I looked down at Amber and got mad at her fearful expression. She was too pretty for tears.

"Which one is your cousin?" I asked, assuming it was the feminine looking guy on the ground getting stomped.

"He's in the red. They bully him, because he's different," she cried.

"Don't cry, pretty girl, hold on," I said.

I pushed my way through the crowd and snatched the guy who was kicking Amber's cousin off of him. I guess he assumed I was breaking the shit up, but my fist connecting with his jaw told him otherwise. He stumbled back and looked at me in confusion. I punched his ass again, and he was out. Weak ass, nigga. I pulled out my guns and pointed them both at the nigga.

"Nigga if you touch him again, I'll body you out here. That's for any of you," I yelled.

The crowd looked mad and shit, but they didn't buck. They didn't want to see me really get down, and I'm glad, because Amber was standing there wide-eyed. Dylan was beside me with his gun daring someone to move so I put mine away and helped Amber's cousin up. He was beat the fuck up, real bad. I could see the crowd getting thin, and a few niggas were mugging me.

"Is there a fucking problem?" I asked to the ones who looked like they wanted to do something.

"Nah, fam," one of them said.

"Chill out on the fam shit," I said, not feeling how quickly he shot that to me.

I walked Amber's cousin up to her, and she hugged him. He winced in pain, but he was good. Hell, even though he got his ass beat, I had to give it to him; he was walking off with his head still high.

"Hey, you two good?" I asked them, as I noticed them walking off.

"Yeah, we only stay about a ten-minute walk from here," Amber said.

"I'll drive you; come on," I said.

Amber hesitated, but her cousin pulled her along. Hell, the way he was limping, he wouldn't make it five minutes into the walk. I hit the alarm on my car and told Amber to get up front. I was kind of mad that her cousin was bleeding on the interior ,but I could get it detailed later. I pulled up to the tattered house and shook my head. I know it was the country, but I expected her to at least live in a nice house.

"So what were they fighting you for anyway?" I asked Amber's cousin.

I could feel Amber watching me, and I smiled a little bit. She probably didn't know how to take me right now.

"He's mad I didn't want to be with him on the down low anymore," the guy said, rolling his neck.

"Aw, hell nah," I laughed, "That nigga talk all that shit in the gym and is out here fighting for his love and shit."

"Jace, you wild man," Dylan said, laughing with me.

The guy didn't laugh, so I chilled, but the shit was still funny. I knew that shit looked too personal. The nigga who beat him up had tears in his eyes and shit.

"No disrespect, though; it was just funny," I said.

"It's cool," the guy said, "Amber, I'm going to go in your house. You know my mama gone act a fool if she see me looking like this and get to praying and shit," the guy said.

I laughed at his ass again. The shit was just funny to me. I looked at Amber when she didn't reply to him and saw her still watching me in a trance. I reached out and touched her cheek softly.

"Why you looking at me like that?" I asked her softly.

"Why are you being so nice to us? What is it that you want?" she asked me with serious eyes.

"Who says I want something? No disrespect, but I don't think it's nothing you can give me that I can't give myself," I said, gesturing towards her house.

She looked embarrassed for a minute. I wasn't judging her; hell, she wasn't grown, so she couldn't change her living situation.

"I got to get out of here and make a few moves, but can I finally get your number, pretty girl?" I asked her.

She hesitated until her cousin spoke up.

"Where is your phone? Hell, I'll tell you her number since my cousin is a deer in headlights right now. It's 870...,"

I took the number and laughed at dude again. I never interacted with gay niggas before, but he was cool peoples. I called the number, and the phone in Amber's pocket rang.

"Ray," she finally said, breaking from her trance. "I didn't tell you to I wanted him to have my number."

"You didn't have to tell me. Hell, we all see you staring at him like he a fucking moon," Ray said.

We all erupted into laughter, and even Amber blushed and laughed. I reached over and ran my hand under her chin again.

"You don't have to front with me. I like you, too," I told her.

She looked down and smiled before opening the door and getting out.

"Thanks for the ride," she said.

"It's nothing. I'll call you tonight," I told her.

"Ok!"

Chapter 12

Lena

I was still miserable as hell. It's been almost a month since we took Nina, and Leo and I stopped talking, and he still hasn't reached out to me. Nina was still in her attitude phase and giving all of us the silent treatment, and Tena was tired of hearing my shit.

"If you love him, just call him. Both of you are being stupid, so hell, you might be meant to be," she last told me.

What was even worse was Reno's ass. He did all this to get Nina back, and it looked like he was dating another chick. I was so tired of being in his house that I wanted to go back home to my parents' house, but I wouldn't be there without my siblings. Dad was always gone, and Mama would have me helping her do some kind of "do it yourself" project that never turned out right.

"Sis, get your ass up and get dressed. Nina has another appointment today and you're coming with us," Tena said.

"She invited me?" I asked, perking up.

"Nah, but you're going to come, anyway. Sis, do you know why Nina forgave me so quickly? It's because I'm not sitting here playing the fucking victim role. Face it, we fucked up, and we apologized, but what's the point of kissing ass? You know she gets off on making you mad right now, so stop the weak shit," I said.

"What if she gets mad when she sees me?" I asked her.

"Oh, she's going to be mad," Tena laughed, "But, so what? Damn sis, we're twenty years old, but it seems like you're twelve sometimes. I don't see how Leo dealt with you so damn long," Tena said.

"Shut up; it's because he loved all this ass," I laughed, standing up and looking back at it.

"Well, act like you know. Get your ass out of this depression shit, and boss back up like your sister did," Tena said.

I was in a better mood since I was getting to go with Nina to check on the baby. I really loved Nina, and it hurt so bad that she possibly hated me. I walked downstairs with Tena, and Nina was already sitting on the couch looking pretty as always. She was dressed in stretch jeans, a mid-sleeve black sweater that showed her cleavage, and black ankle boots. She had a pretty burgundy bag that she was going through before she saw me. Instantly, her face twisted up in disgust, and I stopped walking.

"Lena, come on," Tena said.

I held my head down and kept walking. Damn, why was Nina so cold to me? Tena got the keys to her car, and she had me sit up front while Nina sat in the back.

"Tena, why the fuck is she with us?" Nina angrily asked.

"Because she is. You want to go to your appointment or not?" Tena asked, placing a hat over her curly hair turned backward.

"Well, as long as she doesn't say shit to me," Nina mumbled.

"Nina, I'm sorry, I wish you would-,"

"Lena cut the sob story. Nina knows you're sorry," Tena said, turning the radio up.

I swear, Tena reminded me so much of Reno at times. They were both straightforward and didn't really tolerate a lot of shit they didn't like. I wished I could be that way sometimes.

"Tell Nina who your ex is," Tena said.

"Why?" I asked.

"I already know; some guy named Rio or some shit like that," Nina said.

"No, it's Leo," I said.

Nina was silent for a minute.

"Bitch! You mean Leo, Drake's cousin! How did I not put two and two together?" Nina yelled.

I didn't know if she was mad or happy, so I stayed silent.

"Lena, can you call him?" Nina asked, leaning up and being nice this time.

"I don't think he wants to hear from me. We broke up," I sadly said.

"Bitch, just call him," Nina said.

I wasn't feeling her calling me bitch, but I held my tongue. I called Leo and placed him on speaker. The phone rang and rang until it went to voicemail. I shrugged like it was nothing, but my heart fell into my stomach. It was my first time calling Leo, and I at least expected him to answer. Maybe it really was over. I was sad all over again as we walked into the clinic. I guess Nina finally grew a heart, because she sat beside me after signing in.

"You really love him, huh?" she asked me.

"Yeah," I sighed.

"I don't hate you, Lena. It's just, you remind me so much of the old me. I used to walk around playing the victim. I actually have been playing it since Reno kidnapped me, but I decided that I can't go through life that way. Neither can you, Lena," Nina told me.

I looked at her in shock. That was the most she's said to me all month.

"Nina!" a nurse called out.

Nina smiled at me and invited me back. Tena opted to stay in the waiting room, and I anxiously followed Nina to the back. Even though this wasn't my brother's baby, I was still going to love it just as much as I loved my nephew RJ. After the nurse had taken Nina's vitals, she left us alone in the room.

"Hey, who knows what may happen? If you and Leo get back together and get serious, we could be related in another way," Nina laughed.

"Oh, my gosh, this is so weird. Now that I think about it, this whole scenario is some shit from a movie," I said. "I wish we could be, but Reno-,"

"See, there you go with that shit. Reno used to beat my ass for years, and I still went and found my happiness. I know he doesn't touch you, but you're going to let him come between you and your love. I guess you want your brother to pick your husband, too, huh?" Nina said.

"I just don't want the drama," I sighed.

"Then, you're not ready for a man like Leo. I've been around him a few times, and I know he's not going to baby you while you go back and forth," Nina said.

Before I could respond, the doctor walked in. I was smiling and almost crying happy tears while she got the ultrasound. Nina was almost four months, and she had a tiny belly that I thought was so cute. I started to wonder what kind of mother I would be if the time came. I was always the good girl, the one who walked on eggshells to make everyone else around me happy.

When I met Leo, I was so drawn to the strength in him. He made it clear that he wanted me, but he didn't chase me for long. Every time I started to get scared, he would get mad and finally backed away. I still remember it like yesterday, and I cried myself to sleep for a week until I finally decided to go find him.

****

"Dammit," I whispered to myself.

The sun had just gone down, and I had lied and told Daddy I needed to get tampons. Tena knew what I was up to and opted to ride with me in case I chickened out. There he was, posted in a group of guys in gray sweatpants and a hoodie with his hands down his sweats. It was cold as hell outside, and I could see the air as they spoke. I pulled up to the house I always meet Leo at, and all of the guys stopped talking and looked in our direction. Leo looked so damn good with his cropped curly afro and gold-framed glasses on. He didn't even need glasses, but whenever he wore them, he was that much sexier.

"Tena, he is so freaking cute," I blushed.

"I admit, he is cute," Tena said. "I don't think he's going to walk over here. Go approach him; follow all the way through."

I got out of the car in my leggings, black Timberland boots, and oversized college hoodie. I saw Leo crack a smile, then he ran his tongue over his teeth, as I walked up with false confidence. He walked up and met me halfway in the middle of the road.

"Hey," I shyly said.

"What you doing out here in 30-degree weather?" he asked me.

"You stopped returning my calls," I said.

He didn't speak; he just looked at me. I didn't know what he was thinking, but since I was already this far, I decided to keep going.

"I really do have feelings for you, and I wanted to prove it you, so here I am," I said.

Leo pulled me into his arms and held me close, and I started to cry.

"Stop that, baby," he whispered in my ear. "I'm not going anywhere."

****

"Lena!"

I snapped out of my daydream and looked at Nina.

"Girl, what are you daydreaming about. My appointment is over girl," Nina said.

"Oh, sorry," I smiled.

We walked out of the appointment, laughing, and Tena stood up and clapped.

"It's about damn time you two made up. Now, come on, I'm starving," she said.

When we got back in the car, I took my phone off of the charger, and my heart started beating fast. I had three missed calls and a text message, all from Leo. I opened his text message and smiled big.

Leo: You ready to talk?

Chapter 13

Nina

A woman always knows. Reno was in bed, far away from me, passed out sleeping, and I was lying awake crying. I missed Drake so bad, and I was hurting. I heard Reno's phone go off, and for some reason, curiosity got the best of me. I eased out of bed, tiptoed to the nightstand, and looked at his lock screen. I saw that he had a text from someone named Serenity.

Serenity:I can't sleep. Please tell me you're awake.

I knew Reno had hoes, but I felt like maybe he really liked this one. Sometimes, he would sit across from me at breakfast and smile hard while texting on his phone. I sometimes wondered why he even brought me back. I first thought that, maybe he wanted me that bad, because he would try to have sex with me, but he started to fuck Xena right down the hall. Speaking of Xena, I was nervous now that she was missing. When she was here, she took all of my beatings for me, but after the night she and Reno fought really bad, and he dragged her out of the house, I haven't seen her since. I hoped she wasn't dead. Even though I didn't like her at all, I didn't wish death on her. I don't think Reno thought things, through, because RJ had been so sad lately.

Since I was wide awake, I walked down the hallway to check on RJ. I walked into the bedroom he was in, and I could hear him sniffling.

"RJ, are you ok honey?" I asked, turning on his light.

I noticed that he was actually crying in his dream, and I woke him up. He opened his wet eyes and looked at me sadly. I sat on the edge of his bed and saw him clutching a funny looking bear. It had to be as old as he was.

"Did your mommy give you this bear?" I asked him.

He nodded sadly. "I miss my Mommy. Why did she run away? Was it because I was bad?" RJ asked.

It broke my heart that he felt like her being gone was his fault. Reno was such an asshole sometimes, and he didn't even realize he was making his childhood come alive through RJ.

"If you want, I can be your mommy until she comes back," I offered.

"But I want her to be my mommy too. Why does daddy hurt mommy?" RJ asked.

"Well, RJ, daddy has a lot of issues, but he loves you very much," I said, blinking back tears.

I wondered if Reno would ever know what normal was like. I don't think he's lived a life that wasn't full of drama before.

"I'm scared of daddy," RJ said.

"You don't have to be scared of me," Reno's voice suddenly said.

We both looked towards the door at Reno standing there looking defeated.

"Nina, let me talk to my son," Reno said to me.

I felt RJ clutch my arm, obviously not wanting me to leave him alone with his daddy.

"It's ok, RJ," I said, weakly smiling at him.

I stood up and passed Reno on the way out. He closed the door, and I went downstairs to make a glass of orange juice. I could hear a voice in the kitchen and could tell it was Jace.

"Stop bullshitting. You know you're feeling a nigga. I'll be down there tomorrow to hoop and bring you something," Jace said.

I turned the lights on, and he jumped before realizing it was me.

"Damn, you need to quit tiptoeing around this motherfucker," Jace said.

I laughed, as he walked out. I thought it was cute that little Jace had a girlfriend. I hoped he wasn't like his brother. I ended up eating a bowl of fruit with my glass of orange juice, then sat on the counter, looking at the moon outside. It was big and bright, and for some reason, it made me feel at peace.

"Hey," I heard.

I looked and saw Reno walking in.

"Hey," I said softly.

"I guess the baby is keeping you wide awake, huh?" Reno asked me.

I didn't respond. I was scared to. This was the first time he acknowledged that I was pregnant since he brought me here. He grabbed a water bottle and pulled up at chair right under me. My body tensed as I felt him watch me.

"Let me ask you something, Nina," Reno said.

"Ok," I said.

"Did you ever love me? Be honest," he said.

I took a deep breath and tried to think of how I would word my reply without making him mad.

"Stop thinking so hard and just talk to a nigga. You know like Mrs. Jacob's says in therapy, just open your mouth and talk," Reno said.

I was confused right now. What was this?

"The night you rescued me, I didn't know what to expect. I thought you would want sex from me, but it shocked me when you didn't pressure me. I fell in love with your protectiveness over me, and I was happy until...,"

I stopped talking as I thought back to all of the abuse. Reno has hit me so many times, I lost count of the bruises. I damn near went to every hospital in the state, because Reno didn't want the police to catch on to what was going on.

"Why did you stay with me all of this time?" Reno asked me.

"I was afraid to leave," I said.

It felt like I was hot air balloon and me saying these things to Reno was finally releasing all of the pressure I had inside. I saw his jaw twitch a little, but I was determined not to be mad.

"Not out of love, though?" Reno asked.

"Reno, I will always love you. You saved me and probably saved my life. Who knows what could have happened that night if you didn't rescue me," I said.

"I loved you, Nina, hard as hell. Mrs. Jacobs tells me that I tried to replace you for my moms and shit, but I don't know," Reno shrugged, looking away from me.

I stayed silent as he stood up and leaned against the wall.

"So, how did you and Drake happen?" he asked.

"Reno, I never cheated on you, ever. Drake and I didn't get together until after I left you," I said.

"Why Drake, man? Damn, it could've been any other nigga out here, but you chose my boy from childhood? Nina, that shit was foul," Reno said.

"You beating on me was foul, too," I said, before I stopped myself.

Reno threw up his hands with a chuckle.

"I guess you got a nigga there," he laughed.

The shit wasn't funny at all to me. I got infuriated and stopped biting my tongue.

"You seem to have a new girlfriend, so why am I here? What is your motive?" I asked.

"It's a part of the game. You wouldn't even understand," Reno said.

"You will never be happy causing misery to other people, Reno. Drake and I were happy, and we weren't bothering you," I said, feeling tears pop up in my eyes.

"You think that nigga is just so perfect, don't you?" Reno asked me.

I folded my arms and looked at him. What the fuck did that mean?

"Nina, it's some shit about Drake that you don't even know. He isn't this innocent person you paint him out to be. We were friends for a reason, Nina, remember that shit," Reno said, before walking out and leaving me to my thoughts.

I rubbed my belly and wondered what that meant. I mean, Drake did always come off as perfect, and I always wondered how he and Reno were such great friends. They say birds of a feather flocked together, and Reno did his share of dirt in the streets. I just wondered what kind of dirt Drake had that I didn't know about.

Chapter 14

Reno

I was still in a fucked up mood since finding out the truth about RJ. I damn near killed Xena when she told me that RJ wasn't my son, but Drake's. All this time, I was thinking Drake was my nigga, but he been foul for a long ass time. Xena said the shit like Drake knew it, too, and that's what pushed me over the edge. These two probably were laughing and shit behind my back. Then, he had the nerve to take Nina from me when he wasn't shit his damn self. Yeah, I was getting over Nina, but my anger at this bullshit was deep as hell. I mean, this nigga had me calling his son my junior. Drake is a hoe ass nigga for that shit. Hell nah, I wasn't letting him get Nina back; I would rather her go to another nigga.

I needed to clear my mind before I lost it again, and after talking to Nina and trying to stay calm, I needed a release. I saw that Serenity texted me, so I figured she would still be up since it was only an hour later. I drove to her apartment and called her phone.

"Hello?" she softly said.

"You said you couldn't sleep, and you still sound awake. You good?" I asked her.

"I'm ok. Just a little restless," she sighed.

"Come downstairs, so we can talk," I told her.

"Downstairs? Reno, are you outside?" she asked me.

"Yeah," I said.

"Just come up here," she said.

"Bet," I said.

My dick jumped instantly. The first thing I thought of was fucking her. I couldn't help it; a nigga was backed up. It had been a week since I put Xena out and RJ's teacher who I fucked a while back started acting crazy, so I stopped hitting her off. I parked in a visitor's spot and waited at the door for Serenity to let me in. Her apartment was on some top flight shit, but I liked the fact that she was safe. At least I knew a nigga couldn't catch me slipping out here. When the door opened, I damn near wanted to cry. She had on those short ass workout shorts women be wearing with a tank top that showed the side of her breasts. Damn, her thighs were thick and toned. I could tell she worked out regularly. I guess she read my mind, because she crossed her arms over her top.

"Sorry for my appearance; I know it was cold out and didn't want to have you waiting long," she said.

"I damn sure ain't complaining," I mumbling.

I followed her to the elevator feeling territorial of her.

"You walk around here dressed like this all the time?" I asked her.

"No," she laughed.

"Good, don't have me beating ass in here," I said.

"You are so funny," she laughed harder.

I didn't care about manners on the elevator. She was telling me about her day, but I was staring at those thighs. Damn, I was going to dick her down so damn good, she didn't even know.

"You should wear sunglasses. I can read your mind all in your eyes," she said, softly.

"You like torturing a nigga. I peep you, shorty," I told her coolly.

She laughed at me, as she guided me to her apartment door. When I walked in, I felt like I was in a rainforest or some shit. She had plants everywhere and African art decorating the walls. Yeah, I know some shit about the motherland. I got a relaxed vibe, and I was thinking that maybe I should let her decorate one of my bedrooms. That way, I could walk in and think of her. Damn, I was really in here on some in love shit.

"Sit on the floor with me," she said, sitting down on a yoga mat.

"What?" I said, raising an eyebrow.

"Just sit down," she laughed.

"You different as hell," I commented, kicking my boots off before sitting down.

She wanted me to cross my legs, too, but I wasn't going for all of that shit.

"Give me your hands," she said.

I decided to play her game. Hell, I would damn near do anything she said if it was going to get me some pussy. I gave her my hands, and she closed her eyes and shit like she was Ms. Cleo on TV. I stared between her legs at that fat pussy poking from her shorts, and my mouth watered. Damn, I've never been so anxious to taste a woman before. *Look at me, calling her a woman and shit.*

"Why are you holding onto so much pain?" she asked me.

"What you talking about?" I asked her, confused.

"I feel your spirit. You want to open up and be great, but you're afraid to. You revert back to your past memories," she said.

She opened her eyes and looked at me, and I couldn't take it anymore. I pulled her arms until she leaned forward, and then I reached over and pulled her onto my lap.

"No, Reno, let me up," she said, trying to stand up.

I wrapped my arms around her and held her in place. I was wearing sweatpants, and I knew she could feel how hard my dick was. She was breathing heavy and shit, and it turned me on. I kissed her neck, right above her collarbone, and her nails instantly dug into my arms.

"Oh, shit," she whispered.

I knew I had her. I got aggressive and snaked my tongue up to her ear before biting it softly. By now, she was shaking and moaning like crazy. I would've thought she was a virgin, because she was trembling so hard. I laid her back flat on her yoga mat and leaned on my elbows over her. I looked her in her eyes to let her know it wasn't a game.

"This is going to happen," I told her.

She closed her eyes and shook her head no. I leaned down and kissed her lips softly, before I spit some of her own game back to her.

"I can read your mind, too. You invited a nigga up for a reason, didn't you? And you wore these short ass shorts for a reason, too, didn't you?" I asked her, kissing her right between both collarbones.

"No, Reno, no, I'm not ready. I'm not a sexual person," she moaned.

"Aw, for real," I asked, grinding my dick right where I knew her clit was.

She shook and bit her lip.

"Please Reno, please spare me, I'm sorry. Let's start over," she begged.

She was funny as hell. She was telling me no, as I circled my tongue around her hard nipple poking out of her tank. She wasn't even wearing a fucking bra and wanted to tell me she wasn't sexual. The pussy was dripping wet; I would bet all of my money on it.

"I just want to taste you, baby; can I do that?" I asked her.

Instead of answering me, she covered her face and started saying some motivational shit to herself. I kissed my way down her belly, and then I leaned up and yanked those shorts off. That pussy was pretty, just like I knew it would be. Shit was even shaved for a nigga. Oh, she was ready. I licked her outer lips, and she was already arching her back. I hadn't even tongued that clit down yet. I pulled those lips apart, and she was wet as fuck. Damn, this shit was like a dream. I stuck my tongue deep inside of her trying to coat her juices all in my mouth.

"Oh, Reno; oh baby," she moaned, trying to push my head away.

I grabbed both of her wrists and placed them on her thighs, opening her legs wider, and dove back in.

"Shit, shit, shit! Ooooo, sssssss," she moaned and hissed.

She sounded so sexy, and it got me in a zone. I freed one hand and slid two fingers inside of her. She was so tight, she was gripping my fingers and jumping every time I went in deep. Damn, if she was running like this from my fingers, what was she going to do when I put this dick inside of her? Suddenly, her legs got a force of their own and clamped down on my head. I knew that reaction. I started sucking on her clit like it was the last drop of juice in a sippy cup.

"Oh, god, oh god, Renooooo!" she screamed.

She wet my whole beard up, as she came, and I welcomed that shit. She was sweet as hell, fuck it, she was sweeter than Nina, and that's the only other pussy I ever ate. I finally came up for air, and I felt bad for her. She was shaking and moaning with tears running for her closed eyes. I kissed her lips so she could taste herself. Since I was laying on her again, I knew she could feel my dick poking her.

"Reno, I'm not ready, I'm not ready. Please let me wait," she begged.

"Ok, mama," I laughed, "I'm not into taking pussy. I just wanted you to stop fronting on a nigga. This pussy is mine, you understand me?"

She nodded, and it stroked my ego. I picked her body up, and she directed me to her bedroom. As soon as I laid her down, she curled up and closed her eyes. My dick was still hard as hell, so I did some shit I hadn't done in a long ass time. I jacked my shit off, but it only took me a few minutes. Once I looked at that naked ass and pictured being in those tight walls, I exploded. Damn, I wanted to fuck her, but Serenity made me feel shit I never felt before. She made me think of how my actions would make her feel. The last thing I wanted to do was lose her, so after I cleaned myself up, I undressed, got in bed, and held her from behind. I kept teasing her by rubbing my dick on her pussy lips and clit, but I didn't penetrate her. She did cum three more times off me teasing her alone though. A nigga wasn't even being selfish with her. I waited until she was asleep, and I knew she couldn't hear me before I said the shit out loud.

"I love you."

Chapter 15

Drake

I was somewhat shocked by some of the shit Xena told me. Me and this nigga damn near grew up together, and he was on some real snake shit. I knew it would come out one day, but I didn't think it was going to be this soon. When Xena told me that Reno hasn't really been home and wasn't fucking with Nina like that, a nigga got happy. Shit made me miss my girl and baby even more. Not being able to see her and her belly grow has been pissing me the fuck off. I was ready to get my damn girl back. After getting Xena set up in a hotel, Leo and I left heading back to my mom's house. It was time to figure out what the fuck Reno was up to. We were headed back to the house cruising.

"Aye yo, pull over," Leo said, hopping out the car before I could even comprehend what the fuck was going on.

I slammed on the brakes, but this nigga was already out the car. I watched as he headed towards some nigga who was shaking some girl. I pulled the car over and got a better look at the female and realized it was one of Reno's twin sisters.

"Yo, get the fuck off of her," I heard Leo yell to the nigga that was all on Lena.

"No, Leo. It's ok," she said.

"So, you letting niggas put their hands on you, now?" Leo stepped back and asked.

I had my hand on my pistol ready for some action if Leo needed it, but I was staying out of it until then.

"No, but it's my fault," Lena said.

"How the fuck is a nigga putting his hands on you your fault? Are you really that damn naive?" Leo asked.

"Look, you don't understand what's going on," Lena said.

I sat there shaking my head. That girl is more fucked up than I thought.

"I don't need to understand a damn thing to know that a nigga isn't supposed to put his hands on you. You know what, fuck this. You're more fucked up than I thought," he said walking off.

He got back in the car, and I watched her as she stared at him as he walked away with one sad ass expression on her face.

"What was up with that?" I asked as I pulled off.

Leo didn't respond right away. I looked over at him, and he had his hand on his forehead.

"You was really feeling shorty, huh?" I asked.

"Yea, man, but shorty young-minded. She bad as fuck, but I can't deal with the entitlement bullshit she be on. She chose her brother over me, so it is what it is. Even after she called a nigga out the blue, and we sat down and talked, a few days later, she told me it was too complicated, and she wanted some space. Don't mean I still don't care for shorty. I'm not going to sit back and watch a nigga put his hands on her or any female for that matter," he said.

"I hear you. Now, you see why I gots to get my girl back. She's been the one for me since I first laid eyes on her. Now, she's carrying my seed. I can't let this shit go," I said, as we pulled back up to my mama's house.

Suddenly, she called my cell phone and was yelling.

"What the fuck happened at my house?" I could hear my mother yelling into my phone.

Leo and I looked at each other.

"I'm getting calls and shit from neighbors telling me that a light-skinned nigga been sneaking in my shit, and it wasn't anyone who they

76

recognized. Then, they told me you and Leo went in and came out with a beat up woman. Drake don't play with me; what the fuck is going on?"

"Mama, let me call you back," I sighed.

"I don't know what kind of shit you into, but I will board up a plane and come back home. You were supposed to go get Nina and come back. It's been damn near two months Drake," she yelled.

"Let me call you back, ma, damn," I said, hanging up before she replied.

We walked inside the house ,and I could tell someone had been inside again. Nigga wasn't even trying to hide that he was breaking into her shit. This time, there was a note taped to her TV. I walked over to it and read it.

I know you wanted your bitch back, so I decided to give you the one I was tired of. Stop fucking my old hoes, bitch nigga."

"This nigga is playing games. It's time I play with his ass back," I said handing the note off to Leo.

I called Mama back, because knowing her, she would book a flight on her own and try to jump in the shit.

"Ma, I put you there to keep you safe," I told her.

"I ain't scared of nobody. You know I can handle myself," she said not budging.

"Ma, this isn't the time to be a hardass. You and I both know how Reno gets down. I'm not trying to have you in the middle of this bullshit. He done already came to your house with this shit. You was lucky you weren't there," I said.

"Just like you keep an ear to the streets, I keep one there, too. Don't forget who raised you," she said, hanging up.

"Yo, Auntie is a trip. Let's get the fuck out of here and get this shit rolling. My trigger finger been itching since we found Reno's baby mother," Leo said.

"I'm with you on that one," I said, as we headed back out.

"Nigga, first let's hit up the club. I need a fucking drink," Leo said.

"Bet," I said, as we headed in the direction of the club.

Leo's ass never went to the club, because his crazy ass was banned from all of them. We pulled up and the first person I see walking across the fucking parking lot is Candy. Ever since she revealed that she's been in love with Reno, she's been staying out of my way. I haven't seen much of her lately, and I was happy. I didn't need any distractions.

"Yo, ain't that Candy right there?" Leo asked.

I didn't need to look at him to see where he was pointing to.

"Yea. That's her," I said, nonchalantly.

I really didn't give a fuck about seeing her. We got out and headed towards the door.

"What's good with you, Drake?" One of the bouncers asked when we approached.

"Different shit, different day, but I'm still making money," I told him dapping him up.

"Well, shit. I feel you on that one. Surprising to not see you with Reno for once, especially since he's in there right now," he said.

"Word?" Leo and I asked at the same time.

"Yea. Shit, thought you would've known. You know how y'all roll," he said.

"I thought the nigga was still banned," I said.

"Nah, they decided to be nice for a night since he got his lady with him and shit," the bouncer said.

I just shrugged, paid him, and walked in. Leo and I shared a glance as we both checked our waists for our guns. There was no need to check us out. They already knew the deal. We weren't walking in without them. The club was dark, so you could never really see who was walking in. Knowing Reno he was occupied with a bitch somewhere.

Leo and I walked in and headed straight to a secluded booth that was set up to see the whole club. A waitress came straight to us. We put in our drink orders. We both ordered something light just in case some shit popped off.

"Where's Reno at, ma?" I asked.

"His usual spot watching you talk to me," she said before walking off.

Chapter 16

Lena

I was so happy that Nina was talking to me again. I was beginning to feel lost since I always looked up to her like a big sister. I knew I was getting on Tena's nerves. All she wanted to do was go fuck off on her bitches and leave me hanging, but I wasn't having that.

One of the nights we went out, I met this dude named Chance. He was so cute, with his brown skin. He was tall with dreads, and he had some grills. It was something about him that screamed for me to leave his ass where he was standing, but there was another part of me who was intrigued by him. Since Leo basically said fuck me when I asked him for space, I chopped it up as his lost. I knew he had to be missing me, but I guess I would never find out.

One night, I was in my bed sleeping when my phone went off. I woke up and looked at the time, and it was damn near four in the morning. I looked at my phone, but it went black since I missed the call. I picked it up only for it to ring again with Leo's name flashing across the screen. My heartbeat started racing, and I woke up completely.

"Hello," I answered.

"What the fuck are you doing?" he asked.

"Leo, don't be calling my phone with no bullshit. It's four in the damn morning," I fussed.

"Fuck all that, Lay'Lena. Why the fuck are you letting niggas grab on you? That's why you wanted to take a break?" he asked.

Damn, he called me by my government knowing I hated that shit. I don't know why my daddy let my mother name me that shit. I fucking hated my ghetto ass name.

"Lena. Do you hear me talking to you?" he said.

The sound of his angry voice made me wet. I was missing the fuck out of his dick, and I know he was missing this pussy.

"Look, Leo. We were having a disagreement," I told him.

"Who the fuck was that nigga?" he asked.

"Are you drunk?" I asked.

He was slurring his words.

"I love you, Lena," he said, before the phone hung up.

I pulled the phone away from my ear and looked at it with my mouth open. That was the first time I ever heard Leo say those words. I tried calling him back, but the call kept going to voicemail. I was stuck and confused. I always felt the love he had for me, but I never thought he loved me even though I've said it to him a few times. I smiled, but then it disappeared when I realized he wasn't there anymore.

I didn't remember going to sleep, but when I woke up, I thought I dreamed that Leo said those magical words to me until I felt my phone in my hand. I went through the day in my feelings, checking my phone every five minutes to see if he called or texted.

"Girl, what the hell is wrong with you? You've been moping around all damn day," Tena asked, busting in my room.

"Nothing," I said sadly.

"Bitch, get a life. If it's about Leo, then I'm going to keep saying it. You brought it on yourself. If you want your man, then go get him and stop stringing him along," she said.

"Why don't you have a girl?" I asked, wanting to change the subject.

I was one the verge of crying, and I didn't know why.

"Because I'm not ready to settle down. Plus, I haven't found the right female yet. These bitches only want to act gay to get close to Reno," she said.

"You're feeling somebody, aren't you?" I asked.

I could see it all in her face.

"Nah," she said not looking at me.

"Tena, I'm your fucking twin. I know when you're lying. What's good?" I asked.

"Ain't shit. I done fell for somebody who wants somebody else," she said shrugging her shoulders.

"What you mean?" I asked tilting my head.

"Exactly what I said. I fell for somebody who wants somebody else," she said.

"Damn, how that happen?" I asked.

"I don't even fucking know to be honest with you. I knew she loved a nigga, but I knew she was feeling me, too. I guess I was trying to win her over, but whoever the nigga is, still has her heart," she said.

"Are you going to fight for her?" I asked.

"Nah. I'm not doing no shit like that. If it's meant to be, then shit will fall into place. Other than that, I'm falling back," she said.

"So, I gotta go fight this nigga to get him back, but you won't fight for a bitch that you actually want?" I asked.

"I knew you was going to do that. The difference between my situation and yours is that you had the nigga completely and I didn't have her. I was sharing her ass. She's scared, but I ain't tripping. You have the chance to go get him. You're just fucking scared, because you like being chased. Y'all been dealing with each other for too damn long. Hell, this nigga even used to bring me on the dates back when you were being scary. I even know y'all are going to get back together," she said.

"And how do you know that?" I asked with my arms crossed.

"Because this is some bullshit, and you know it. You're going to see what I mean," she said walking out.

She thought she was slick trying to avoid telling me the whole thing but whatever. My phone went off and I looked at it so quick I gave myself a damn headache. I unlocked my phone seeing that it was a message from Chance to meet up with him. I rolled my eyes knowing I really didn't want to, but I wasn't trying to hear his mouth.

I got up and got dressed. I headed downstairs seeing Reno and Nina on the couch watching a movie. I stopped and watched them in awe. For the first time, Nina actually looked comfortable being back here. I smiled looking at them. Was Nina feeling Reno again? It reminded me of when I first found out Nina was living with us.

****

I walked into the house from school. Normally, Tena and I would walk home together, but her ass had got caught up with her little girlfriend and left me to walk alone. I wasn't tripping, though. It was hot, and the boys were out. I knew, if Tena was with me then they wouldn't approach me. And just like I thought, I was able to get four boys' numbers that day.

I walked in the house, and it was quiet. Reno's truck wasn't parked out front, so I figured it was in the garage or something, but I didn't hear or see him anywhere. I went up to my room and got undressed. I had my earphones in my ear dancing when I saw my bathroom door opening. I looked to see some random bitch walking out. I was used to Reno bringing bitches home, but none were ever allowed in our rooms.

"Who the fuck are you?" I asked pulling my headphones out of my ear ready to box this bitch.

I had no respect for his hoes, because Reno switched them up like clockwork, but this one was kind of pretty.

"Uhh, hey, I'm Nina," she said with a little smile.

"And what the fuck are you doing in my bathroom? You bitches get an inch and want to take a whole fucking walk," I said shaking my head.

"Reno told me to use this bathroom until he got the one in the guest bedroom fixed," she said.

"So you've been all up and through this damn house, huh? Why the fuck are you here?" I asked getting irritated.

"Um, Reno is helping me out," she said.

"Helping you out how? We don't do charity cases around here," I told her.

"I'm not a charity case. I was having problems at home when my mother put me out and Reno picked me up and brought me here. I um, I met your dad, and he agreed," she said sadly.

Now, I felt bad all of a sudden.

"Oh, shit. Damn. Sorry to hear that," I said loosening up some.

I sat on the bed and patted the seat beside me. Nina told me the rest of her story, and the rest is history. I've loved her as a big sister ever since.

****

I really wanted to know how in the hell she ended up with Drake now. I've never seen her and Reno like this before. Even though I've always loved Nina for Reno, I never thought she was the one for him. She always seemed to be faking it to me sometimes. She could keep him calm, but she would never stand up to him once he started putting his hands on her. I always felt bad for her, but I always thought of what Reno wanted before what was right. After all, he was my brother, and we all knew he had his issues.

I walked out the house realizing what everybody had been trying to get through to me. My happiness is more important than somebody else's. I've been so worried about what Reno would think of me and everybody else that I forgot about myself. It's time I finally think of myself. It's time I get my man back. I pulled my phone out and called Leo.

"Ugh," I heard when the phone picked up.

"Damn, girl," I heard Leo's voice.

"Ahhhhhh," some bitch moaned.

I hung up the phone as tears ran down my face. I was officially done with Leo. I felt disrespected. He couldn't possibly remember what he told me early this morning. It was time for me to move on.

Chapter 17

Jace

I don't know what got into Amber or who got in her ear, but she finally came around, and I was actually enjoying her company. We started hanging out after I took her and her cousin home. I tried not to judge her every time I dropped her off at home, but I was feeling some kind of way that her brother had her and her folks living like that when he had mad bread.

Reno kept asking for information, but I wasn't getting much out of her. Either, she didn't know anything, or she was good at holding onto secrets. We were out one day when a phone conversation she had changed the dynamic of everything that was going on.

"Hello," she answered her phone.

We were out at a park, walking around enjoying the breeze. I had to keep readjusting my dick, because she had these tight ass shorts on and a shirt that showed off her belly. I could see a hint of a tattoo that was on her back. I'm not sure if she had a couple or just one, but it looked like the shit wrapped around her stomach. I couldn't stop taking glances at her ass. That shit was so wide and phat. I just wanted to grab it and hold onto it. That shit had me hypnotized.

"Uh-yea. Why?" she asked, taking a glance at me. "Man, are you serious?" she stopped and folding her arms while glaring at me. "Let me call you back," she said putting her phone back in her pocket. "Is there something you need to tell me?" she asked.

"Naw, why? Who was that?" I asked.

"Are you Reno's brother?" she asked.

Fuck. How the fuck did she find that shit out? There's no way I can tell her the truth, so I did what I felt I needed to do. I leaned in and kissed her like I've been wanting to since I laid eyes on her. She tried pushing me away, but I wrapped my arms around her then went down to her ass squeezing it tightly.

"Mmmmmmmmm," a moan escaped her lips.

That shit had my dick brick hard. I pushed her away.

"Look, I'm going to be honest. I had been coming around for a reason, but that's not what I'm on now. I swear, I'm feeling you," I told her.

I bitched up quick. I don't give a damn how you fucking look at me. This girl is fucking beautiful and smart. I want her worse than a fat kid who needs to lose weight to join the basketball team. Shit was that damn serious.

"Why did you lie to me?" she asked. "I heard rumors that Reno and my brother aren't speaking."

"Technically, I didn't lie. I may have led you on under false pretense, but I didn't lie," I said, kissing her neck.

"Fuck you. I don't deal with deceitful ass niggas. Take me home, Jace," she said, pushing me away and walking off.

"Amber, come on, man," I said, jogging behind her. "Ok, look, if I was on some bullshit, I could've lied about who I was, bashed you in the fucking head, and kidnapped you. I'm being real right now, and I kissed you. I don't even kiss on bit- I mean girls," I pleaded.

"Take me home, now!" she demanded.

"No," I said back.

Fuck that, she kissed me back like she wanted a nigga, and I knew she was probably in her feelings. If shorty was that damn loyal to her brother, she wouldn't have let me do that shit. She looked up at me in disbelief with her mouth open, and I grabbed her and kissed her again.

This time, I knew she wanted me. She dug her nails into my back and was moaning while I sucked on her tongue softly.

"I can't do this with you; my brother won't let me," she whispered.

"Fuck your brother," I said, not trying to be rude, but needing to make a point. "You see how he got you living? I wouldn't have you living like this."

"It's not that simple. My mom was his dad's side chick, and she doesn't work; she just collects checks and gambles," Amber said, sadly.

"But that shit makes me respect you even more, because you go a job," I said.

"This is complicated," she sighed.

"Don't worry about that shit. You just let me worry about it. Until then, just don't change on me, Amber. Honestly, I was sent to make sure Drake wasn't up to no shit for my brother. I'm not planning to hurt him," I lied.

"If you hurt me, Jace, I'll fuck you up," Amber threatened me, playing in my dreads.

"Why would I hurt your pretty ass?" I smiled at her.

Kissing on her had me horny as fuck, and the way she kissed me back let me know she felt the same. I hated that we weren't in my town, because I couldn't take her anywhere, and I didn't want to fuck with the hotels out here. That's the easiest way to get caught slipping. Fuck it, Little Rock airport was less than two hours away, so I could book a room there for the night. I walked her over to a nearby bench sitting her down on my lap.

"Spend the night with me," I whispered in her ear, as she sat on my lap scrolling through Instagram.

"What?" she laughed, "How?"

"Don't worry about that; just say yes," I told her.

"Jace, I'm only sixteen. I can't spend the night with you; my mama won't let me," she said.

She never said she didn't want to, so I came up with another plan. Shit, her gay cousin was cool, and I knew he liked me for her so I let him in on it.

"As long as I get my own room and $100," he rolled his neck, as he got in my car.

"Damn, you don't play no games," I laughed.

I pulled out my knot and peeled off $100.

"Dammit, I should've asked for two," he said.

"Here, man," I said, giving him another bill.

He did some funny ass walk up to the fucked up house with Amber and I sat in the car waiting. The lie was simple. I was their classmate, and the school had a game in Little Rock so they were going to ride with me to it, and we would go to a friend's house after. I knew my mama wouldn't go with that shit, but Amber assured me that her mama wouldn't care as long as she was out of her way. They came back out, and Amber was carrying an overnight bag. I ran my tongue across my teeth thinking about how I was going to fuck that little petite ass up.

****

"You bullshitting me, right?" I asked her.

"Why would I lie about that?" Amber softly said.

"So you want me to be your first?" I asked.

She nodded shyly. All that smart mouth she had was gone behind closed doors. Here we were, naked under the covers, and she had tensed up when I slid a finger inside of her, then confessed to being a virgin. I never fucked a virgin before, and I didn't want to hurt her, but damn, I wanted the pussy extra bad now knowing another nigga hasn't been in it.

"Don't just nod, open your mouth and say it. Say you want me to be your first, so I can believe you," I told her.

She looked up at me and pulled my head down to kiss her. Her ass was being hardheaded, but I had something for her ass. I massaged her clit and she started moaning.

"Oh, my god, that feels so good," she moaned.

I slid my finger back in her and she tensed up again.

"Tell me. Stop stalling, because I'm ready to taste you," I whispered in her ear.

She shuddered when I said that and finally said the magic words.

"I want you to be my first," she whispered.

"Relax and trust me," I told her, but she didn't relax one bit.

Her ass was jumping and shaking as I kissed my way down between her legs. I lost my virginity at twelve to a twenty-year-old substitute at my school, and I've been fucking bitches outside of my age group since. I never went down on any of them since Reno told me you only do that shit to your main bitch, but Amber was growing on me. I didn't know if she could be my main just yet, but dammit, I was about to find out if this pussy was good. I didn't want her to know I was new, so I just started freestyling. I went straight for her clit with my tongue since that got all the ladies wet.

"Ahhhh, Jace, oh my god," she moaned, clamping her legs shut around my neck.

Damn, she almost decapitated my ass with those sexy ass legs. I laughed as I loosened them up. I was feeling myself now. I went back to what I was doing, making sure to hold her legs down, and she was crying and screaming at how good it felt. I pulled back, but her moaning "don't stop" made me dive back in. Suddenly, she screamed real loud, and her legs went limp. I knew she was cumming, so I stuck two fingers in her to feel that shit. Damn, she was dripping wet, and she even tasted good in my mouth. I had to slide in her shit right now. I put a condom on and positioned myself over her.

"Is it going to hurt?" she asked me.

I looked down at my dick and smirked. Shit, I might hurt shorty for real. Every bitch I've been with struggled to take it and would run if I beat their shit up.

"I'll be gentle," I promised her.

I couldn't even get the head in before she winced in pain and cried out for me to stop.

"Look at me, Amber. Just look in my eyes and take it," I whispered, slowly sliding in while I had her attention.

She was a good girl just like I knew she would be. She scratched the fuck out of my back and held me tight until I got it all in, but once I started kissing her and fingering her clit, she was moaning in pleasure. I was trying to think of anything that was not about sex so I wouldn't bust so damn early. I wasn't inside for a good five minutes when she moaned in my ear.

"Jace, it can be yours if you want it," she moaned.

Fuck! I kissed her real hard then pulled out as I nutted early. That's how good her shit was. Fuck that, I was going to go back in for round two.

"Damn ,baby," I breathed, falling on top of her. "Shit."

****

"Boy, you going soft on me for a bitch? Not any bitch, but that fuck nigga Drake's sister?" Reno yelled.

"Man, chill the hell out, bro. I told you, she don't know shit about what he doing. I don't know who told her who I was, but she don't even know that you beefing with Drake," I lied.

She didn't know until I confirmed it, but she had an idea. Reno was my big brother, and I looked up to that nigga, but even I knew he was fucked up in the head. Especially, when he didn't take his medicine, and I would bet money he was way off it right now.

"You gone try to save the hoe, ain't you?" Reno chuckled.

"Bro, chill out," I said, not feeling him calling her a hoe.

"Bitch only known you, what? A few weeks, and she giving up the pussy she claim was untouched?" Reno laughed.

I didn't respond to him. He wasn't there; he didn't know shit. I confirmed the shit was real when I saw the blood on the sheets after I finished round two and fucked her to sleep. It made me feel some type of way that she went through that pain for me. It made me feel like, maybe I found a girl that wasn't just a throwaway to me. Fuck what Reno was talking about. I was keeping that girl for myself.

Chapter 18

Leo

"Lena, stop playing these damn games with me! You see I'm blowing your shit up so answer me back, please," I said to Lena's voicemail.

I didn't know Lena could be so cold. This was the last time I was letting my guard down for a bitch.

"Man, she not answering," I told Drake.

"The fuck you do to her?" Drake asked.

"I ain't do shit. She been tripping lately," I shook my head.

Lena giving me the cold shoulder was fucking up the plan. We already figured out that Reno had a new bitch and his attention wasn't on Nina. Plus,the twins were driving her around, so we had the perfect plan to get Nina back. The only thing was convincing them, which I thought would be easy, but Lena was on the bullshit again.

"These bitches, man," Drake laughed, balling up his fist. "They'll make a man make some dumb ass moves."

I agree to that shit. Right now, Drake and I were supposed to be in Atlanta getting this money and stunting on them niggas. Instead, we were back in Little Rock trying to check niggas and get our women back. This shit was crazy.

"Man, she gone make me go find her ass," I vented as I pressed redial.

This time, she answered the phone and was crying, so I instantly softened up.

"Lena, what's wrong?" I asked her.

"Fuck you, Leo; you are just like the rest of them," she suddenly spat.

Drake looked at me, and I took her off speakerphone and put the phone to my ear.

"Lena, what the fuck you talking about? What I do now?" I asked her.

"I heard you, Leo. I heard you. Not only were you fucking some bitch, but you answered the phone to let me hear it," she cried.

"Lena, I didn't-," I started saying then suddenly stopped and thought back.

It was a few days ago when I fucked that random bitch in the backseat of her car. I remember looking at my phone afterward and seeing that it was on my call log. I asked her about it, and she said she rejected a call. I was too drunk to investigate. That bitch hit answer instead.

"Lena, let me explain," I began.

She was silent, so I tried to think of the right words to say before I said them. She hadn't hung up the phone so that was a good sign.

"Look, Lena, I'm not perfect, and I know I fucked up, but I meant what I said to you. I swear, on everything that shit was real, Lena," I told her.

"I don't believe you," she whispered.

"Lena, I saw you with that other nigga, and it made me want revenge," I lied.

The truth was, I hadn't fucked her in a long ass time and needed to get rid of some pressure, but she didn't need to know that.

"Leo, I've never cheated on you, ever," Lena said.

That shit made my heart smile. I knew she was a good girl. She was just naive as hell when it came to her family.

"Lena, we gone get past this shit, baby, but look, I need your help with some shit. It's about Nina," I said.

I told her the whole plan, and after some convincing, I got her to agree. By the time I hung up, I had a headache.

"It's a go," I told Drake.

"About damn time. Damn, I need my girl back, so I can get back to this money," Drake said.

"Can we put this Reno nigga out of his misery now?" I asked, feeling pissed.

I blamed him for all this shit. Had he not taken Nina, I wouldn't have gotten mad at Lena for helping him, and we could be good right now. I could be deep in her guts right now. I know that's her brother, but fuck him!

"Yeah," Drake said, rolling a blunt.

I knew it would hurt him to take his childhood friend out, but shit, that's life. Sometimes, a motherfucker can be with you 24/7 and be your enemy. We sparked the blunt ,and after we got high as hell and relaxed a little, Drake said some wild shit.

"I think Candy needs to be hit, too. Shorty told me she in love with Reno the other day," Drake said.

"Fam, you tripping! That bitch could be setting us up right now!" I snapped.

"Nah, she don't want Reno to know we've been fucking. She think she can change his ass," Drake said, shaking his head.

"Still, I don't trust these hoes out here. How you know she not gaming you?" I asked.

"Shit, you never fully know, but I'm just gone sit tight and watch her ass. We still need this spot to hide at until when we get Nina," I said.

"How you know she not gone flip when she see Nina in her shit?" I asked.

"Did you not hear what the fuck I said? She in love with Reno. Shit, she gon' be happy as fuck to see I got Nina out the way," Drake said.

The shit didn't make sense to me, but fuck it. If Drake thought he knew these women, then he probably did. Who am I to say different? Once we killed the blunt, I decided to go make a few plays. I was still under the radar, because as far as I knew, Reno didn't know me. Amber hasn't been calling me back since I told her that Jace was Reno's brother. At first, I panicked, but I got word that she was at school and work, so I knew she was just dodging me. I drove down to my hometown and asked the streets first.

"Yeah, your cousin low-key, but she been fucking with that dreadhead. He broke up a fight with Ray and everything," my old partner Ant told me.

"When this happen?" I asked him.

"A few weeks ago," he said. "Shit, I seen his car at the gym a while ago."

"Bet," I told him.

I headed to the gym, and as soon as I walked in, I spotted Amber holding a book but smiling at the game going on. She didn't even look up and notice that I walked in.

"You in love or some shit?" I asked, leaning over and pulling the book out of her hands.

"Leo! You scared the hell out of me," she exclaimed jumping back some.

"I told you to watch the nigga, not fall for him," I said.

"Who says I fell for him?" she replied.

"So, what dirt do you have on him, then?" I asked her

"I don't think he has any ulterior motives, cousin," she said, sounding stupid as fuck.

"Amber, you really think this nigga just woke up one day and wanted you? You can't be that damn naïve," I angrily said.

"You don't know him. You just don't want me to be happy," she yelled.

"Get your shit, and come on," I told her, noticing that Jace had stopped hooping and was walking towards us.

"Leo, stop, I'm not off work yet," she said looking around.

I walked over to her manager and got her attention.

"Mrs. Robinson, Amber is going to work half a day today. Family emergency," I told her.

"Oh no, is everything ok?" Mrs. Robinson asked.

"It will be," I assured before walking off.

By now, Jace was trying to talk to a crying Amber as she gathered her books. I mugged the fuck out him and grabbed Amber's arm.

"Aye, man, what the fuck?! Why you grabbing on my girl and shit?" Jace yelled, jumping stupid.

Suddenly, my crew from back in the day walked up behind me, and we outnumbered Jace and his boy twelve to two.

"Your girl? Nigga, if you don't get your young ass up out my face with that bullshit. Amber, go get in the car and wait for me," I said, never taking my eyes off of Jace.

He stood, mugging me back with just as much hatred as I was giving him.

"This is my city. Take your ass back to Little Rock and don't come back in my gym little nigga," I threatened him.

"Man, fuck you! Amber, Amber!" he yelled, ignoring me.

"I'm sorry, Jace," Amber said, sadly.

I almost felt bad for a second. These two were caught up in our shit.

"What the fuck?! Amber, who is this nigga to you?" Jace said, brushing past me to walk up to her.

It took everything in me not to knock his ass out, but I didn't want to make the situation worse. We already had a plan for his brother, and now, I was thinking about adding Jace to the list. Fuck it!

Chapter 19

Reno

"Nah, baby, it's not like that. I've just been busy," I told Serenity, as I watched Nina walk around the house smiling and rubbing her growing belly.

"I guess I understand. If you need space, I can fall back," Serenity said.

"I don't want you to fall back. Just wait on me," I said.

"How is that fair to me, Reno? I have a life to live, too. I haven't seen you in almost two weeks. I miss you," she pouted.

"What else do you miss? Do you miss how I made you feel?" I asked, leaning against the wall.

Nina shot me a look that said she heard me. I didn't give a fuck; her days of getting this tongue were over since she let Drake hit.

"I do, but most of all, I miss you. I miss your vibe and your energy. I feel like we can be positive together, baby. Baby?"

I was hearing Serenity, but my attention was diverted when I saw my dad walk into my crib. All these years I've lived here, he has never come over to my place.

"Look, baby, let me call you back," I said, hanging up the phone.

I didn't give her a chance to reply before I hung up the phone and walked into the living room.

"Lena, Tena, and Jace!" he yelled.

"Pops, what's going on?" I asked, seeing the crazed look on his face.

"Daddy, what's wrong?" Lena asked Coming down the stairs.

"You and your sister stay down here with Nina. Jace and Reno, let's talk in the office. I got some shit to address," he said.

I saw Nina looking scared as shit, and for a moment, I wanted to go hug her and comfort her like I used to, but then I remembered that she was Drake's bitch, not mine. I led the way to my office, and we walked in and shut the door. I had new furniture, so no one knew about the day I fucked my office up. My pops lit a blunt and took three long puffs before he sat on the edge of the table.

"I'm only going to say this shit one time and one time only. The next time I have to hear from the streets that my sons are knee deep in some beef and kidnapping shit, I'm going to personally fuck the both of you up," he said.

We both sat in silence as he continued.

"Reno, what kind of weak ass shit you on? You brought that bitch to live with us all those years ago and you let her fuck around and get pregnant by Drake? You don't know how to check a bitch? And why the fuck is the bitch still pregnant? You should've killed that bastard and beat that hoe silly," he said.

I saw Jace look wide-eyed at what he'd just heard. He never saw this side of him before. Hell, I learned how to beat a bitch's ass from my father himself. He used to beat my mama silly.

"I'm not letting her keep that baby, and I'm not sparing Drake,either," I said.

"So, what the fuck are you doing then, because if you can't handle the shit, I can. You and I both know this is some bullshit," he said.

"I got the shit under control," I said, pulling on my ear to calm myself down.

"I regret having a weak ass son like you sometimes. You letting this hoe make you look weak out here in these streets. Break that bitch down and make her wish she never crossed you every time she sees you," he said.

"Chill out," I said, throwing my hand up to leave.

"Weak motherfucker. Just like your weak ass, crackhead mother. Jace, pack your shit. I'm getting you out of here before you pick up on his weak shit," he said to my back.

I don't even remember turning around and tackling my pops off the table. All I remember is punching him in the nose, breaking his shit instantly.

"Come on, Reno, stop it bro," Jace said, pulling me off of him.

I pushed Jace off of me and stood over my father. He wiped at the blood pouring from his nose and laughed.

"But you won't beat that pregnant bitch's ass," he laughed.

Pop! Pop! Pop!

We all stopped at the sound of gunshots. I looked at Jace who was looking at me wide-eyed. Without thinking, I grabbed my gun from under office table and my dad got off the floor and pulled out both of his pieces. We forgot all about the beef as we all realized one thing. Gunshots were fired and the girls were all downstairs.

"Ahhhhh!" I heard Lena scream.

I took off in front and ran to the stairs. There were five masked men, but they didn't see me yet. I saw one of them grabbing Nina, who was cowering in the corner.

"Nigga, put my bitch down!" I yelled.

In that split second, he looked up at me, and I saw Tena from the corner of my eye pull out her gun and shoot. Fuck! That was a dumb move! She missed, and bullets started flying everywhere. I saw her go down, but I wasn't sure if she was hit. We ran down the stairs, ducking bullets and firing back at them. One of the gunmen had Nina at gunpoint against the wall and suddenly we all stopped.

"Nigga, you already know what this is," Drake said, pulling his mask off his face.

"Bitch ass nigga, you really ran up in my shit?" I laughed in disbelief. "Over this bitch?" I asked, pointing my gun at Nina.

Drake stood in front of Nina blocking my shot. I knew I wouldn't shoot her, but I damn sure felt like shooting Drake right in the damn head.

"All of y'all shut the fuck up," my dad yelled. "Drake, you know what the fuck this is. You hurt anyone in this bitch, and you'll forever be on the run. I'm the fucking boss out here. Lena and Tena, where y'all at?"

"Over here, Daddy," Lena cried.

"Go upstairs, and don't call the police. We gon' settle this shit like real fucking G's tonight," he said to them.

Lena hadn't moved yet. She was staring at one of the masked men, and I was about to intervene until she spoke.

"Leo?" she asked.

"It's cool, baby. Just go upstairs and let us handle this," he said, not even looking at her.

Baby? Who the fuck was this nigga and how the hell did Lena know his name? I know my sister wasn't on no snake shit.

"Nigga, you the one who was talking all the shit the other day, huh?" Jace bucked.

I held him back, and the guy took his mask off and smirked at Jace.

"You already know what it is," he said.

"How the fuck you know my daughter?" my dad asked.

"Ask her," he laughed.

"Nigga, I'll shoot your fucking head off," I said, walking up on him.

"Be easy, son," my dad said, stepping in front of me. "Lena, take your ass upstairs with Tena now!" he yelled again.

Once my sisters were gone, he pointed one of his guns at the man holding Nina.

"Nigga, let her go, and get the fuck out of my son's house. All of you extra niggas get the fuck out now, or I'll pop off the next shootout, and I won't miss this time," he said, pointing the second gun at Drake.

Drake mugged him for a minute before nodding.

"Black, let her go. Ace and JJ, go get the car ready. Leo, guard me from the door," Drake said.

"You sure, fam?" Leo asked.

"Nigga, you got two seconds," I said.

"It's cool, fam," Drake said.

Once it was only us four in the room, including Nina, my Dad went and grabbed her by the arm.

"Now, it seems like this bitch right here is the reason we all got a problem. So, let's hear her talk. Nina, what do you want to do?" he asked her.

Nina was standing there like a dumb ass deer in headlights. I could see Drake getting confused, and it made me laugh. Bitch didn't even know who she wanted.

"Baby, really?" Drake asked her.

"I want you, Drake," she cried.

"Damn, it took you long enough," I laughed. "You sure you don't miss sleeping next to me at night?"

"Leave it alone, Reno. So, Nina, my son rescued your broke, rejected ass, I took you in my home, let you eat my food, didn't charge your ass a dime, and now you want to fuck his homeboy? Damn, son, I thought this little hoe was going to be different," my dad said, throwing her at Drake.

She tripped and almost fell until he caught her.

"That shit is nothing ,Pops. Nina, you mean to tell me you still want this nigga after he got Xena pregnant and let me name the baby after me. This bitch nigga didn't even step up to the plate for his own son, but you want to have his baby and shit. I mean, we all know that

Xena was a fucking hoe, but for him to let her pin the little nigga on me is some fuck shit," I said with a smirk on my face looking at Nina.

Nina's mouth dropped, and I saw Drake look at her. She looked at Drake, and I could see the hurt in her eyes. I was amused until I realized that I hadn't seen that look on her face in years. For a while, when I hurt her she didn't show any emotion. Her eyes would be blank. The look in her eyes showed pain and betrayal. It was as if he ripped her heart out of her chest. It was at that moment that I realized that Nina really didn't love me anymore. Drake really had her heart now.

"Oh shit, he didn't tell you? Damn, Drake, you was just gone lie to her, huh? At least I never lied about the shit with you, Nina," I said in my feelings.

"Drake, RJ, oh my god, RJ is your son?" Nina yelled with tears in her eyes.

"Baby, we can talk about that later? Look, just go to the car with Leo," Drake said, reaching for her.

"You asshole! I hate you!" Nina screamed at him. "I hate both of you," she added, pointing at me, too.

"I love you, too, sexy," I winked at her.

"I hate to interrupt your little soap opera bullshit, but if Nina is going to go with Drake, let that bitch go. Drake, understand you will see me again for crossing me and my son," my dad said.

They turned and walked out, and I was standing there in disbelief.

"So, that's it? What the fuck? So, we just gone let them niggas leave like that?" I asked.

"Reno, dammit son," my dad said, adjusting his nose with the dried up blood around it. "You so fucking dumb sometimes. You don't go to war over no bitch. You don't love the bitch and you know it. You want to get that nigga where it's going to hurt him; hit his pockets. You see, I've been keeping tabs on him, and I know who his new plug is, well was. Once they ride the fuck off into sunset back to Atlanta, that nigga will find out he don't and won't have a way to eat," he said.

I understood what he was saying, but shit, I still wanted to body this nigga. Fuck Drake and fuck Nina, too. He left with the twins, and Jace and I started taking shots, trying to stop myself from running out and killing Drake. I knew it was only one person who could calm me down, so I drove to Serenity's place. I guess she was waiting on me, because she was standing outside fully dressed and looking sexy. I got out and walked up to her, and she looked guilty as fuck.

"Reno, what are you doing here?" she asked.

"I need to talk to you. I need you to calm me down before I do something crazy," I told her.

"Hey, is this hoodlum bothering you?" a male voice said.

I turned around and saw some aphrodisiac motherfucker standing there looking at Serenity. It all made sense. This must be who she was waiting on. I balled my fist up and knocked the shit out of him. He fell back, and I started beating his ass. I could hear Serenity screaming for me to stop. I heard the police sirens pulling up. I heard them tell me to stop. I couldn't stop. I was in that mind frame again.

"Reno, please!" Serenity cried, as the police tackled me.

I started fighting back, and I felt the volts and shocks go through me. These motherfuckers pulled the stun gun on me. It only made me more angry, and I got one cop around the throat.

"Sir, stop resisting, stop resisting!" I heard them yell.

Pow! Pow!

"Shots fired. Suspect is down!"

"Noooo!"

Chapter 20

Nina

"Nina, stop. Calm down!" Drake said to me, bear hugging me in the backseat.

I was still kicking and trying to get free. As soon as we got in the car, I started attacking him. I couldn't believe this shit. Drake fucked Xena, too, and RJ was really his? I couldn't take this anymore. It's like everything in my life was one big nightmare. I wanted out.

"Let me go!" I screamed.

"No, Nina. Not until you calm down. Stop overreacting before you hurt my baby," he said.

He held me tighter, and I started to get physically tired from trying to fight against him. I finally gave up and started crying in his arms. The hole I felt in my heart was so big, I didn't think I could ever love again. I just couldn't forgive Drake for this one. It was just too much.

"Nina, I'm sorry, baby," he kept, whispering in my ear.

I grew numb as we dropped people off and finally drove to a hotel. I heard Drake telling Leo that he was going to put me on a plane in the morning to Georgia and go back to finish Reno. He carried me in the lobby with me straddling his waist. To onlookers, it looked like I was hugging on my man, probably about to go have rough ass sex. My face was cradled in Drake's neck, and I was crying. Once we got on the elevator, he put me down and backed me against the wall.

"Nina, please stop crying. I love you, Nina. That was the old me, but I'm different now," Drake begged me.

I didn't respond; I just looked at him through tear-stained eyes. As we walked to the hotel room, I thought of what I really wanted in my life. Could I really depend on the men around me? I zoned out as Drake stripped my body nude and walked me into the bathroom. I stood and watched him run me a bubble bath. I cried again as I looked at him. This was supposed to be my knight in shining armor. I was supposed to be in my happily ever after stage right now.

"Come here, baby," Drake said to me.

I walked over defeated, and he helped me get into the bubble bath. He washed my body and kissed all over my tear-stained face. I saw the regret in his eyes and wanted to hug him and say it was ok, but what Reno said stuck in my head. Was Drake really going to keep this from me? I thought we told each other everything, so why would he not tell me this? I just didn't know who to trust anymore. Drake pulled me from the bath and wrapped my body in a towel before letting the water out.

"You ready to talk?" he asked me.

I shook my head no, and he sighed. He picked me up and carried me to the bed, and the next thing I knew, he was kissing his way down my body. I tried to fight him, but ultimately, my body lost to him. He slid his fingers inside of me and sucked my clit between his lips.

"Oh, god," I whispered, as I rode the waves of pleasure he gave me.

He got me right to my peak, then slid into me in one stroke. I moaned out loud, and he covered my mouth with his and gave me deep and slow strokes.

"I'm sorry," he kept whispering in my ear.

I lost count of how many times I came. All I know is, I closed my eyes and fell asleep with him still stroking me. Hours later, I woke up in the dark room with Drake holding me close to him. I remembered everything that happened, and I started crying again. I slid out of bed and dressed in the clothes I came in. When I looked back at Drake, he was watching me.

"I need some ice," I said.

"I'll go get it," he said.

"No, baby; it's just down the hall," I said, grabbing the ice bucket.

"Ok, well when you get back, let me give you a massage," he offered.

I smiled weakly and walked out the room. Once I was gone, I jogged to the elevators and hurriedly pressed the buttons. I decided that I didn't want to be with Drake right now. I was going to catch a ride to my mama's house for advice. Once the elevator dinged, I got on, and it closed just in time for me to see Drake walk out the room and look at me. *Oh, shit!*

I was frantic as it made it to the bottom, but I relaxed once I knew that I would make it before Drake made it to me. As soon as I got to the lobby, I saw a few people, but an older man stood out to me. I couldn't place his face, but he looked familiar to me. Maybe he was from my old neighborhood or something. He seemed to be looking for someone, but right now, I needed him.

"Excuse me, sir, I need help," I said, running up to him.

"What's wrong, ma'am?" he asked me in a caring voice.

"I need a ride to my mom's house, but I lost my wallet. I will pay you if you take me; it's not far from here," I told him.

"Are you running from someone?" he asked me.

"Yes," I whispered.

He grabbed my hand, and we hurried out of the lobby.

"Nina!" I heard Drake call for me, and I froze in fear, but the man pulled me along. As we walked to the parking lot, my heart suddenly dropped. I tried to turn back, but a gun was pointed at me as he approached me.

"Bitch, scream, and I will kill you," he said.

He picked me up and threw me in the backseat of an SUV.

"Nina! Nina!" I heard Drake scream.

Why did I leave? Why couldn't I just stay in the room with Drake? Now, there I was, being kidnapped again, this time by Reno's father.

"So what, you were about to leave Drake and fuck with my old head now?" Reno's father asked, cracking up.

It was then that I noticed that the old man was the gardener for Drake's father. How could I have not recognized him? I lay back in the seat, and I gave up for real this time. I wasn't even free 24 hours, and there I was being taken away again. I know I was mad at Drake, but I still wanted him. That man was my heartbeat, and I loved him to death.

"Why are you doing this to me?" I asked when I got tired of crying.

"Because you influenced my son in the wrong way, and I'll be damned if I let you get away with it," he told me.

"I did nothing to Reno," I said.

"You called the police on him that day. You let them fucking doctors convince my son that he was crazy and shit. Before you came along, he never was this weak," he said.

I sat there and thought about the time he just spoke of.

****

Reno and I had just come from a party. He was so drunk that I had to carry him into the house. He couldn't walk straight without falling. Carrying his big ass wasn't fun at all, but I was happy to be bringing my baby home with me. The second we stepped foot inside, he threw up right in the foyer.

I walked him upstairs, took his clothes off, and put him in the bed. He was knocked out snoring. I didn't even change out of my dress. I went back downstairs and cleaned his mess up. I was in the middle of cleaning it up when my phone rang. I went in my clutch that I left by the door and took my phone out. I could see that it was a number I didn't recognize.

"Hello," I answered.

"Where is our boo?" a female asked.

I heard laughing in the background, so I knew it was one of Reno's bitches playing on my phone.

"And who might that be?" I asked.

"Don't play dumb, boo? Everybody know that's community dick," she said.

"Listen here, bitch. I don't give a fuck what Reno does outside of this house. I do know one thing, though. I have his heart, and he comes home to me every night. All you bitches get is a little bit of his time and some money thrown at you. I don't give a fuck about you calling my phone with this bullshit. I know what's up, so try again, boo," I told her, wiping my face.

I was so sick of doing this with his bitches. I'm bold over the phone, but my heart breaks every time they call me. He knew I was fragile. He knew what I had been through in my life, yet he's another person taking advantage of my heart. I had nowhere to go, though, so I depended on him.

"You may have his heart, but I have that dick on lock. So tell me. How does my pussy taste?" she said laughing.

"I could ask you the same thing," I said.

I could hear her breathe in to reply, but I was knocked upside my head out of nowhere. My phone flew from my hand, hitting the floor shattering. I fell to the floor right in the rest of Reno's mess. Reno looked down at me with the most evil set of eyes I had ever seen in my life. I didn't even recognize him.

"Reno, baby," I started saying.

Reno bent down and picked me up by my throat. I tried prying his hand away, but he landed a mean blow to my mouth causing blood to fly from my mouth. I was dazed some, but I knew what was happening.

"So, you being sneaky, huh, bitch?" he asked through gritted teeth.

"What are you talking about?" I managed to get out through my bloody mouth.

"You in my house talking to another nigga? What? I don't treat you good enough? Do I not give you enough money, put you in the best clothes, have you driving the best cars?" he asked.

All I could do was nod my head. I was trying to keep from swallowing the blood, but I knew if I spit it out, and it got on Reno, he would get even madder.

"I picked your ass up off the streets and this is how you repay me?" he asked.

His eyes were so dark, I didn't know who he was. This wasn't my Reno. I did what I knew would keep him at bay if I could get away. I kicked him in his dick, then he dropped me immediately. I ran to the bathroom, closing the door, and locking it. They had emergency phones throughout the house. I had grabbed one on the way to the bathroom and called 911.

When the cops came, it was hard watching them escort Reno off the property. I hated that I had to call them, but I didn't know what else to do. When Reno's father came downstairs and saw what was happening, he was pissed. He cussed out every officer that was there and then cussed me out once they left.

"You stupid, bitch. Now you done started some shit," he said, before disappearing back into his room.

I didn't understand what he meant by that. I had cried myself to sleep not knowing what was to come. I had just found out I was pregnant.

When Reno finally came home, things had changed. Reno was so mad at what happened that he beat the damn baby out of me and didn't even know it. I later found out that his parents knew all about his condition, but his father refused to believe that Reno was that way. He wouldn't let him take his medicine so that he could be ok. I used to sneak and give them to him without him or anyone knowing. I was the one who suggested counseling. He was against it at first but realized that he needed it.

****

I knew it was a fight I couldn't win, so I gave up. Reno's father always openly spoke against our therapy sessions. A few times, he tried to blame me, but Reno would always curse him out, and we would leave. Eventually, our trips to his father's house became rare, and when I did come with him, it was times that his father wasn't there. We drove for what felt like hours before we pulled up to a normal-looking house in a country town.

"Tie her up and take her around the back, and into the house," I heard Reno's father say to a group of men who approached the SUV.

My heart dropped, and I instantly started kicking and screaming. I was punched in the mouth and then my mouth was duct taped. I felt blood filling my mouth, and I had no choice but to swallow it. It started pouring down raining as they hog tied me and placed a sheet over me. I cried, expecting to be killed as they carried me to my fate. We went into the house, past an older looking woman smoking a cigarette, and into a back room. My body was thrown on the floor, and I feared for my baby. I hoped I didn't hurt him or her. The men untied me and snatched the tape from my mouth before unlocking the many locks on the closet the door. Once the door was opened, I was shocked to see another woman inside. She was standing in alarm and was looking afraid. I looked her over and wondered who she could be. She had a very light complexion, and she looked so familiar to me. I could tell that she was being fed and her clothes looked old, but not extremely old.

"Go in the fucking closet," they said, pushing me in.

Once they closed the door, it was pitch black, and I started to cry again. It wasn't until we knew they were gone that the woman spoke to her.

"Are you Nina?" she asked me.

"Yes," I said through tears.

"I heard them talking about you. You were Reno's girlfriend, right?" she asked.

"Yes," I mumbled.

"I'm his mother," she revealed.

My heart nearly stopped. She couldn't be! Reno's mother was dead.

Chapter 21

Lena

"I'm not a traitor!" I cried.

"Shut up! Shut up right now! How long have you been fucking Drake's cousin?" my father asked me.

"I'm not telling," I said folding my arms and looking away.

The tears were falling down my face at rapid speed. Daddy had been yelling ever since they left the house. He had us all in the living room sitting there wondering what the hell was his issue.

"The fuck you mean? What did we teach yall?" he had the nerve to ask.

I rolled my eyes.

"See, that's the thing. We're not kids anymore. We're grown. It's time we live our own damn lives. None of us have been in a decent damn relationship besides Reno, because of what you taught us. Loyalty and family coming first had damn near ruined my life. I'm not telling you a damn thing about him. All my life I've done whatever you wanted me to. I've gone out of my way to prove to you that I'm all about family. Not anymore, starting today. You're on your own. I'm living for me now. I found someone who loves me for me and not what I have between my legs," I told him before getting up and walking away.

"I don't know how I ended up with the weakest kids ever. Family is the most important thing to anybody. All that other shit will come later. We're about family and money," I heard him say.

"We're the most dysfunctional family ever so whatever you're talking about doesn't even matter," I said walking up the steps.

I headed straight to my room. I knew what everyone had been trying to tell me. Even though Leo and I hit a little rough patch and have been going back and forth, he's the first man I knew I actually wanted to be with officially. He has done nothing but show me the utmost respect. He loves me like no other. Hell, he loves me better than my own father.

I lay across the bed after grabbing my phone. I went through it for a while trying to gather the courage to call Leo. I needed to find the right words to let him know that I chose him and always will choose him. I was dialing his number when I heard clapping out of nowhere. I looked up to see Tena standing there looking silly.

"What the hell are you clapping for?" I asked sitting up.

"It's about damn time," she said.

"About damn time, for what?" I asked.

"You finally stood up to Daddy, hell for yourself. It's about damn time. I've been waiting on this moment for years. I don't think it came at a better time. You better work," she said laughing.

"Shut the hell up. I realized that I couldn't keep doing that shit forever. It's time I live my life for me and nobody else. I love Leo even if we aren't speaking right now. I just need him to know that I choose him and that I'll never choose Reno or anybody else ever again," I said.

"I feel you. You inspired me to do the same," she said pulling out her phone.

"What the hell are you doing?" I asked.

She didn't respond right away. Seeing her phone made me think about mine. As soon as I looked down at it, I saw that a phone call was ending. I went to the call log and saw that I actually dialed Leo's number. I wasn't sure if I wanted to be mad that he hung up the phone or happy he heard what I said.

"Hello," I heard a female's voice causing me to look up Tena.

"Listen, I love you, and I want you to be mine. I'm not taking no for an answer. You know you love me, too. I don't care about the shit you've been talking about. That nigga don't love you back, and you know it. He couldn't care less about your ass. You spend more time with me, anyway. If you didn't feel anything for me, then you wouldn't let me love on you the way that I do. I can tell you feel the same way about me as I do you. I'm tired of trying to hide my feelings or us, so let's go ahead and make it official," Tena said.

I sat there with my mouth open. I've never known Tena to ever keep a girl or confess her love to one. This right here is some new shit, but I was happy that we were both finally going after what we wanted. I could see the struggle within her day in and out. We were so worried about pleasing Reno and Daddy. Tena wasn't as bad as me, but she had her ways of doing what they asked.

The female sighed. "T, you know that what we have isn't right. It was never supposed to be like this," she said.

"Candy, I don't want to hear that bullshit. You and I both know that you want me just as bad as I want you. I can feel it, and I know you can, too. Stop fronting. Reno doesn't want your ass. He has his own problems that he's dealing with," Tena said.

My mouth dropped again when I heard that. Tena was bold as hell, but I didn't think she was that damn bold to steal a girl right from under Reno's nose. Crazy thing is, she's right. He wouldn't give a damn no way. No one other than Nina ever mattered to Reno. Whoever this chick is got another thing coming if she thinks she can get Reno for herself.

"T, I can't. You know I'm in love with him. It wouldn't be right," she said.

"You sound stupid as hell right now. Reno doesn't give a fuck about you. I'm the one who's been there every time he's fucked you over. Just let that shit go and be with me," Tena said, sounding like she was begging.

119

I could see her heart crying. It was written all over her face that she was hoping this girl gives in, but for some reason, I could tell that she wasn't.

"Hello," Tena said.

"Look, I do love you, but I just can't. I'm sorry," she said before hanging up.

Tena didn't take the phone away from her face right away. She just stood there looking out into space for a minute. Then, all of a sudden, her eyes shifted to me. I got up, walked over to her, and hugged her. I could see the fight leaving her body. I felt bad for her. We stood there embracing causing me to think back to a time when Tena thought she was in love before.

****

"Man, Le, you gotta meet this chick I've been dealing with. She's all that and some, and she got some fire ass pussy," Tena said, busting into my room.

Lately, she had been leaving me to walk home from school by myself. I didn't know what the hell was going on, and she wasn't trying to tell me, either. Tena could be so secretive sometimes.

"Who is she?" I asked, looking up from my homework.

"Her name is Remy," she said looking off.

"Ok, where you meet this one?" I asked.

Tena had a habit of meeting females and not dealing with them for too long before tossing them to the side. She would tell me I needed to meet them, and I never would because something would happen, and she would be done with them before I could even remember their name.

"She's outside right now. Come meet her," Tena said, excitedly.

"She's outside right now?" I asked with my eyes raised. "Girl, are you crazy? You know Daddy will have a fit if he sees her in front of the house," I said.

"I ain't worried about all that. Look, I've been dealing with this girl for a long time. I think she's the one," Tena said all happy and shit.

"Wow. Seriously? How long have y'all been dealing with one another?" I asked, getting up and following her outside.

"For a hot minute," was all she said as she led the way.

As soon as we stepped outside, we saw Reno leaning into a window of a car.

"The fuck?" I heard Tena ask.

She stormed over to the car. I stood in that spot and watched what was about to go down.

"How the fuck you know my girl?" Tena asked Reno.

Reno stood up and looked at Tena before laughing.

"Your girl? T, she a hoe. I done fucked her plenty of times, and so has my niggas. If she your girl, then you wifin' a hoe," Reno said laughing.

I looked at the girl who had embarrassment written all over her face. Tena stood there with a 'What the fuck' face. I couldn't believe what was going on.

"I'm sorry, Tena. I didn't want you to find out like this," the girl said.

"Damn, was you feeling shorty that bad?" Reno asked, amusingly.

"This is some bullshit. Get the fuck away from my house, bitch. Don't ever call me, text me, tweet me, DM me, none of that shit. Fuck you, bitch," Tena said, walking off.

"Damn, sis, my bad," Reno called out after her.

I watched as Tena ran past me back into the house. I turned back around to see that neither Reno or the girl cared that they'd just fucked over Tena. They just kept talking, then he eventually took her to the guest house where I'm sure he fucked her then sent her on her way. I walked back into the house to go check on Tena, but when I got to her room, she had locked her door.

****

For days, Tena wasn't herself. Once she got out of her funk, she had sworn love off. Even though it wasn't that long ago, it's still a little surprising watching her confess her love to yet another woman Reno already has caught up in his web. It's like they have the same taste in women or something. I felt horrible, but I knew she would bounce back from this like she's done everything else.

I watched as she quietly left out the room. I laid back down and debated on whether I should call Leo back or wait on his call. I don't know how long I was laying there, but my phone started ringing scaring the hell out of me. I picked it up and saw that it was Leo. I smiled before answering.

"Hello," I answered.

"Meet up with me," he said.

Chapter 22

Drake

Seeing Nina again with her big belly made my heart smile. She was wearing her pregnancy well. She didn't look like she was gaining much weight, but I could see that she'd gotten a little thicker in the thighs, wider in the hips, and her ass was a lot fatter. I was happy as hell to see my girl, but mad as fuck I had to go through all this shit to get her.

The fact that Reno's father let us go wasn't surprising. He thinks he's smart as hell, but he's really dumb as fuck. He always thought he was the shit out in the streets, but in reality, he only had shit on lock because he had the best product in town. A lot of people didn't like fucking with him, because he was fucking crazy. See, Reno's father has told Reno that he got his bipolar condition from his mother, but he's been in denial for forever. Reno gets it from him. His mother was perfectly normal. He never wanted anyone to know, but I did. Reno doesn't even know that information. He went to high school with my moms, and she knew all about his condition since she was a student worker in the office.

Watching Nina's face as Reno told her the truth about RJ damn near broke my heart. Even though I have known for years, I wasn't going to continue to deny my son. I was mad as hell that she found out that way, but it was out there now, and there wasn't shit I could do about it. I think she was madder at the fact that I slept with someone who was once her friend, rather than the fact that RJ was my son. I know she's going to continue to love him regardless of who his father is.

I swear, Nina could be so damn stupid sometimes, but I loved her too much to say anything. I was happy to have her in my arms again until her ass decided to leave. Running after her was like running after a child sometimes. I understood why she did what she did, but she should've known that it wasn't such a bright fucking idea to do it at that moment. Watching her get taken away again hurt me even more than the first time. I'm actually scared this time. I never saw Reno as a threat, but his father, on the other hand, was another story. I wasn't 100 percent sure, but I recognized his voice. Plus, my gut feeling was telling me that the man who grabbed Nina was Reno's father. I stood in shock as they drove off. I real-deal bitched up and felt like my heart was ripped out of my chest. I was too drained to give chase to the truck.

"Sir, do you want me to call 911?" a woman in the parking lot asked me.

"No," I sighed and turned around.

I had to get back to the room and get my phone, wallet, and gun. Once I had all the shit I needed, I left and went in search of Reno. I knew he had something to do with this, and I wasn't about to sit around waiting for some phone call. When I pulled up to his spot, I was surprised that the door was unlocked. Thinking it could be a trap, I pulled my gun out and walked in. I cleared the living room and kitchen, and just when I was about to give up, I heard movement. I looked up to where I heard it again and aimed my gun at the shapely figure in the dark.

"Please sir, don't shoot me, please," a sweet voice cried out.

"Who's up there with you?" I asked her.

"It's just me; I swear on my life," she frantically explained.

"Where the fuck is Reno?" I yelled.

"He's still in jail. He sent me here," she nervously explained.

"Come down here," I said, not believing shit she said.

Reno was just here hours ago. She was a ball of tears, as she walked down the stairs and up to me. I couldn't help but look her over. She was breathtaking, and she seemed sweet. She wasn't Reno's type at all. I looked closer and realized she was the girl with him in the club. I grabbed her when she got close enough and pulled her towards me.

"If I find out you're lying to me, I'll blow your fucking brains out, bitch," I said.

She was nervous and crying, but I didn't give a fuck. Right now, Nina was missing, and I would lay anybody down to get her back. I walked through the entire house, and just like she said, it was empty. I went back to the living room and made her sit down with the gun still pointed at her.

"Why the fuck is Reno locked up?" I asked.

"I, he, please sir, can you not point that at me?" she cried.

"Nah, now hurry up and tell me before I get mad," I said.

"He beat up my ex, and the police were called. He kept resisting and they finally shot him," she said.

"So what, you here robbing him or some shit?" I laughed.

"No, he got a bail, and he needed me to come get the money," she explained.

"Well, let's go bail this crazy motherfucker out. You got the money?" I asked her.

She nodded and pulled it from her clutch. Shit still wasn't adding up to me, and right when I was about to kidnap her for revenge, she said something that changed everything.

"I'm on your side, Drake," she whispered.

I looked at her with a raised eyebrow. I didn't take her for the hoe type.

"What? You trying to fuck or something?" I asked.

She drew up her face as if I offended her to the highest degree and shook her head. "Tamara, Nina's cousin, is my friend from college. She told me about this situation with Reno taking Nina from you, and she hired me. My mother is Reno's therapist, and my job was simple. Get Reno to fall for me and take his attention off Nina," she said.

"So, you're one of them bitches who get paid to set niggas up?" I asked, not feeling the thought but feeling relief that she was at least in my corner.

"First of all, I'm not a bitch, and secondly, no. I wouldn't agree until she told me about how much Nina loves you and how afraid she is of Reno. I'm here for Nina, and unfortunately, you too," she said, looking me up and down in disgust.

"Let's go bail him out and find Nina. She got taken again, and I know he was behind that shit," I said, grabbing her by her arm and pulling her up.

"Wait a minute. When did she get taken again?" she asked looking me.

"An hour ago, if that," I said.

"Reno's been locked up at least 4 hours. He couldn't have taken her," she said.

"Man, I know how his ass works. He never wants to be outdone. He got somebody to snatch her again," I said, getting mad all over again.

All I could think was that Nina was somewhere not being fed and being beaten with my baby inside of her. Just thinking about the what-if when it came to my baby was making my blood boil.

"Fuck! I'll murder all of them," I vented.

"Please, Drake, calm down. I can help you, but you cannot act off pure rage or we will lose this war. I have a plan," she told me.

As we drove down to bail Reno's crazy ass out, she told me her plan. I wasn't too sure if I should trust her just yet, but I had no other choice. We pulled up to the jail, and I watched as she got out and headed inside. I sat there thinking about everything that was going on. If I didn't love Nina so much, I damn sure wouldn't be going through this shit right now. As soon as Reno walked out and saw me, he started talking shit.

"I know damn well you didn't bring this bitch nigga with you," Reno yelled walking up on me.

"Nigga, how you think she got here? You stay needing me to help you with your shit, you dumb motherfucker," I yelled not backing down.

"No, no, stop it. Reno, baby, calm down. Look at me," Serenity said running to stand between us.

"So what, you fucking this nigga or something? How you know him? Man, watch out," Reno said, trying to push around her.

"Calm your crazy ass down and listen to her," I said, walking away and getting in the car.

I watched her calm his wild ass down in seconds. Whatever hold she had over him, it was deep, because Reno's crazy ass grabbed her and started kissing her. Damn, she was good at whatever she did. By the time they got inside the car, Reno's whole vibe was different. I was halfway down the street before he spoke again.

"So Nina is gone again?" he asked me.

I glared at him through the rearview mirror. What kind of game was he playing? I knew for a fact he was involved.

"Yeah, and I'm positive your pops took her," I replied, forcing myself to stay calm.

"Hell nah, nigga you seeing shit. She probably got took by another nigga she was fucking behind my back since she was already fucking my so-called boy and shit," Reno chuckled.

"Reno, baby, stop that," Serenity said, grabbing his chin and making him look at her.

I'll be damned if he didn't stop and soften up.

"You better get your pops before I do, nigga," I simply said.

"Yo, make a U-turn at this light," Reno said.

"What?" I said.

"Just do it, damn. We gotta drop Serenity off," he said.

"No, baby, I drove to your house," she said.

"So, how the hell you end up with Drake?" Reno asked, looking at her like she was crazy.

"Cause I came over about to start another war thinking you had Nina again," I told him.

"Look, man, I don't know where the fuck that bitch-," he was saying.

"Reno," Serenity butted in.

"My bad, I don't know where Nina is. But shit we can both head to my pops' place, cause I wanna know why the fuck he got her, too," Reno said.

"Yeah, that's exactly what the fuck we gone do," I said.

"Stop flexing, nigga," Reno said.

"Fuck you," I said.

"Nah, go fuck Nina, nigga," he said.

I gripped the steering wheel trying not to pull over and jaw his ass. This shit was taking all of my patience, but I needed Nina back. Once we got to Reno's place, I called Leo and filled him in.

"Man, don't trust that snake ass nigga. I'm following you over there with my people. This could be a set-up," Leo said.

"Good looking, fam," I said before hanging up.

After Reno watched Serenity pull off, he went into the house and came back with two guns and two blunts already rolled up. He got on the passenger's side and looked around the car for a minute.

"What?" I asked.

"Damn, I ain't know you were still fucking Candy," he laughed.

Chapter 23

Reno

"Man, I know you ain't call this nigga?" I said, sizing his ass up as he walked up on us.

I watched the nigga my sister was fucking with walk up on the car and damn near snapped.

"Right now is not the time! I'm not trying to hear this shit," Drake said in anger.

"Nigga, fuck you, too," I said.

"What up, fam?" this nigga said, sliding in the backseat.

He mugged me the same way I was mugging him, and I was tempted to punch him in his shit.

"Is there a fucking problem?" he asked me looking me up and down.

"Hell, yeah, it's a fucking problem! How long you been fucking my sister?" I asked him.

He just gave me a sly smile that made me mad even more, while patting Drake on his shoulder.

"Hey, D, you better check your mans," he said.

"Drake ain't gotta check shit!" I bucked at him.

"Man, both of y'all chill the fuck out. Let's not forget Nina is still missing. Reno, call your pops and tell him we on the way right fucking now!" Drake said.

"Soft ass," I mumbled, feeling salty at how he was acting about this Nina situation.

Seeing her look at him how she did back at the house fucked with my head, too. She never looked at me like that. I didn't think the bitch had it in her. I shook those thoughts out of my head. Besides, Serenity was a badder bitch in my opinion. I chiefed on a blunt the whole ride to my pops' mansion. We parked up the street, and I called Jace to get my access.

"What's up, bro?" Jace asked, answering the phone.

"Unlock the gate and door, and don't say shit," I said.

"Cool, I got you," he said.

We heard the gate buzz and watched as it opened. I guess this nigga Drake was really in his feelings because this nigga didn't even wait until the gate was fully open before he took off up the driveway. We all hopped out quick and jogged towards the house. It was quiet when we walked in, but I knew the twins were wide awake. They never went to sleep until around two am.

"Where Pops?" I asked Jace.

"I don't know. He left with Jasper, and we haven't heard from him since," Jace said.

"Leo?" Lena asked, from upstairs in the dark.

"Damn, you got night vision or some shit? And shut the hell up before you wake her up," I said, referring to Michelle.

Lena and Tena both approached us and Lena and Leo had this long staredown.

"Leo, was I just a pawn in your game?" Lena asked.

"Lena, baby, you know better than that," Leo said, on some real playa sounding shit.

"Man, cut that shit out. Lena, we not here about you; we're looking for Nina," I said.

"What do you mean? Drake, didn't you run in my brothers shit guns blazing and take Nina back? What? You lost her again already?" Tena asked.

"Your bitch ass pops took her!" Drake yelled.

"Nigga, yell at my sister, again, and see what happen?" I jumped in.

"What's up? I'm tired of your ass, anyways," Drake replied, walking up.

Leo stepped in between the both of us and stopped us.

"This shit not solving nothing, and Nina is still missing," he said too calm for me.

I reluctantly backed down, because he had a point. It was strange that my pops was out, because he never was the type to be in the streets late at night. He had too much to lose.

"Where is RJ?" I asked them.

"Michelle put him to sleep hours ago. He's been asking about you," Lena said.

I had too much going on so I left my son here, but now I wasn't feeling him being over here. I went up the stairs without saying another word and walked into the room where RJ was sleeping. I shook him awake and he lit up.

"Daddy!" he cheered.

"Come on little man, you're coming with me," I said.

"Yay! Is mommy here too?" he asked.

"Nah," I replied picking him up.

Ever since I put Xena in Drake's mama's house, I hadn't heard a thing from the silly bitch. I started packing RJ's clothes and we went back downstairs.

"Drake!" RJ cheered.

I instantly felt anger as I sat back and looked at the two of them. I never noticed how fucking identical to each other they were. Even though he looks so much like Xena, now that I know the truth, I can see the resemblance. This whole situation was fucked up, and I felt myself about to flip the fuck out, but I reminded myself that RJ was there.

"We out. Once Pops shows up, call me," I told Jace.

"I got you, bro," he told me.

Once we got back in the car Drake was driving, I sat in the backseat with RJ. He was talking about some shit at school, but I was thinking about some deeper shit. How much could I trust Drake? His whole fucking existence around me was questionable as fuck. Here I am sitting next to my son that really is his son, riding in a car of a bitch I fucked first but Drake came behind me to fuck. Now we're discussing how to find Nina, the woman I used to claim as my main bitch, who is Drake's bitch now. Maybe, Drake was a wolf in sheep's clothing this whole time. This shit wasn't looking too good, no matter how you put it. We pulled up at my house, and I told Drake to follow me inside. He stayed downstairs while I put RJ to sleep.

"Hey, where's a bathroom? I gotta piss," Leo asked, when I came back downstairs.

I didn't even know he walked in. My mind got to plotting before I answered him.

"Yeah, I got one down here," I said, leading him to the downstairs bathroom.

I remembered thinking it was stupid to have a bathroom that locked from the outside when I first got this place, but now, it came in handy. I locked Leo in, pulled out my gun, and walked up on Drake who was looking down at his phone texting. He didn't know what hit him as I rushed him against the wall and put the barrel to his temple.

"Give me one good fucking reason why I shouldn't blow your brains out? Nigga, you been plotting on me since day one!" I said through gritted teeth.

Chapter 24

Leo

I was washing my hands when I heard this big ass bang. I turned the doorknob, and that shit wouldn't turn. What the fuck? I started banging on the door, and then it hit me. Reno's bitch ass locked me in the bathroom. How the hell was I caught slipping this damn hard? I knew he tried to off Drake before, but since Drake was so trustworthy of him this time around, I thought why not. Now, my cousin could be in danger, and I'm stuck in the damn bathroom. I started kicking at the door, but it wouldn't give way, so I gave up and pulled out my gun. I shot a hole through the door near the handle and kicked in an even bigger hole. Who the fuck has wooden doors in a big ass house anyways? I cut my damn leg pulling it out of the hole, but I got the door unlocked. I rushed out and saw Reno and Drake on the floor struggling to reach a gun. I ran up and kicked the gun away and pointed mine at Reno.

"Nigga, don't make me do it," I threatened Reno.

I broke them up and stood between them.

"You still plotting? You locked me in the fucking bathroom and out here trying to kill my fucking cousin? Man, let me off this snake nigga once and for all, Drake," I said.

"You too pussy to shoot me," Reno said snidely.

"Ask your sister if I'm pussy when I'm knee deep in hers," I shot back.

"Nigga, I'll-," Reno started saying.

I knew what I said would get to him, because he tried to run up on me, but Drake held him back. I laughed at how mad he got knowing that he couldn't take me on his worst day. I grew up boxing, and my record was undefeated.

"Fuck you trying to off me for nigga?" Drake asked Reno, still maintaining his hold.

"Nigga, you a straight sellout. You wanna be me so bad you gotta fuck all my bitches and copy my ways?" Reno yelled.

"You got me fucked up," Drake said, letting him go and squared up again.

They started fighting blow for blow, and I lit up a blunt and let them. Sometimes, niggas just have to fight it out. After I had felt like they made their point, I broke it up.

"Alright, so are yall gone fight all night or are we gone come up with a plan?" I asked them.

Reno nodded and said some crazy shit. "If I find out my Pops is behind this shit, let me murk him. This shit been a long time coming," Reno said.

"Reno, you know if you touch your pops, his whole empire will come after you," Drake said.

"Fuck that. I still feel like he behind the shit with my moms, and I been hating the nigga since. This the last straw for him," Reno vented.

"Just calm down; we gon' set this shit up right. You remember that white boy Alex? We can have him trail your pops and put bugs in the house. Have him go by when the twins are there alone or some shit and say he's checking the internet connections or some shit," I said.

"Yeah, I know of dude. He like a computer nerd or something," Reno nodded.

Just like that, we got to setting shit up, and for the moment, our personal beef was dead. I left with Drake and called Lena. My phone had twenty missed calls from her.

"Leo, this is crazy. All of this drama is going on and Nina is gone again, and-," she was saying.

"Lena," I simply said making her shut up.

"Yes," she said, sniffling tears.

"Marry me," I said.

I heard her burst into tears, and Drake damn near slammed on the brakes as he jerked his head to look at me.

"Look, Lena, life is too short, and the shit that's going on is showing me that it can be a lot shorter. Let's do this baby. I just left your brother's house, and he's cool with it," I lied.

Drake laughed and shook his head at me. Yeah, a nigga was lying, but I wasn't gaming. I wanted Lena bad. Real bad.

"Say something, baby," I said, when she stayed silent for too long.

"Leo?" Tena's voice said into the phone, "Did your hood ass just propose to this girl over the phone with no ring? Come harder if you want my sister." With that, the phone hung up, and my heart started racing.

"I gotta get a ring fast," I told Drake.

"Fam, you real wild. I thought you didn't like Reno," he asked me.

"I don't like that fuck nigga, but I love his sister," I said.

"Man, shit is getting crazier and crazier, but shit, if you need a ring, I know a guy. I'll take you to him after this bullshit blows over," Drake said.

We made it back to Candy's place, and shit got even weirder. That Xena bitch was sitting at the kitchen table looking all cracked out and shit, and Candy had an attitude.

"What?" Drake asked Candy.

"Drake, you are an asshole. You have a son you don't claim, and you put your baby mama out on the street?" Candy asked.

"What? Man, both of you miss me with that shit. Xena, you fucking crazy for lying and trying to start some shit, and Candy, you're crazy for believing the shit. I'm going to sleep," Drake said, walking to Candy's bedroom.

Candy smirked as her eyes roamed my body, but I wasn't paying her ass any mind. Drake walked back out with an attitude.

"Bitch, what the fuck?! You packed all my shit?!" Drake yelled.

"I need the keys to my car and house please, you man beater!" she yelled.

Drake threw the keys at her and went to grab his bags. Candy just poured herself a glass of wine while Xena walked out with her head down. I went outside behind her to curse her ass out when she reached up and covered my mouth.

"Ssssh! Just follow me down the street and chill please. I have a plan," she said.

Drake walked out going off, but I motioned for him to be quiet. We walked up to a Honda Accord, and Xena unlocked the doors and let us inside.

"Xena, I'll break your fucking neck! What kind of shit is that?" Drake yelled.

"Candy was plotting on you. I went to get my hair done, and she happened to be there. I overheard her saying how you get money, and she was going to trap you with a baby, so I showed her RJ and told her bad things so she would leave you alone. Fuck, Candy, I have a plan to get Nina back, and I know who has her," Xena said.

"Who has her then?" I asked, getting tired of the extra shit going on.

"Reno's dad," she said.

"See! I knew I wasn't fucking crazy!" Drake snapped.

"It's a set-up. He knows that she is the reason that Reno is going to therapy, and he's never liked Nina. She told me this back when we were still friends. He wants to kill her off in hopes that you and Reno will link back up," Xena explained.

"So, how the fuck do you know all of this shit?" I asked Xena, as she lit up a blunt.

"If you would shut the hell up, I can finish the story," Xena snapped on me.

I waved her off and hit the blunt when she passed it to me.

"His dad is fucking my homegirl. I put her on him and told her to milk his pockets, but I didn't know she would milk his mind, too. He pillow talks like a motherfucker, and she turns around and tells me everything. The only downfall is I don't know where he's holding her," Xena said.

"Fuck it, I say we kidnap that nigga and flip the script," I said, ashing my blunt.

"And, then what? He might have some niggas holding Nina. Man, fuck! They got my future wife and shit. I swear to God if anything happens to Nina and my baby, I'm going to lose my shit," Drake snapped, punching the dashboard.

"Don't worry fam we gone get her back."

Chapter 25

Nina

"So you've been held captive here all these years?" I asked Reno's mother.

"No. I've only been here for a few months. When I didn't die after Bernard shot me in the chest, the doctors asked me if I knew who did it. I lied and said no, but they knew it was him. A sweet little nurse raised about $400 for me to leave town once I recovered, and I took the first thing smoking to California. It hurt me to know that my son was at a funeral, grieving over an empty casket he thought had me inside of it," she said.

"An empty casket?" I asked.

"Yes, ma'am. Anything is possible when your cousin owns a funeral home. That's exactly how Bernard got rid of me. He killed me in his firstborn's mind," she sadly said.

"Reno loves you. He always talked about you," I told her.

"My beautiful son. He was the best son a mother could ask for. He would try to cover for me as hard as he could, but you know a child can only hide so much. I really hate that he had to go through that with me considering his mental state," she said.

I assumed she was talking about him being bipolar, but I wasn't sure, so I didn't ask. Instead, I just rubbed my belly and tried to ease my nerves. I was starving, and I knew it wasn't good for me or the baby.

"Is that my grandchild?" she asked me.

I shifted uncomfortably before answering. "No, we ummmm, we aren't together anymore," I told her.

"I see. I just assumed it was since I heard them say you were with him," she said.

"Do you think we will make it out of here?" I asked her, changing the subject.

"I have faith in God," she said.

That didn't answer my question, but I was too sleepy to combat her. I lay down on the uncomfortable wooden floor and got as comfortable as I could before closing my eyes.

***

"You have to be stronger for the baby. If you give up, so will the baby," Reno's mother told me.

I was dry heaving after waking up to extreme hunger pains. I panicked when she told me that getting food every day wasn't guaranteed, and only given on the days the old lady holding us hostage was feeling sympathetic. I needed anything to cure the gut-wrenching hunger pains I was having. After what felt like forever of me crying and gagging, the closet door finally opened.

"What's wrong witcha? Is you sick?" she asked, kicking my hand slightly.

"She's carrying a baby, Charlotte," Reno's mother confirmed.

"Shut up! Acting like you know me and shit, and I can see that she's pregnant," Charlotte shot back.

"I do know you, Charlotte," Reno's mother shot back.

"Just for that, you aren't eating tonight. I'm sure your crackhead super powers will kick in. Nina get up and follow me," Charlotte said.

She watched me with impatient eyes, as I picked myself up off the floor as fast and best as I could.

"You just all belly. My little relative needs to be fed," Charlotte said.

I'm sure she assumed that this was Reno's baby, but I wasn't going to correct her. I needed food bad and didn't want to upset her. I followed her to the kitchen, and my belly instantly began to churn. She made a pot roast with carrots and potatoes, cabbage, and dinner rolls. I sat at the table as she stirred the pot of cabbage.

"No, go wash up first. Filthy people don't sit at my table," she said with her back turned towards me.

I stood up, but I was still confused. Where did she want me to go? I was being held hostage in this house. I've only seen the closet.

"Well, what are you standing there looking foolish for?" she snapped.

"I um, I don't know where to go," I said.

"Down the hallway and to the left," she said.

I found my way to the bathroom and sighed. It was semi-clean and very tiny. I located a washcloth and started to clean my body using the sink while standing in one spot. I didn't want to get inside of the tub with the ring around it. Once I felt clean, I redressed in my same clothes and went back into the kitchen. My plate was now sitting on the table, and I dug in greedily. She just watched me eat in delight.

"Reno was my favorite nephew," she grinned, lighting a cigarette.

I paused eating and wanted to ask her not to smoke around me, but she gave me an evil look as if she read my mind.

"I taught him all he knows. You can thank me for the way you've been satisfied," she said.

"Huh?" I asked.

"You're carrying his baby, so I know you've had the dick. I was his first," she laughed.

I suddenly got sick and stopped eating. What kind of sick shit was this? Reno's auntie used to fuck him? I felt my eyes water with tears at the thought as throw-up was about to fly out my mouth.

"Oh, so you think I'm some sick, old bitch? I was adopted into this family, so we aren't blood. Besides, it was better he lose it to me than some fast ass little girl. At least I wouldn't bring him an STD or a bastard baby," she continued.

I felt the tears slide down my face as she rolled her eyes. It all makes sense now. The reason why Reno is so promiscuous is because he was molested by someone he trusted.

"Don't act all high and mighty because you're fucking him now. I've been breaking these boys in for years so young ladies like you can benefit from it. I ain't the first one, and besides, Reno never complained about it, either. You fucking up my mood with all that damn crying. I guess you do belong in that closet with his hoe ass mama," Charlotte snapped, snatching me up.

Once she returned me to the closet, I pulled my knees to my chest as best as I could, but that didn't work, so I just sat there and cried while Reno's mother ate the leftovers from my meal Charlotte brought and threw at her. What kind of evil had I done in my life to deserve that treatment? I couldn't imagine God being real right now.

"She likes you," Reno's mother said.

I just looked at her with my tear-filled eyes. I didn't care what that old bitch liked; I didn't like her.

"This could be our only hope. You have to befriend her. Get close to her and figure her out. Once you do, Nina, listen to me, you make a run for it. Don't worry about me. If it's God's will, I'll be alive when the police come find me," she said.

"No, I'm not leaving you. You have to leave with me! I can't do it by myself," I cried.

"Listen, you have to be stronger than that. Think about your baby. If you don't make it, he or she won't make it, either," she told me.

I nodded knowing that she was exactly right and sat up straight placing my hand on my belly. I rubbed my belly and felt a surge of energy. I had to see my Drake again. I felt so stupid for running from him like I did and back into danger. I didn't even care anymore that Xena was his baby mama. I loved RJ like he was mine, anyway.

"You seemed upset when you came back in. Can I ask what it was that made you that way?" she asked me.

"When we make it out alive, I'll let Reno tell you," I said.

"That's the spirit. I have a good feeling about you being here. We will make it out," she said.

Chapter 26

Jace

"That little bitch has been a problem since the day Reno brought her ass home. Now, one thing I don't do is let bitches come between my money and business. She has to go," I heard my pops say.

Jasper stood with his hands behind his back and nodded.

"We must hurry, boss. The quicker we kill her, the quicker Drake and Reno will get over it," Jasper said.

I was holding my breath as I held my phone out to record the conversation. I knew I wouldn't get caught, because I never got caught. I've been sneaking to my father's office to eavesdrop ever since I was little. I always thought he was the coolest man on the planet, and I wanted to be just like him. When he would have the big bosses over, I would sneak downstairs and listen to them. I imitated how they walked, how they talked, and even took note of how they plotted to kill people. I was standing there in disbelief as they discussed how they were going to kill Nina.

"That other bitch can get offed, too. I'm sick of her being around. I've been wanting to keep torturing her for daring to cross me," Pops said.

Buzz! Buzz! Buzz!

Fuck! Amber started calling a nigga, and I knew they heard it. I had to think quick. I answered the phone and knocked on the door.

"Hey, baby," I said to Amber.

"Hey, baby, why haven't I heard from you tonight?" she asked me.

"My bad, beautiful; I fell asleep," I lied.

I knew Jasper was at the door stalling and listening, so I knocked again. I wanted to give the illusion that I was clueless to the meeting that was going on. Finally, Jasper opened the door, and my Pops walked up behind him.

"What you want, son?" he asked me.

"Hold on, baby," I said to Amber, "Pops, I need you to let me out. I need to go make a quick play," I said.

"Jasper, let him out," he said.

I turned to walk off, but he called and stopped me.

"Son?" he said.

"Yeah?" I asked him.

"Stay away from Reno," he said in a warning tone.

I nodded, but I got curious as hell. Why would he want me to stay away from Reno? I played it cool and nodded again before I walked off.

"Baby, I'm back," I said to Amber.

We had talked for a little bit about her day before I asked her if I could call her back. She was mad, but I would make it up to her like I always did. I immediately called Reno, but he didn't answer. I decided to send him the audio anyways. I knew, once he heard it, he would call me back fast as fuck. I sat at the desk in my room trying to make sense of what was going on when Tena burst into my room dressed like some nigga instead of a female. I swear, I sometimes thought my sister was going through a phase, but the older we got, the more she started fucking with females. And they were some fine ass bitches, too.

"So, are you going to tell me what the hell is going on around here?" she asked me.

"Sis, what the hell you talking about?" I asked turning around and looking at her.

"I'm not fucking stupid, Jace. Nina is missing, again. Drake, Reno, and Leo came in here looking for Dad, and you were at his office door just now recording him talking. Do I need to keep going here?" she asked, moving her hands around.

I sighed and debated on if I should tell her. I knew she wouldn't go behind my back and tell dad. Plus, if shit went wrong, we had another person who knew what the fuck was going on. I figured it wouldn't hurt to let Tena know what I knew.

"Ok, Tena, but don't tell Lena. You know how she is," I told her, looking in her eyes, so she would know I was serious.

"Ok, ok, I won't say shit. Now, spill the beans," she demanded, quickly.

"Ok, sis. Pops took Nina, and he's planning on killing her," I said.

"Get the fuck out of here," Tena said, waving me off.

"Ok, I knew you wouldn't believe me so listen to this," I said.

I played the whole recording to her and her mouth dropped in shock at what she just heard. She shook her head and started pacing the room in anger.

"Look, Nina isn't a saint, but she doesn't deserve to fucking die," Tena yelled.

"Sis, calm the fuck down before he hears you," I said.

"What is so special about Nina all of a sudden that everybody is fighting over her?" Tena asked.

"Easy, she is in the middle of business. She is the reason why Reno and Drake fell out, and you know Pops not having that shit. Really, if you ask me, Nina is fucked up in the whole game," I told her.

"So, because she got tired of Reno beating her ass and finally stood up for herself, she's fucked up?" Tena argued.

"Nah, she's fucked up for going to his best fucking friend," I explained.

"Some friend Drake is, but it takes two to fuck and create a whole baby," Tena chuckled.

"Well, however shit goes down, Reno is still my brother, and I'm going to ride for him," I said.

"Speaking of, where the fuck is Reno?" Tena asked.

"I don't know; he didn't answer his phone when I called him," I said.

Lena came bursting into the room crying before Tena could reply.

"I'm going to do it, sis. I'm going to say yes," she said.

"Do what?" I asked.

"Oh, gosh Lena, not right now," Tena said, throwing her hands up in the air.

"No, it's time I go after what I want. I'm always the one who tries to please everyone and end up unhappy," Lena vented.

"Sis, what the fuck are you talking about?" I asked her.

"Leo asked me to marry him, and I'm going to do it," she announced, smiling.

"Yeah, with no ring and over the phone. How romantic," Tena sarcastically said.

"Hell, nah. First off, that nigga a fucking lame," I said, still not feeling him after he came at me that day. "Sis, you really letting a nigga propose to you with no ring and shit? Where is the wedding going to be, at the courthouse downtown? Man, you do some silly ass shit, sometimes," I said.

"Fuck you! You're just like him," she said.

"Just like who?" I asked.

"Reno! That's who!" she said.

"Fuck out of here," I said shrugging her off.

"No, fuck you. You don't want anybody happy just like him. I'm finally fucking happy for once, and I'm doing this for me," she said with so much conviction.

"I don't give a fuck. You whack for accepting a proposal without a ring and over the phone, and he's even whacker for doing it. I thought you had standards when it came to niggas," I said, shaking my head.

"I've always had standards, but the relationships never got anywhere, because I was always running to y'all rescue whenever y'all needed me for something. Not anymore," she said, shaking her head.

I still wasn't feeling this Leo, nigga. He just comes out the blue one day and is fucking my sister and telling me I can't fuck with his cousin. Nah, he had me fucked all the way up.

"Man, all of this shit is crazy. Is this what love will do to people?" Tena asked, shaking her head.

"Both of you chill out. Reno is calling," I said with my phone in my hand.

Tena went to close the door, and I answered, placing him on speakerphone.

"Bro, what is that fucked up shit you just sent me?" Reno yelled.

"It's exactly what you just heard, bro. No bullshit; I was right there, and I heard it with my own ears," I said.

"On some real shit, Pops gotta go!" Reno said.

"No, Reno, just calm down," Lena said.

"Nah, sis, fuck that nigga. He always has treated me like a fucking black sheep. Just because he's a saint to you doesn't mean he looks that way to everybody else," Reno barked.

"Bro, I'm with Lena. I know Pops is fucked up in the head, but he's still all we got. Your moms died and ours left and never came back for us," Tena voiced.

"So, it's fair that he can do all this fucked up shit to us and get away with it? Nah, see that's that weak shit. If y'all really fucking with me, then we can all come up with a plan together," Reno said.

"Ok, this may be bad timing, but can you all fill me in on what is really going on?" Lena voiced.

"Hold on, Reno," I said.

I played the recording for Lena and watched her eyes open wide in shock and mouth drop. She was the closest to him than all of us, because she was so damn docile and never went against him. I almost thought she would walk out of the room and break, but she dried her tears and put on a straight face.

"This shit is wrong. I'm in," she said, standing up straight and looking me in my eyes.

"That's love, sis. Now, I'm already one step ahead of the game! I got Alex placing bugs in the house in the next day or two, but he'll be disguised as an internet guy. Make sure Pops is not there, but if he is, stall him. Hopefully, we can find out where Nina is," Reno said.

"But it's only one catch. Pops only talks business in his office," Tena said.

"True, but I got another plan. I need y'all to be in on this one together. I got mini-tracking devices that I need to be planted in all the cars. If I do it, he'll suspect something, so you all have to do it," Reno explained.

"Ok, bro, we got it. Oh, yeah, Pops told me to stay away from you and shit," I told him.

"Fuck him! He's saying that because he knows he did some fucked up shit to me," Reno said. "One more thing, Lena!"

"Yes, bro?" she said.

"Leo straight. I don't want to see my sisters dating, but if you do have to date someone, choose him. He's straight up real, and as much as I hate to give him props, you need a real nigga to break you," Reno said.

"Thank you, Reno!" Lena cried.

"You, too, Tena. You need a real nigga to turn your ass back straight," Reno joked.

"Fuck you," Tena spat.

"Nah, but for real. I don't know what's going to happen, but I love all of y'all. I know I ain't been the best big brother, but shit, I ain't the worst, either," Reno said.

"That's love, bro. We don't judge you, and you know that," I said, low-key referring to his mental illness.

It used to be hard trying to be close with him when he would always spazz out and get sent away for the weekend to our aunt's house down in the country, but he was the only brother I had, and if he told me to squeeze the trigger on anybody for him, I would. Including my own father!

Chapter 27

Reno

As soon as I hung up the phone, the doorbell rang. I looked at the clock and saw that it was a quarter after eight in the morning.

"Who the fuck is this?" I mumbled.

I didn't want RJ waking up yet, because he would be ready to bounce off the walls. I went to open it before they rang the doorbell again, and I was greeted by the sweet scent of strawberries and big, curly hair. Serenity smiled at me and held up a Whole Foods bag.

"Can I come in?" she asked me.

"Hell, yeah," I said.

She was looking good as hell in some yoga pants and a Nike pullover, and her ass was bouncing so much, I wondered if she had on any panties.

"I wanted to come make you an electric meal and take away some of your stress," she said.

"You coming to do voodoo on me?" I laughed.

"I don't need to use voodoo. I'm confident in my own abilities," she smiled.

"I can relieve some stress on you, though," I told her, as I grabbed her waist from behind and made circles on her neck with my tongue.

Her knees buckled, and she softly moaned.

"You remember how that tongue made you feel?" I whispered in her ear.

"Oh, Reno, stop please," she moaned.

"Is that how you'll moan my name when I'm deep in this shit?" I asked her, grabbing a handful of her ass.

"Please, Reno," she begged.

I let her go and laughed. She wanted the dick bad, but I wasn't about to be the first one to break. She needed to learn how to submit to me a little bit. I watched her open a few cabinets before she finally got the blender Nina used to love so much.

"How did you know I had a blender?" I asked her.

"Women's intuition," she said.

"Yeah, ok," I laughed.

I watched her make a green smoothie and chop up some vegetables before steaming them.

"I love your kitchen," she complimented, smiling back at me.

"I see," I smirked, walking up behind her.

I started kissing her neck and was about to slide my hand in her yoga pants when RJ's cockblocking ass walked in.

"Can we go to Playtime Pizza?" he asked me, while staring at Serenity.

"Playtime Pizza isn't even open yet," I told him, pulling the straw he was chewing on from his mouth.

"Daddy, who is that?" he asked, pointing to Serenity.

I almost got choked when he called me Daddy. I don't give a damn what happens, RJ is still my son, and Nina and Drake aren't just walking away with him.

"I'm Serenity," Serenity kindly said, while kneeling down to RJ's level. "What's your name?" she asked.

"Reno, like my daddy, but I got another name, too! It's RJ!" he said, getting all hype and shit.

"Calm down, little man; you must think Serenity is pretty," I laughed.

"Yep, she's pretty like Nina. I miss Nina, Daddy. Is she ever coming back?" RJ asked looking at me.

"I don't know," I mumbled. "Go upstairs, and get out of these bed clothes," I told him.

The vibe was weird, and I thought Serenity would be mad, but she wasn't. She walked up to me and grabbed my face in both hands and kissed me. I grabbed her chin and took control of the kiss until she pulled back and whimpered from the freaky way my tongue was sliding in and out of her mouth. I rubbed her face and was stuck for a minute. Was I really going soft for a female that wasn't Nina?

"You're scared of me, aren't you?" Serenity asked me.

"Nah," I replied.

"Yes, you are. I feel the nervousness in your energy," she insisted.

"You just catch a nigga off guard, but nah, I ain't nervous," I told her.

"Reno, you can trust me. I'm here for you and only you," she smiled, leaning in to kiss me again.

It's crazy, but I trusted the fuck out of her ass. That's the only reason why I even told her about the secret key to get in my spot when I was arrested. A nigga hasn't even slid inside of her yet, and I was already thinking about cuffing her.

"Why are you staring at me like that?" she laughed.

"I want you to be mine, for real! No other niggas popping up or you having your own place," I said, meaning every word.

"Reno, don't you think it's too soon? I mean, we haven't even known each other for six months yet. Plus, I wouldn't want to invade you and your son's space," Serenity said.

I instantly regretted the offer. What if she wasn't feeling my ass like I thought? I let her go and took a couple of steps backward.

"What?" she asked me.

"Nothing. So you trying to put me on a diet or some shit?" I joked.

"Reno, what's wrong?" she asked again.

"Nothing, fam," I replied.

"Fam? Ok, so is that how you're going to start viewing me now?" she replied, getting an attitude fast.

I thought that shit was sexy. She wasn't so cool and collected right now.

"You don't have to stunt for a nigga. You not on what I'm on, but it's cool, baby," I said, walking behind her and popping one of the strawberries she had in my mouth while smacking her ass.

"Reno, everything doesn't have to be done your way. Ok, let's just talk about this like reasonable adults," she said, watching me as I purposely ignored her.

RJ walked back in just in time, and I walked over to him picking him up.

"Little man, what kind of cereal you want?" I asked him.

"Apple Jacks!" he cheered.

I proceeded to make RJ his Apple Jacks and made a bowl for myself while Serenity poured her drink in a cup and leaned against the counter watching me. She was pissed, but she was trying hard to play it cool. Her exterior was starting to crack, and I was getting a kick out of the shit. I don't understand why females always felt like they were in control of every damn thing. I see that I'm going to have to break her just like I did the rest of them.

"You can sit down if you want to," I told her, looking up at her with innocent eyes.

I saw her look at me with an expression I couldn't read before sitting back down. I entertained RJ while she pretended to be enjoying her smoothie. Once RJ finished eating, I told him to go watch TV and walked over to Serenity.

"Why you get so cold on a nigga?" I asked, sincerely.

"I apologize. I guess I just expect too much from you," she softly said.

"Too much like what? What am I not doing? I take you out all the damn time, we talk every day, you pretty much know where I am all day, so what the hell else do you need?" I asked.

"You don't open up to me. It's like you're closed off. Sometimes, I think it's because you're not really feeling me, and that's the reason why I said no to your offer. I don't want to move in here and get comfortable just for you to say never mind to me and not pay me any attention once I'm here," she said.

"What the fuck you mean I don't open up? I tell you damn near everything," I said.

"Yeah, but it's one thing we don't talk about," she said in a low voice.

"Man, whatever. I'm going in here with RJ," I said, waving my hand at her and walking off.

She was trying to get in my head and shit like her damn moms. I hated when she did that. I told her all the time that she didn't have to worry about Nina, but she always found a way to bring her ass up. I turned the game on for RJ and was kicking his ass on the 2K when Serenity finally walked in the living room. She stood off to the side, so I motioned for her to come to me. She was fine as fuck to me, even when she was on that bullshit. I let her sit on my lap, and she wrapped her arms around me while resting her head on my shoulder. I kissed her forehead and she smiled a little.

"Can we work on that part?" I asked.

She held me tighter and nodded her head.

"So, what's the first step?" I asked her.

"Make peace with your past while you still can. Drake needs you, and you need him, too," she said, softly.

Chapter 28

Lena

"Daddy?" I called out.

My father took his glasses off and smiled up at me, as I knocked on the door of his office.

"There goes my favorite child. Come in," he said, smiling.

I kept my innocent face on, as I walked in and sat across from him.

"What's on your mind?" he asked me, intertwining his fingers.

"Daddy, how will I know if a man loves me?" I asked, innocently.

He chuckled and sat back in his seat. Then, his expression turned to anger.

"Come here, Lena," he said.

I did as he said and walked over beside his chair. He reached up and grabbed my face by my chin and pulled me down to him.

"So which one of these weak ass niggas are you fucking and you let get in your simple-minded ass head? You want to go against everything I ever taught you and be a fucking whore, just like your mother? Remember, that's the reason she left all of you with me, to go be a whore for that young nigga," my father roughly said.

I flinched and held back tears as bits of saliva hit my face.

"So, who are you fucking? It's that Leo motherfucker, huh?" he asked searching my face.

"No, Daddy, I'm still a virgin, I swear," I lied, showing him my purity ring he gave me. "That's why I came in here. I think he wants to have sex with me before he marries me and I-," I started babbling.

"Fuck him then, Lena. All he wants to do is fuck you and tell the whole city that he fucked Bone's daughter. Don't be so fucking naïve, Lena," he said.

"Yes, father, Goodnight," I said.

I walked away from him and headed out his office but stopped when I heard him speak.

"Goodnight. Remember, Lena, you are my chosen child. You have to remain loyal to me," my father said.

"Yes, sir," I said with my head down.

I walked out of his office and went upstairs to my room. When I got inside, Jace was pacing back and forth anxiously, and Tena was in the mirror brushing her hair back into a ponytail.

"I did it," I said.

"Where did you place it?" Jace asked me.

"In the chair across from his desk. Inside of the seat cushion," I said.

"Ok, so how are we supposed to hear if someone sits their wide ass in the seat?" Tena asked me

"Jasper, never sits. That's a good placement," Jace said.

"I don't know, you sure you couldn't find any other place? Maybe like under the desk or even his chair?" Tena asked, smartly.

"Yeah, but he would've seen that shit. Damn, can't you just be happy I went through with it?" I vented.

"Yeah, sis, I'm happy. I'm sorry," Tena said, "So, what did you and the old man talk about?" she asked, calming her attitude.

"I asked him relationship advice, and he basically called me a whore," I said.

"As if he isn't," Tena replied, with even more attitude than she had before.

"Well, I'm about to go move around a little bit. You two need something?" Jace asked, walking towards the door.

"Yeah, get me some Playtex," Tena said.

Jace burst out laughing in hysterics. I looked at him like he was immature until he calmed down.

"Sis, you on your period? I forget gay girls have those," Jace joked.

"Fuck you, bro," Tena laughed, putting her middle finger up.

Once Jace left, I got serious.

"Tena, do you believe Dad when he says those things about Mama?" I asked her.

"I mean, nah. Not for the most part, but sometimes, it kind of makes you wonder. She just left us and never showed her face again. She stopped calling after a year, and then we never heard from her again," Tena said.

"I sometimes think Dad did something to make her leave. Remember how she used to cry all the time before she left?" I said.

"Who knows. I don't think about the shit anymore so it doesn't matter to me," Tena shrugged.

We dropped the topic and sat in silence until I got up the nerve to tell her my next revelation.

"I accepted Leo's proposal," I blurted.

"Really! Awwww Lena, where is the ring?" she asked.

"Um, he hasn't gotten it yet. Well, I don't think. I haven't seen him," I told her.

"What?!" Tena said a little too loud for my liking.

I looked towards the door to make sure Daddy wasn't coming or had even heard us.

"Will you shut the hell up? Yes I did. And, to be honest, I don't care about a damn ring. I don't need a ring. I just want him," I told her.

"You're serious about him, huh?" she asked.

"I am," I said, nodding my head.

"I guess I can't be too mad at you, then. As a matter of fact, I'm happy for you, but his ass better have a ring soon," she said, laughing, while walking over to me and hugging me.

"So, are we going to sit back and watch all this go down, or are we going to help them get Nina back so shit can go back to normal?" I asked.

"And that's why we're twins. Let's go," she said.

Chapter 29

Drake

How the hell Reno knew I was fucking Candy, I had no idea, and the nigga wasn't trying to tell me, either. It was crazy that we were able to finally come together again and come up with a plan to get Nina back. I wasn't sure what Reno's reason was for getting her back knowing he had another bitch, who I might say was bad as fuck, but I just hope this nigga wasn't on some bullshit. When Leo proposed to Lena, I was, but wasn't, shocked. I knew that nigga was in love. We all have always been the type that, when we're done, we're done. Ain't no coming back or chasing a bitch. We move the fuck on.

Finding out that Candy was on some bullshit wasn't too surprising. I should've known that when she confessed her love for Reno's crazy ass. I guess Xena got a heart all of a sudden. She may have been a hoe, but her ass was never dumb streetwise. After running some more shit down to us, we dropped her off at a hotel. Leo and I pulled up in a cut and smoked a blunt while talking.

"What the fuck are we going to do with Candy?" he asked.

"You already know. I'm already planning that shit now," I said, exhaling.

I was pissed off that Candy was trying to play me, but she was the one that was going to be mad in the end. I sat there quietly thinking about my girl. I was missing her like crazy. I still wanted to smack her upside her head for taking off on me, but I knew I wasn't going to stop until I got her and my baby back safe with me.

"You thinking about her?" Leo asked out of nowhere.

"Yea," I replied.

"I can't wait until this is over. I need my girl back," he said.

"You really feeling this chick, huh?" I asked looking at him.

"Yea, man. I'm not the type to change a bitch, but I can already tell that she really wants a nigga. Plus, nigga, you know me. I don't chase, I replace," he said.

"Marriage, though?" I asked.

"Nigga, you got a lot of fucking nerve questioning me. I may be fucking with your enemy's sister, but I ain't fucking his girl," he said.

"You got that, but I told you some of the shit we've been through. We got years on this shit," I told him.

"Years of back and forth. You've had her momentarily, and she scary as fuck," Leo said.

"Damn, nigga. Why you going in on my girl like that?" I asked.

"Because nigga, I'm trying to figure out what it is about this chick that got you and Reno both going crazy over her. Is her pussy that damn good? Like, what's really good with this chick?" he said.

"I can't explain it, and that should be enough. It's not even about her pussy. We just have a connection that I've never had a with any female before. The shit is just deep with us when she's not on some bullshit," I said, looking out the window.

"I guess I feel you. I can't explain the shit either with shorty. I just know she's the one, fam," he said. "Ay yo, ain't that Bones shit right there?" Leo asked, pointing to a car riding past us.

I looked in the direction he was pointing, and sure enough, it was.

"Well, ain't this some shit," I said starting the car back up.

I didn't turn my lights on as I pulled out behind him making sure to keep my distance. I pulled my phone out and called Reno.

"The fuck you want, nigga?" he said when he answered.

"Kill the shit, nigga. I just happened to see your pops out here, and I'm following him," I informed him.

"The fuck you at?" he asked.

I could hear noise in the background. It sounded like he was moving. I told him where we were at, but something caught my attention. There was another car out here following his father as well.

"You got eyes out here already?" I asked.

"Naw. Why?" he asked.

"Hold up," I said, putting my phone down and pulling over.

I watched as the car went by and I saw that it was his brother Jace. Leo and I looked at each other and smirked. I put the phone back up to my ear.

"Looks like little brother is trying to step up in the big leagues," I said.

"The fuck you talking about?" he asked.

"Your brother is out here following your pops," I said.

"Aww, shit. Man, keep an eye out for him. Don't let shit pop off. I'm on my way," he said, hanging up.

"I ought to fuck with this young nigga," Leo said.

"Naw, don't do that. If he wants to play with the big boys, let him. We'll watch from afar," I said.

We creeped back out and headed in the direction we saw them both going when we were led to a warehouse.

"I ain't never know this shit was out here. This the perfect spot for some shit to go down and nobody hear shit that's going on," Leo said.

"Word," I said agreeing.

I parked off on the side making sure neither one of them saw us. We watched as Bones and his wannabe ass muscle got out the car and walked up to the door. They walked up all casual like they weren't holding somebody hostage. They walked in, and not long after, they were walking out. Leo and I looked at each other. I think we were thinking the same thing. *Where the fuck is Nina?* After we had left the warehouse, we took another long ass drive to a normal looking house out in the country. We parked all the way down a path and Jace parked a few yards away, not knowing how to be incognito at fucking all. Bones got out with Jasper.

"What the fuck is really going on?" Leo asked.

"I'm wondering the same damn thing," I said, still looking in Bones direction.

Chapter 30

Nina

I wasn't feeling good at all as I lay in the closet. I didn't know how long it had been since I got there. All I knew was that my baby wasn't doing well. I was cramping bad, and all Reno's mother would and could do was pray for me. This crazy bitch wasn't trying to feed me like I wasn't pregnant. All she would do was talk fucking crazy about her fucking Reno. I just sat there and rubbed my stomach when she would let me eat. Slowly, but surely, I was getting to know Reno's mother and what was really going on. To say I was shocked was an understatement.

All we could do was talk. We had nothing else to do. I don't know if there was anybody else in the house or not. I swear, my mind was playing tricks on me, or maybe I was becoming delusional, but I could've sworn I would hear more than one voice. And every time I would get Reno's mother to shut the hell up to listen real good, the voices would go away. She would have the nerve to look at me like I was crazy.

I knew I had to do something before my baby died, because I wasn't getting the proper nutrients for he and I. I wasn't getting any sleep at all, and my baby was way too uncomfortable. After Reno's mother prayed for the umpteenth time, I just laid there as comfortable as I could get. I started rubbing my stomach since the little one was active. I was dying to know what I was having. I wasn't even sure if I had missed my next appointment or not. I could barely think. I started humming and immediately my baby calmed down causing me to smile.

"Are you ok?" his mother asked.

"I am, now, but I'm still hungry," I said, weakly.

She sat up and looked at me. Shaking her head, she stood up and banged on the door. She didn't stop until we heard feet getting closer.

"What the fuck are you banging like that for?" Charlotte yelled, when she snatched the door open.

"This girl needs to eat. I don't give a fuck how you feel about me, but she's with child. She or the baby might die if you don't feed her," his mother said getting in her face.

"You better back your whore ass up. Come on, child," Charlotte said, picking me up and dragging me along.

I don't even remember hearing the closet door close. She dragged me all the way to the kitchen throwing me down into a chair. I tried to get a good look at the house, but it was bare.

"Why are you doing this?" I mustered up the nerve to ask.

"Hell, why not? Bernard said he would give me $50,000 to do this. It's easy money," she said.

"Do you really believe he will give you the money?" I asked, rubbing my stomach.

I could feel myself getting weaker and weaker.

"Hold on, child. I'm making your plate now," she said. "He already gave me half the money," she said, confidently.

I didn't believe her. If I didn't know anything about Reno's father, I knew he was cheap. He only spent money when it came to his business. He didn't even give the twins or Jace any money. Reno took care of them. I sat there not believing a word she said.

"How long has his mother been here?" I asked.

She turned around with my plate and walked over to me looking at me. Something about the way she was looking wasn't sitting right with me. I didn't dwell on it for too long as she placed my plate in front of me. I didn't waste any time digging in.

"You sure are asking a lot of questions," she said.

168

"I just want to know what's going on, and why I'm here," I said, looking up at her for a second.

"Look, don't ask questions you don't want to know the answers to," she said, rolling her eyes.

"But I want to know. I think I deserve to know. I haven't done a thing to Mr. Bernard. I could understand Reno taking me again, but not his father. Does Reno even know about this?" I said.

"Chile, shut up. Shut up," she said quickly.

"Why can't you answer me?" I asked.

I don't even think I was worried about eating anymore. I looked at Charlotte intensely and could see the beads of sweat forming on her forehead. She wouldn't even look at me anymore.

"What are you hiding? What do you know?" I asked.

"You know what? You better eat up, or I'll take your ass back to that closet, and you'll starve to death," she said, pointing at me.

"Am I supposed to die here or something?" I asked.

"That's it. Back to the closet," she said, standing up quick.

"Wait, no, please. My baby," I said, holding my stomach.

"Hurry the hell up. When I come back, you better be done," she said, walking off.

I watched, as she walked off and hurriedly finished my food. I got up trying to be as quiet as possible. I made sure to look in the direction she went with each movement I made. I was glad that my baby was cooperating. I headed towards the direction I saw her go, and I heard voices.

"She's starting to ask questions," I heard her say.

"I don't give a fuck. She'll be the least of our worries soon. Did you do what I asked?" I heard a male's voice.

I recognized it instantly as being Reno's father.

169

"Yea, I put it in her food. It shouldn't be long before taking effect. I hope the baby makes it. You know this isn't right. She and the baby are innocent," she said.

"Fuck her and that baby. She's been a problem since day damn one. This is long overdue. While you're sitting there worrying about that bitch, you need to be checking on her. Don't call me again until it's done," he said hanging up.

I turned to walk away when I felt a gush of wetness and pain shoot through my stomach.

"Ahhhh," I screamed before falling to the floor.

Everything went black before I even hit it.

Chapter 31

Jace

I walked out the house and knew I needed to do something. I couldn't sit around and wait for shit to go down or wait on Reno's call. I needed to prove myself. I could already tell that his plan to get information from Amber were dead now that he and Drake were working together. I was truly trying to figure out why they both wanted Nina back so bad. Reno's been fucking with a bad bitch. I don't see why he even cares about Nina anymore.

Drake knows he's dead ass wrong for what he did to Reno. Niggas don't do that to their so-called brothers. That's when you gotta watch your back of snakes like that from then on. I don't see how Reno hadn't killed Drake already, but I must admit I love this cat and mouse chase that is going on.

I was truly surprised about my pops, though. I always knew he moved funny, but it seems that he's gotten worse over the years. I still remember some of the fucked up shit he used to do to us, and I still wonder to this day what happened to my mother. I remember like yesterday the day she left. I was young then, but now that I think about it, something fishy was up with that situation.

****

"Jace, baby, come here," my mother called out to me.

I was doing my usual of playing the game while my sisters were off doing who knows what, and Reno was running the streets. My pops was nowhere to be found at the moment. I got up and walked to where I heard my mother's voice come from.

"Yes, ma'am?" I said when I found her.

She was sitting on the bed, Indian-style, with a bunch of photographs in front of her. I climbed on the bed and sat beside her. I could see the tears forming in her eyes.

"What's wrong, Mama?" I asked.

"Listen to me, baby, and listen to me good," she said, grabbing my chin making me look at her.

I nodded my head and waited for her to say what she had to say.

"Your father is a very bad man, and Reno is headed in the same path as him. I want you to do everything in your power to be a good boy. Go by everything that I've ever taught you. I'm not sure when it's going to happen, or how, but I won't be here, and I won't be back," she said.

"What do you mean, Mama?" I asked.

"I can't answer that. Just look after your brother and sisters. I'm sorry you were born in the messed up world with an even messed up father. Just remember everything that I taught you. When you get older and think about all of this, you'll understand. The most important thing to remember is to never follow in your father's footsteps. Always watch how he moves. I love you, son," she said, kissing me as tears ran down her face.

"I love you, too, Mama," I said

I was confused as fuck and didn't know what the hell she was talking about. I thought she was tripping. She pushed me off the bed, and I went back to playing the game without another thought. A few days later, my parents were arguing, and I mean hard. As usual, Reno was running the streets, but for once, Tena and Lena were home. We all happened to open our doors and step out into the hallway at the same time.

"What's going on?" Lena's naive ass asked rubbing her eyes.

It was late as hell.

"They're obviously arguing," I said, as soon as their door flew open, and Mama was walking out with a bag in each hand.

"If you walk out that door, don't bother coming back," my father said standing in the doorway.

"Trust me, out there would be a whole lot better than being here with you,"
my mother stopped and said with so much hatred.

Tears were running down her face. She walked up to Lena and Tena,
dropped her bags, grabbed them, and held them tight.

"Yea, you better hug them tight, cuz' if you walk out that door, you'll never
see them again," my father said, pointing towards the stairs.

My mother didn't bother replying, nor did she look at him. I don't know
how long she held onto Tena and Lena, but it seemed like forever before she kissed
them and walked over to me. She stopped in front of me and looked at me trying to
smile.

"Mama, please don't leave," I said, hugging her tightly.

"Remember what I said, baby," she said, ignoring my plea.

She grabbed me and hugged me so tight I couldn't breathe, but I didn't care.
Her touch was everything at the moment. She kissed me on top of my head.

"Remember what I said. I love you," she said before walking away.

We would get calls from her, but our conversations would be short. The calls
didn't last long before we stopped getting them altogether. For a good while, we would
ask Pops what was going on, and he would never say. Eventually, we stopped asking.
I can't and won't say we stopped caring, but life went on. I don't know what
happened to my mother. Ever since then, my pops had been moving even more funny.
It didn't take long for him to get rid of Mama's stuff. It was like she never existed. I
remember, after a while, he said something to me.

"Son, don't trust any bitch. All they want is your money and dick. There
isn't a bitch out here that's loyal. Not even your mother," he said, before walking
away from me.

****

As I followed my father, I was sitting and wondering what
happened to my mother. It was time I got to the bottom of things. I
didn't know where my father was going, but I was damn sure going to
find the hell out. I wanted to call Reno, but I felt the need to prove

myself to him that I could handle shit on my own. The closer I got, the more anxious I became.

"Fuck!" I yelled, realizing that I didn't even have a gun on me. "Just fucking great," I said.

I saw another car heading in the same direction but didn't think anything of it. I had my mind on getting to my father and finding out what's really good. My phone rang, and I knew it could only be Amber.

"Yea?" I answered.

"What the hell have you been doing? Why aren't you calling me back or replying to my texts?" she asked going straight in.

"Baby, I've been busy with family stuff. Look, I'm busy right now. I'm going to have to call you back," I said.

"I'm sick of this shit. If you're going to be with me, then you need to have time for me," she said, smartly.

"Girl, get the hell out of here with that bullshit. When I first tried to holla at you, you didn't want shit to do with me. I'm keeping it real with you instead of lying to your ass again. I got some family shit going on. Some real shit that's taking up a lot of my time. I'm going to need you to work with me here. I don't give a fuck what you do, but what you're not going to do is stop talking to me. I put myself on the line to be with you so chill with that noise," I told her irritated as fuck.

We pulled up to the second destination of a house that looked familiar as hell. I watched my pops and Jasper get out and go inside.

"Whatever," she said, smacking her lips.

"Whatever my ass. I promise, as soon as I get some free time, we'll be back to us. Can you just hold on a little longer?" I said, trying to smooth things over, as I tiptoed out of the car.

"Ok, I gue…" she was saying.

POW! POW! POW!

"Oh, shit," I said ducking.

I dropped my phone, and I could hear Amber calling my name. I was too scared to look up. I don't know how long I was ducking, but when I finally got the nerve to peek, I heard footsteps. I slowly raised my head only to see Jasper standing in front of my car.

"What the fuck?" I said to myself.

"Get the fuck in the car," he demanded.

I could still hear Amber calling my ass, and my other lined beeped. I looked down to see Reno calling me. I tried to move indiscreetly, but fast enough to answer the phone.

"Don't you fucking move," he demanded, pointing his gun at me. "Don't make me shoot your ass like I just did your weak ass father," he said, walking towards my side of the car.

"The fuck?" I said again.

I hit the answer button as soon as he reached for my car door.

"Yoooo, what the fuck is going on?" I could hear Reno ask, as soon as the call picked up.

"Your whole family is fucking stupid, but the one who is the most stupid is your father. Why did he really think that I was going to let him slide with what he did to my sister? You should've stayed your ass at home youngin'. I loved you, nephew," Jasper said, before raising his gun up at me.

POW! POW!

"Ahhhhhh," Jasper said, right before falling to the ground.

"Come on, Jace. Let's get you and your father to the hospital," I heard Drake say coming out of nowhere.

I just so happened to remember that Reno was on the phone, so I picked it up quickly.

"Hello!" I yelled frantically.

"Jace, what the fuck is going on?!" he yelled back.

Drake snatched the phone from me and pushed me in the direction Pops and Jasper were at.

"Ya boy not ready. He almost got himself shot," Drake was saying dissing my ass.

POW! POW! POW! POW!

I felt a sting in my back as I flew forward. "Oh shit," I heard before my back started burning and my vision got blurry.

Chapter 32

2 Hours Earlier

Lena

"Uh, sis, where are we going?" I asked, as soon as we got in the car.

"That's a damn good question," Tena said, as soon as she sat down. "Let's ride around for a minute until we figure it the hell out," she said.

"Should we call Reno or Jace first?" I asked.

"Now, why the hell would we do that when we're trying to help out? You know damn well they don't even want us out the house," she said, getting comfortable.

"True," I said, starting the car up.

I took off, and we drove in silence. I don't know what was going through Tena's mind, but I couldn't get Leo off my mind. Every time I think about him, I start smiling. I can't believe I agreed to marry him. All the times I thought about it, and it's actually happening.

"Yo, pull over," Tena said out of nowhere.

"Huh?" I asked.

"Pull over," she said, looking real hard out the window.

"What's up, sis?" I asked.

"Just pull over," she said.

I could tell by her body language that she was getting mad. I pulled over and watched as she hopped out before I could even put the car in park all the way.

"Wait, Tena," I called out after her, but she kept walking.

I finished parking the car and hopped out following behind Tena.

"Candy?" I heard Tena call out.

There were a group of females standing outside looking like they were up to no good. There it was, late as hell, and these bitches out here like it's the afternoon or something.

"Tena? What you doing here?" a female turned around asking.

She kept looking back at the group of females as we walked up.

"Yo, why you haven't you been answering my calls?" Tena asked.

"I told you what the deal was," Candy tried saying, discreetly, trying to pull Tena out of earshot.

"What are you trying to hide?" Tena asked, snatching away.

"Can we talk about this at another time, please?" Candy practically begged.

"Yo, Candy. What's good?" I heard a familiar voice say.

"Reno?" Tena and I asked at the same time.

"The fuck y'all doing out here?" he asked, looking in our direction as he pulled up on us.

"Shit, we was just riding until Tena seen somebody she knew," I informed him.

"Who y'all know?" he asked, looking between us and the group of females.

I watched as Candy tried to slowly move away from Tena.

"Candy, you handle that or no?" Reno asked, when neither of us replied.

"Ummm, I'm still working on it," she tried to sound all sweet and shit.

"Y'all know each other?" Reno asked looking back and forth.

"Yea, we been fucking," Tena said blatantly.

"Fucking?" Reno asked looking at Candy.

Candy put her head down in shame.

"Oh, shit. You been sucking on my sister? Get the fuck out of here. You go both ways?" he said amused.

"No! It's nothing like that. You weren't available like I wanted, and we ended up meeting. Things just led to more. I swear, it didn't mean nothing," Candy said pleading.

"The fuck you acting like that for? If you like pussy, you like pussy. Shit, if that was the case, we could've been having threesomes. Not with my sis, tho," Reno said still amused.

"So, you not mad?" Candy asked looking at Reno.

"The fuck would I be mad for? You not my bitch," he said laughing.

Candy's face dropped. "Are you serious? After everything I've done for you, you can honestly say you don't care not even a little bit about me?" Candy asked, looking, and I'm sure, feeling, offended.

Reno looked around before his eyes landed back on Candy.

"Everybody and their momma knew who my girl was. That's on you that you wanted to help me out. I hope you didn't think just because you was giving me some ass and doing the shit I asked you for that you would be my girl. You bugging. And now I find out you been bumping pussies with my sister. You really bugging," Reno said.

I looked at Tena, who was just standing there. She was really stuck. Hell, I was, too. I couldn't believe that the nigga this chick was dissing my sister for was my brother the whole time. This shit was crazy.

"Sis, was you feeling this bitch?" Reno asked Tena.

Tena looked at Reno, and I could see that her heart was really broken.

"Damn, sis. I wish I would've known you was feeling her. I would've backed off. Hell, I didn't even know you knew the bitch. Her shit is good, though, but you don't want or need no bitch like her. I'll hook you up with somebody," Reno said, as his phone rang.

"You really out here trying to front on me?" Tena finally opened her mouth.

"Look, it's not like that," Candy said, shaking her head.

"Then, what is it like, because I know you've been feeling me like I've been feeling you, regardless of Reno" Tena said.

"Aye, sis. Nah, fuck that bitch. She ain't even worth it. If a bitch can't keep it real with you, then you don't need to fuck with her. Let's go," Reno said.

I walked over to Tena and pulled her away. She didn't put up a fight, but I did have to drag her some. We quietly got in the car and drove away. I could tell she didn't want to talk about it. We got to Reno's house, and we headed straight to our rooms. I was lying across the bed almost asleep when the door opened and in walked Tena.

"What's wrong with me?" she asked sitting on the bed.

"Huh?" I asked sitting up.

"Why can't I find love? Or why do I find love in the wrong people?" she asked.

"Now, you know you're asking the wrong person, but all I can say is it happens to the best. I guess it's called trial and error. You go through hell to be ready for heaven. Your time is coming, but in the meantime, work on yourself, sis," I said with my hand on her back.

"Where the hell did you get that from?" she asked looking at me.

"I just said shit people been telling me for years. Sounded good, huh?" I asked, laughing.

"Should've known, but thanks for trying," she said, reaching over and hugging me.

Chapter 33

Reno

Chilling with Serenity and RJ felt so natural. More natural than when it was with Nina. I wouldn't really be around to be honest. We played the game together and watched movies for the rest of the day.

"Stay the night?" I asked.

It was getting late, and I didn't want her on the road by herself. She looked at me, and I knew what she was thinking.

"I won't try anything. I promise. You can sleep in one of the guest rooms if you like. It's just late, and I honestly don't want you to go," I told her, rubbing my face against her.

"Please, Serenity. Can you stay?" RJ asked out of nowhere.

I was shocked my damn self. I was being selfish when I asked. I wasn't even thinking about him. I stopped moving and looked at Serenity. I knew it was a wrap then. I tried to hide my smile, but it wasn't working.

"Sure. I'll stay," she said, smiling.

She turned and looked at me and gave me a look that said she wasn't happy about it.

"I swear I didn't put him up to that," I said, backing away and putting my hands in the air.

What the fuck is wrong with me? I thought to myself. *Why am I pleading myself to her?* I couldn't believe my actions, again.

"Look, you can go upstairs and get comfortable. I need to make a run real quick, and I'll be back," I told her.

"What about him?" she asked.

Damn, I keep forgetting about him for some reason. It's her, because I never act like this.

"RJ, go get ready for bed," I told him.

"Serenity, can you help me?" he asked.

I looked at Serenity, who looked at me with questionable eyes. I shrugged my shoulders but was happy.

"Sure, sweetie. You go do what you have to do and get back," she said to me while holding her hand out for RJ.

He turned everything off and grabbed her hand leading her upstairs. I got up and headed towards the door when my phone rang. Seeing that it was Drake, I contemplated answering, but quickly, made my decision when I thought of Nina. When he told me he saw Jace out there, I knew I needed to get his ass out of there before he fuck some shit up, but I had to check on something before heading to where they were.

Seeing Tena and Lena there was a surprise, but I knew all about Tena and Candy. Candy's ass is stupid and reminds me of Xena. She's always looking for the next come-up, but I never thought that she would use Tena. It's fucked up that she used my sister. It's even more fucked up that she thought I would want her ass. I couldn't let them know that I already knew what was up, so I played that shit off real smooth.

I may be slowly getting over Nina, but other than Serenity, I'll never want another woman, especially somebody like her. That bitch will let me do anything to her sexually, and will do anything I ask her to do. Silly bitch. I knew I hurt her feelings, but I didn't give a fuck. What I asked her to do was actually going to be the last thing I needed from her, because I was cutting her off. I knew she had fallen for somebody else but wouldn't admit to it. She fucked up big time with Tena thinking she was going to get with my sister and I sit back and allow it. This shit is a game, and this shit happens every day.

After dealing with Candy, I headed back to the house. Lena and Tena followed me home, and as soon as we got inside, Tena went straight to upstairs. I knew she was in her feelings, and that I was going to have to talk to her. I headed to my room and saw Serenity and RJ knocked out on my bed. Shit was a cute ass sight. I pulled my phone out and took a picture. I had to shake my head at the soft ass shit I was doing when it came to her.

I took my clothes off and got in the bed with them trying not to wake them. Serenity started stirring, but quickly stopped moving. RJ was in the middle of us. I was in a deep sleep when my phone started ringing, so I picked it up to answer it.

"Yeah," I answered the phone seeing that it was Jace.

All I could hear was the sounds of Jace struggling, so I got out of bed careful not to wake Serenity.

"Hello!" he yelled frantically.

"Jace, what the fuck is going on?!" I yelled back.

There was silence before I heard another voice.

"Ya boy not ready. He almost got himself shot," Drake said.

POW! POW! POW! POW!

I heard a bunch of commotion before Drake finally got on the line again.

"Yo, get to the hospital. Your pops, Jasper, and Jace got shot," Drake said sounding winded.

"The fuck? I'm on my way," I said.

I threw my clothes on while Serenity was still sleeping. I ran into the room where the twins were spending the night and told them we had to get to the hospital. I told them to meet me in the car. I was out the room before they got out the bed. As soon as they got in the car, I rushed to the hospital not caring about any police. They were going to have to catch me today. I knew Jace's ass wasn't ready for this shit. I don't know what the fuck he was thinking. We pulled up, and I didn't care about parking. I hopped out leaving the car in the emergency parking.

"Reno, you can't leave the car here," I heard Tena say.

I wasn't trying to hear that shit. I ran inside and went straight to the desk.

"Oh, my God. Look who it is. How do I look?" I heard one girl from behind the desk say to another girl.

Both of them bitches were ugly as hell.

"Look here, I don't have time for your ugly ass trying to hit on me. I'm looking for my brother," I said, brushing them off.

"Look, Reno. There goes Drake," I heard Lena say feeling a hand on my shoulder.

I looked at her and saw the direction she was pointing, seeing Drake talking to a doctor. I was about to head in his direction when something caught my attention. I watched as Nina was being rolled in the opposite direction of all of us. At first, I thought I was tripping, but I would know Nina anywhere. Now, I was standing there torn on which direction I should go. Did Drake already get to Nina before I could help? Why didn't he say shit about her over the phone?

Chapter 34

Drake

Watching Jasper pull out his gun and shoot Bone was the last thing I expected to see following them. Then, to watch Jace go down was even more crazy. Leo and I picked him up and went to the car that Bones and Jasper drove in since we were close to it. I could see all the blood that Bones had lost and prayed he wasn't dead, because I wanted his blood on my hands. Once we got Jace in the car, we quickly put Bones in, being careful to not let them touch each other. Fuck Jasper; he could bleed out for all I cared.

We got to the hospital in no time and had them rushed to the back. After attempting to clean the blood all over us, we were finally able to relax, but I knew I had to make the calls. I knew Reno was going to go the fuck off when he got here. I spoke with the doctor who briefed us on the situation, and a few moments later, everyone else showed up. I don't know what the hell was going on with Reno, but as soon as the doctor walked away, and I turned to head back to my seat, I saw Lena and Tena standing by the entrance, and Reno walking in the opposite direction. I walked over to the twins.

"Hey. When did y'all get here? Where is Reno going?" I asked.

"We just got here, and I don't know. He just took off in that direction in a hurry," Lena said, looking in the direction Reno went.

"What's going on?" Tena asked.

"Jace and your Pops got shot," I said, solemnly.

"What?!" they both damn near yelled at the same time.

"Calm, down. They're in surgery now. Come on," I said, walking them over to where Leo was sitting.

Leo stood up when he saw us. The moment Lena saw him, she ran right into his arms and cried. He held her tight, and I wrapped my arm around Tena, who looked to be in a daze. I wasn't sure if it was for both of them or just one of them. We all sat there and waited. Lena and Tena were so out of it that they didn't even ask what happened, and I was actually happy about that. I don't think I could tell them what I saw. It wasn't a pretty sight.

While waiting, I couldn't help but think about Nina. I was wondering how she and my baby were doing and was hating the fact that this was pushing me away from trying to find her. Right after we went to the second house in the country, the gunshots happened before I could investigate. Bones went in with Jasper, and when they came out, Jasper got to blasting. I don't know how long we were sitting there, but I do know that Lena and Tena never stopped crying. Hell, none of us moved a muscle while we sat there. I just so happened to look to my right and saw the doctor coming our way.

"Y'all, the doc is coming," I said, looking at Tena and Lena.

They hopped up quick meeting the doctor halfway. The doctor looked at me, and I gave him a head nod.

"What you think he gone tell them?" Leo asked.

"I don't know, but I sure hope Bones ain't the one that's dead," I said, looking at him.

I turned back and looked in their direction to see what I could try to make out on what he was telling them. It wasn't long before I saw both Tena and Lena's legs buckle.

"Oh, shit," Leo and I said running over to them before they fell.

"What's going on?" I asked.

"They didn't..." Lena started but sirens and alarms started going off.

"Code red. We have a code red in room 1127. Paging, Dr. Harris," we heard come over a loudspeaker.

Shit was loud as hell. The doctor just took off running without even saying anything. Leo and I looked at each other wondering what the hell was going on. We walked the girls back to the chairs. Lena buried her head into Leo's shoulder while Tena leaned her head on mine. We let them calm themselves down.

"What did the doc say?" I asked curiously.

"They're both in a coma," Tena said zoned out.

"Damn," I replied.

I really wanted to say ain't this a bitch. Now, we gotta wait to find out what happens to them, and whether either of them were going to wake up. We sat there and waited for the doctor to come back when Reno finally appeared looking for us.

"Where the fuck you been?" I asked hopping up.

"Fuck you mean! Where the fuck is Jace and my Pops?" he asked.

"They both in comas," I plainly said.

Reno looked at me like I was telling the sickest joke.

"Fuck man, this fucking up the plans on finding Nina!" I exclaimed.

"Fuck you mean? Nina just got pushed down that hallway," Reno said, pointing in the direction of Labor and Delivery.

"Reno, stop smoking fucking crack," I said.

"Motherfucker, are you deaf? I know what the fuck I saw. I tried to follow behind her, but they put me out," he yelled.

I put my hands on the sides of my head and looked at him for a minute. This nigga was tripping. What did he mean Nina's ass was in here?

"Reno, I swear to God if you on some bullshit, and Nina ain't here-,"

"Man, fuck that shit you talking," Reno said, waving me off and walking back to the information table.

I followed behind him with a sinking feeling in my stomach.

"Aye, what room is Nina in?" he asked, interrupting the nurse's conversation.

"Nina who?" one of them asked.

"The only fucking Nina you've know Reno to cuff," he said back.

She rolled her eyes then looked on the computer screen.

"She's not in a room yet; she's having an emergency C-section," she said.

"Emergency what? The baby barely even six months! Aye, I need to get back there, and see my baby," I yelled.

"Your baby?" they both asked in shock, looking from me to Reno.

"Yeah, let me back!" I said, attempting to go through the doors, but the shit was locked by a security pad.

"I'm sorry, sir, but I can't let you back there. She is under strict regulations. I wasn't even supposed to tell you that she was here yet," the girl who first answered me said.

"If something happens to my baby, Reno I swear to God your Pops is done," I yelled.

"Nigga, calm your fucking ass down before you make a case that don't need to be made," Reno bucked back, getting in my face.

Just then, Reno's phone rang, and I saw that it was Serenity.

"Hey, baby," he said in a shaky voice. "I'm at the hospital. It's not me. It's, shit man, it's my pops, my little brother, my Pops best friend, and Nina-,"

Reno dropped the phone and walked over to a group of police officers in a daze.

"Sir, you need to step back," one officer said, trying to restrain him.

He bum rushed his ass out of his way like a rag doll and continued his journey to the person they were protecting.

"Reno! Bro, what are you doing?" I heard Tena yell, and I pushed past the second officer.

"Sir, get on the ground now!" an officer yelled with his gun pointed at him.

"NO, Officer! Please don't shoot," the person they were guarding said.

"Do you know this man?" a female officer asked her.

"Yes, he's my son."

Chapter 35

Leo

Drake's phone kept ringing and the caller ID that only said "S". I usually didn't answer his shit, but with everything going on, it could possibly be important. It rang again for the 10th time, and I finally answered.

"What up," I said.

"Drake?" a soft, angelic voice asked.

"Nah, Drake is busy at the moment, but this his cousin Leo," I said, wondering who the fuck this could be.

"Hi, Leo, I'm Serenity, Reno's girlfriend," she replied.

What the fuck? I know Drake wasn't doing the game like that, was he? Damn, he was just begging for Reno to kill him at this point.

"Listen, I am on your side. I was sent by Tamara, Nina's cousin to help Drake find Nina by getting close to Reno," she explained.

"How I know you not bullshitting?" I asked, not ready to just openly trust her.

"Good question, you don't, but if you speak with your cousin, he will explain everything. Besides that point, I wanted to know if Reno was with or around you? He isn't answering my calls," she asked.

"Nah, I haven't seen him," I lied.

Like I said, I didn't know this chick like that, and right now, everybody was suspect.

"Ok, I will keep trying him. Thank you, Leo," she said.

"No problem," I said.

Once I hung up the phone, I looked over at Lena. She was curled up on the couch with her head resting in Tena's lap. I watched her from afar and wondered what the fuck it was about her that had me doing the shit I was doing. Before I met Lena, I had three other females. Sexy ones with their own money and careers, too. No doubt, I could see Lena being just as good as them when she graduated, if not better, but something about her innocence caught me off guard and made me want to be around her all the time. I was just about to walk up on them when an older, attractive woman walked in and broke down in tears.

"Where is he? Where is he?" she asked the information desk.

I wasn't standing too far away since I took my phone call in the hallway, so I could hear everything.

"Who are you looking for?" a nurse asked her.

"My love, Jasper Valentino," she cried.

Oh, she must have been that snake ass Jasper's ole lady. I was looking at the diamonds on her wrists, fingers, and ears, trying to figure out how Jasper had her so iced up. Damn, Bone was paying his flunky out the ass. Just then, the twins spotted her and jumped up.

"They all got shot," Lena cried.

She fell into the woman's arms and started crying again, and I moved from my hiding position. I grabbed Lena in my arms and calmed her down in a way that only I could.

"This is my stepmother Michelle," Lena told me.

"Stepmother?" I asked.

"Yes, she's my father's wife," Lena explained.

"Nice to meet you," the Michelle bitch said.

"Nice meeting you, too," I said playing along.

Shit was turning into the Twilight Zone around here. Reno's ass spazzed out, and then Lena later told us that, the woman he thought was dead most of his life, really wasn't. Drake's ass went off so much about his baby that they finally let him down the hallway to stand outside of where Nina was. Now, I just found out that Bones' wife is most likely fucking his boy Jasper. I wouldn't believe none of this shit if I wasn't currently in the middle of it.

"We should call Serenity," Lena suggested.

"What for?" I asked her.

"Because I know she's awake by now with RJ and wondering where Reno is," she explained.

I didn't want to tip her off that Serenity could possibly be against her brother, so I relaxed a little.

"Cool," I simply said.

While Lena called Serenity, I pulled Tena to the side. I knew Tena was a bit more level-headed, so I wanted to pick her brain a little bit.

"T, let me ask you something?" I asked her.

"What's up?" she asked me.

"Your stepmoms cool and shit? You ever peeped some foul shit about her?" I asked, not really one to filter my tongue.

"Honestly, I don't fuck with her like that. She tries to judge my lifestyle," Tena said.

"I might still be high, but I was standing on the side over there and she came in asking for Jasper Valentino and calling him her love and shit," I told her.

"Jasper? Oh shit, I forgot he was in here. I have to ask about him," she said, attempting to walk to the desk before I grabbed her.

"Nah, T, it's some snake shit going on with Jasper," I told her.

"What do you mean, Leo?" she asked me, looking at me a little funny.

"There goes the doctor!" Lena yelled in the background.

I turned to see her running up to the doctor with Michelle closely behind her. Tena ran off before I could tell her what I meant, so I just shook my head and followed behind her.

"Mr. Russell has woken up, but-," the doctor was saying.

"But what?" Michelle asked, cutting him off.

"But, he seems to be suffering from amnesia. When he fell, he hit his head, and it took some part of his memory. We have talked with him some, and he seems to only remember his son Reno and a Janay Russell," the doctor said.

"Janay Russell. That was his first wife. She is deceased," Michelle said.

"Deceased you say?" the doctor asked with big eyes.

"Yes, she died years ago of an overdose," Michelle said.

"Who the fuck is Janay Russell?" I whispered to Lena, already having a feeling that it may have been the woman who said Reno is her son.

"She was Reno's mother," Lena said.

"The woman who was being escorted by the police and shit?" I asked.

"It looked like her. At least, from the way Reno always described her. Dad never saved pictures of her, so I've never seen her before, honestly," Lena explained.

"But she looked just like Reno. I wonder if it really is her, and if so, why would she fake her death?" Tena asked, walking up to us.

"Where is Michelle?" Lena asked, looking around.

"She went back to see Dad first," Tena said.

"Or maybe Jasper," I mumbled.

"Jasper? Oh no, all of this chaos, and I forgot he was here," Lena stated.

I shook my head and exchanged a look with Tena. My baby was a bit more innocent ,and I wasn't ready to let her know about Jasper yet. We stood in silence, each in our own thoughts for a while until my own phone rang. It was someone I hadn't spoken to forever it seemed.

"Hey, Mama," I said, answering the phone.

"Hey, Mama, my ass. What the hell is going on, and when can we come home? Now, I love being out here in Atlanta and not paying any bills in this massive house, but your auntie is getting on my last nerves, and I miss my own house in Little Rock. Now, if you all don't find Nina soon, we may have to come help you fools," she vented.

"Mama, chill out, please. Nina has been found, and she's in labor with the baby," I told her.

"What? She's about to have my grandbaby? This early? Oh, lord, we have to get down there," Drake's mom's started yelling.

"Dammit, will you two calm down and listen to me. Nobody is going anywhere until we straighten all of this shit out. Damn, women and their need to always-,"

The phone was taken out of my hand by Lena, and I smirked at her taking charge.

"Hi, this is Lena, Leo's girlfriend. Yes ma'am, he certainly is. I have no idea why he hasn't told you about me, but I would love to meet you. Oh, yes ma'am, everything is going to be ok. He just likes to be overprotective and wants to make sure everything is ok. Yes, ma'am, and you, too."

Lena ended the call and walked up on me close.

"There is a way to do things to get the result you want," she smiled at me.

"Oh, yeah?" I asked her, pulling her against me, so she could feel how hard my dick was.

"Baby," she whined.

I ignored her and looked her in the eyes. She had no idea how bad she just turned me on.

"Lena, you mine, you know that shit, right?" I told her.

"Yes, baby, I know it, and I'm proud to be yours," she whispered.

"Who are you loyal to? Tell me right now," I asked her.

"You, baby. I trust you," she said.

I searched her eyes for any signs of doubt and saw none. I looked around and saw that Tena was busy texting, and I thought of an opportunity.

"Did you drive your car?" I asked her.

"Yes," she nodded.

I pulled her to the ER parking lot, and she hit her alarm. We barely made it inside the backseat before we were ripping each other's clothes off. I was glad she had her windows tinted black. She climbed up on my lap, and I held my dick in place for her to slide down on.

"Ahhhh, shit baby," she cried, as I pushed up into her, losing patience.

"Shit, I missed you," I moaned. "Lena, you can't let a nigga down, baby. I don't put rings on just anybody."

"I'm yours, baby, all yours," she replied, leaning down to kiss my neck.

Chapter 36

Nina

"I'm so scared. Please tell me if my baby is ok," I cried.

"Ma'am, you have to be still, ok? The doctor is stitching you back up," a nurse told me.

"I want my baby," I cried, meaning it for two people.

I wanted my newborn baby and my baby Drake, bad. I was miserable without either of them by my side. Since the C-section was so last minute, I felt every bit of pain. When my baby was pulled out, I heard a tiny cry, and then it sounded shaky. The doctors told me it was a girl that I had yet to name, because I was so distraught. Exhaustion finally took over me, and I fell back and went to sleep.

***

"Steve, I'm going to go with lingerie!"

"Lingerie!"

Ding!

I opened my eyes and saw that Family Feud was playing. I blinked a few times before finally coming to and realized I was in a hospital bed. I heard light snoring, and my heart started beating fast. I knew those snores from anywhere. I slowly turned my head to the left and saw Drake sound asleep in the chair beside me, and I, instantly, burst into tears and thanked God that it was him and nobody else. I was back with my baby.

"Nina, baby, what's wrong?" Drake asked me, waking up.

"Baby, I'm so sorry I tried to run away. I feel like this is all of my fault. I love you, baby. I'm sorry," I cried.

"No, Nina, stop that; it's not your fault. Look at me, baby," he said, getting up and sitting on the edge of my bed, "None of this shit is your fault. We all had secrets, and you were the only innocent one who ended up catching hell from it all," Drake told me.

I just stared at him with tears running down my face. I finally felt at peace again. He leaned over and removed a piece of hair from my face.

"I named her Destiny," Drake told me. "It's probably not the name you wanted, but when I looked at her fighting, I knew this shit was destiny. All those years, I watched you with Reno and wished you were mine. All those dreams I had of making love to you, and now you're finally mine. This shit was destiny, baby, and Destiny is living proof. I'm going to do you right, because no one else in this world ever has," Drake said, getting teary-eyed.

I reached up and wiped the tear in his eyes before it could fall. I held his head in my chest and let him get his emotions out while I cried with him. We were in the middle of embracing when I heard someone at the door.

"Come in," I said, assuming it was a nurse.

Reno's mother walked in, and Drake paused. I could see him looking at her trying to see if it was real, and I knew that was the confirmation that she was indeed Reno's mother.

"Hello, Drake. You have grown into a handsome man," she smiled at Drake.

"What the fuck?" Drake mumbled, looking back at me.

"She wasn't really dead, baby," I explained.

Drake stood up and hugged her so tight I almost got teary-eyed.

"Reno isn't going to believe this. Wait a minute, where is my partner at?" Drake said, shocking me completely.

I hadn't heard him call Reno his partner in years.

"They had to sedate him. He flipped out when he saw me. My baby boy couldn't believe it," she cried. "Drake, I am so glad my son has you as a friend in his life. You have always helped take care of him."

Drake cleared his throat, awkwardly, and I looked down. If only she knew. Suddenly, I felt guilty again. The reason for Drake and Reno falling out and all of this beef going on was ultimately because of me.

"Your minute is up," a police officer said.

"Yes, sir," Reno's mother said.

"Hold on, why are the police hounding you and shit?" Drake asked, getting defensive.

"They said it is procedure. They have to be certain I didn't fake my own death," she explained.

Once she left the room, Drake leaned against the wall and stared at me for a minute, and I shyly stared back. I wish I knew what he was thinking, because suddenly, I got the feeling that maybe he was regretting everything.

"What, Drake?" I asked out of fear.

"You're beautiful," he said.

I blushed and looked down. He did still love me!

"You want to see her?" he asked me.

"Yes, I do," I said, looking up and getting excited.

"Ok, cool, let me grab a nurse," he said, walking out.

Once he left, I looked up at the sky and smiled.

"Thank you, God!"

I was never too heavy in the church, but after this, I was going to be a faithful attendee in someone's church. I can't believe I got kidnapped and twice at that!

"Well, hello, Ms. Nina, so glad to see you are feeling better. Are you feeling up to seeing your beautiful daughter?" the nurse asked me while walking in.

"Yes, ma'am, and thank you for being so nice to me during my labor," I said.

"Oh, honey, it's no problem. I knew you were in pain and wanted to help you," she smiled.

Drake helped me into a wheelchair, and I was wheeled down to the NICU. After sanitizing my hands, she let Drake and I back into a small room. As soon as I laid eyes on Destiny in the tub with IV's all over her, I cried out of fear. I was afraid that my baby was too small. The nurse showed me where I could stick my hand in and rub her and I felt my heart grow bigger than it ever had.

"My baby, oh my gosh, Drake, I just had a baby," I cried.

I couldn't believe something so tiny and perfect came out of me. Destiny cooed a little and gave me a big yawn, and my heart swelled a little more.

"She's perfect, isn't she?" Drake asked.

"Yes, baby, she is," I said.

He walked behind my wheelchair, leaned down, and kissed my cheek.

"Life has been hell not knowing if you two were safe. Nina, if we ever have any problems or disagreements, don't run from me, please. Just talk to me," Drake begged me.

"I'm done running. Everything I've ever needed and wanted is right here in front of me, and it's been in front of me for years," I told him.

We watched Destiny for a little while longer before Drake wheeled me back to my room. Once we got inside, he placed me back on the bed and sat at the foot of it, massaging my feet.

"What's on your mind?" he asked me.

"Let's talk about RJ," I said.

Chapter 37

Jace

"Do you know your name?"

I blinked, as I struggled to focus on where I was. Once I saw the board in front of me, I knew I was in a hospital.

"Can you hear me?"

I looked over at the annoying ass nurse beside me who was talking to me while looking through my chart.

"I said, can you-,"

"Yeah, man," I replied, cutting her off.

Her voice was annoying as hell.

"Oh, my gosh, you're awake! Do you know your name?" she asked me.

"Jace Russell," I told her.

"That's right, and Jace, how old are you?" she asked.

"What's up with all the questions?" I asked, trying to raise my voice, but it cut out some.

"Here, drink some water," she told me.

She put a straw to my lips, and once I swallowed, I felt pain in my back and stomach.

"Aw, fuck," I grimaced.

"I knew that pain would kick in eventually," the nurse laughed. "Your family is worried sick about you. Let me go alert them you are awake."

As I sat there, I slowly started to remember the events that led up to the present situation. Jasper shot my pops and then tried to kill me. What the fuck was really going on? Jasper damn near raised me and was always quiet in nature. Who knew the nigga was a snake in hiding?

"Jace, oh my gosh, you're awake," Lena said, walking in the room.

"Bro, you scared the fuck out of us," Tena said, walking in behind her.

Leo and Michelle entered last, and all the women started gossiping while Leo fell back and gave me a look. I wondered how much he knew about what was going on.

"Aye, let me holler at Leo in private everybody," I said.

"In private? Why?" Lena asked.

"Baby, it's a man thing; you wouldn't understand," Leo said, grabbing Lena and kissing her.

I still wasn't used to seeing this nigga kiss on my sister, and I felt some type of way, but shit, I was fucking his little cousin, so I couldn't get too mad. Once they left, Leo pulled up a chair and sat beside me.

"How much do you remember about what happened?" Leo simply asked.

"Shit, every fucking thing. How the fuck did you and Drake end up out there with us?" I asked, trying to sit up. "Ahh, fuck!"

"Be easy, young blood. A bullet went through you. The real question is what the hell were you thinking going on a mission with no backup? What if Jasper did y'all both and left the bodies there? We would still be searching for you right now," Leo said.

"Man, dead that shit. Everybody is still suspect, including you and Drake," I said.

"Stop trying to beef all your life and listen the fuck up. If it wasn't for Drake, I wouldn't even be on your side, and if it wasn't for the fact that I'm about to cuff your sister, I wouldn't even give you the game. Check your fucking emotions and open your eyes. You knee deep in some shit that can take your ass out in the blink of an eye. The only person shooting around this bitch is Jasper, so that's who the fuck you need to watch," Leo said.

He was right, but I didn't want to give him the satisfaction of agreeing with him. Instead, I changed the direction of the conversation a little bit.

"Where the fuck is Jasper at, anyway?" I asked Leo.

"Shit, somewhere around this bitch laid up. I popped that snake ass nigga after I seen him trying to take you out," Leo said.

"Where's my pops?" I asked.

"He's up, but they say he can't remember shit," Leo said.

"I'll let him know then," I said, successfully sitting up this time.

"Nah, he don't remember shit at all, probably not even you. He didn't even know who the twins and were," Leo said.

"Fuck you mean?" I asked.

"He hit his head when he fell and fucked up his brain," Leo explained.

"Man, fuck Jasper. I want to dead him right now," I said.

"We gone get him, I promise you that," Leo said.

"Man, why the fuck isn't Reno here?" I asked, getting pissed off.

"Be easy; your brother got a lot of shit going on right now, but he's here for you," Leo said, standing up.

Leo went to get the twins and Michelle and left. Michelle was weirdly being overbearing. As far as I was concerned, she could chill on all of that, because I wanted to talk to Tena and find out why she was mugging Michelle so tough.

"Your poor father, bless his heart! He doesn't even remember anyone but Reno. I just don't know what I'm going to do. Well, I will leave you all here while I go check on him," Michelle said, leaving the room.

Once she left, Tena vented.

"That bitch is up to something. I don't know why I've never picked up on it before, but her vibe is weird right now. It's almost like she's happy about what's going on," Tena said.

"Why you feel like that, sis?" I asked her.

"When has she ever been so damn affectionate with any of us? She's usually stuck up and being a bitch, not giving a fuck about us," Tena said.

"She's right, Jace. Michelle is a bit dramatic right now," Lena said.

I stayed silent, as I thought back on some shit that I've never spoken about.

***

"Man, why you acting like you so scared to tell me? How wet are you right now?" I asked Stacey.

"Jace, you are so bad. I told you, I'm not ready for sex yet," she replied.

"Man, alright," I sighed, standing up and stretching.

I put the controller to my Xbox down and headed downstairs to get something to drink. It was almost three in the morning, so everybody was asleep, or so I thought. I heard voices, as I walked to the kitchen, but something told me to keep quiet and listen.

"I just can't stand it anymore. He is disrespectful, and he doesn't even try to hide his infidelity," I heard Michelle cry.

"You knew all of this was going in. Remember, you were his side woman for over ten years," Jasper's voice jumped in.

"But once his last wife was out of the picture, I thought it would be me and him," Michelle cried.

"You and I both know that is not how it works. I bet you wish you had taken that date offer from me instead of him now, huh?" Jasper said.

"Sometimes I do," Michelle said.

"Just stay close to him. Figure out where everything is, and you'll make it out better than the last two," Jasper said.

"I just want to be loved," Michelle said.

They got silent after that, and since I wasn't able to see them, I had no idea what caused the silence.

"Thank you, Jasper. You make me feel loved," Michelle said.

Her voice grew closer to where I was, so I ran into the living room and hid behind the couch until the coast was clear.

***

"Man, fuck that bitch!" I finally said.

"Now, we're on the same page. I have a plan," Tena said.

"I'm down, but first, let me borrow somebody's phone," I said.

"Here," Tena said, handing me hers.

I dialed Amber's number. She didn't answer, so I left her a message.

"Call this number back, pretty girl. You know you miss a nigga," I said, smirking.

I gave Tena her phone back, and Lena started smiling.

"Baby bro, you have a little girlfriend?" Lena asked.

"Yeah," I said, waving her off.

"Who is she?" she asked.

"Man, y'all gone flip out," I laughed.

"Better not be Candy," Tena said.

"Who the fuck is Candy?" I asked.

"Ignore her ass. Now, come on with the info," Lena said.

"She's Drake's half-sister," I said.

Tena and Lena both looked shocked.

Chapter 38

Lena

"What's on your mind?" Leo asked me.

"A lot," I replied, keeping my eyes on the soft waves from the Arkansas River crashing against the rocks.

"Hell, I'm not a mind reader, so you have to tell me something," Leo said.

"Shit got crazy, baby. I wasn't expecting all of this," I sighed.

"Yeah, it did get crazy, but where is your head at? You all in, or what?" he asked me.

I turned and looked into his eyes. As crazy as the world was around me, everything felt so right and calm with Leo. If you were to ask me did I trust him with my life, I would unflinchingly say yes.

"Lena?" Leo asked again.

"I'm all in, baby. I'm all in," I said.

It's been a week since the shootings, and Nina has been found, but life was just as hard. My father didn't know who anyone was outside of Reno and his mother, plus he was being investigated for the kidnapping and hostage of Reno's mother. He was now in a holding cell awaiting trial. Jasper ended up being paralyzed from the waist down and is still in the hospital. Jace is home now, and he is pretending to not remember Jasper trying to kill him and his father.

Then, there was Reno, and he was a mess. My poor brother has had the craziest life these days. First, he loses his longtime girlfriend to his best friend, then finds out his son is really the son of his best friend, and now, he finds out the woman he thought was dead all these years is really alive. The only good thing was that he had Serenity around. She has been here for him every step of the way, and I've even noticed her trying to patch things back up with Drake and Reno.

"I want to do the honors," I told Leo.

"Lena, I'm not letting you kill nobody. You're not ready for that type of shit on your conscious," Leo told me.

"Baby, I'm more than ready. I feel like I have to do this," I said.

Leo pulled me into his arms and kissed me.

"Nah, little thug, as long as you have me as your man, you'll never have to touch a gun to pull a trigger," he said.

"Let's change the subject. Leo, let me ask you something, and be very honest with me," I told him.

He just looked down at me until I continued.

"What do you do for a living? To have money?" I asked him.

"I sell drugs," he shrugged.

"Ok. That was honest," I said, being shocked at his honesty.

"You already knew that," Leo said.

"I figured," I corrected him.

"No, you knew. Don't ask questions that you already know the answer to. You know I don't like that," Leo said.

I rolled my eyes and moved away from him. He pulled me back in his space and forced me to make eye contact with him.

"Don't start that shit, Lena. You know I love you, baby, and you know I'll do whatever it takes to make you strong. Don't go through life being so naïve when you know better, because people will manipulate the fuck out of you if you're not careful," Leo said.

"I understand, baby," I nodded.

"Come on, let's go get something to eat," he told me.

We held hands and walked the Big Dam Bridge. I blushed at the way people openly stared at us and felt prideful that I was with Leo. I still remember when we first got together and how scared I was at the fact that he could be cheating on me. Now, I had him all to myself.

Once we got to the bottom of the bridge, Leo pointed out a guy with a camera.

"Come on, baby, let's take a picture," Leo said.

"Baby, no; we don't know him," I laughed.

"Hey, my man, how much for a picture of me and my lady?" Leo yelled out to him, ignoring me.

"Oh, no charge. I'm just practicing to build my portfolio up," he said.

"Baby, people are looking," I whined.

"Come on," Leo said, positioning me by the rocks.

I ignored all the people who were watching us and started taking pictures with Leo. It was actually kind of fun.

"Ok, I want some of my girl by herself," Leo said.

The photographer had me do a series of poses looking out at the water. Finally, he got on the rocks in front of me with his back towards to the water, and I got confused. I didn't think the background would be as nice with random people in it.

"Lena," I heard Leo's voice say from behind me.

"Yes, bab-,"

I stopped talking as soon as I saw him. Everyone in the background was smiling, and a few were even crying at us, but none harder than me, as I burst into tears. Leo was on one knee, holding a cute black and silver box.

"Lena, come here, baby," Leo said with his hand out.

My legs felt broken, but somehow, I managed to walk up to him. He grabbed my hand and kissed it, looking up at me. I was crying super hard by now.

"Lena, I know you already said yes to me, but this time, I wanted to do it the right way. Lena, will you marry me?" Leo asked.

"Yes, baby, yes," I sobbed.

He opened the box, and I saw the most beautiful ring. My hand shook, as he placed it on my finger, and everyone clapped around us.

"I got it," the photographer said.

"Baby, this was a setup?" I asked.

"Look at you, catching on already," he winked at me.

The first thing I did once we got in the car was called Tena.

"Sis, guess what I'm staring at right now?" I asked her.

"The sun? Hell, I don't know," Tena said.

"No, stupid. A big shiny diamond ring," I announced.

"He finally gave you a ring?" Tena asked.

"He did, and it's huge girl!" I bragged.

"Shit, well send me a picture or something," Tena said in a not so happy voice.

"Tena, I promise you will find the right person soon. You're bomb as hell, girl. You're smart, beautiful, and most of all, you have money. What girl wouldn't want that?" I asked her.

"A lot. Face it, Lena, I'm a lesbian, and a woman who likes women doesn't have a lot of options. Most women are only doing it as an experiment," Tena vented.

"The world is changing. Just trust me, sis. Give it some time," I told her.

We made small talk for a little longer before ending the call. I quickly sent her a picture of my ring. I dialed the next number, and then took a deep breath.

"What you over there scared about?" Leo asked me.

"I really miss my friendship with Nina, and I want to make things right. She was like a sister to me," I told him.

"Well, then, call her, but baby, you can't be mad if she doesn't want to be your friend. Hell, it's life, and some people don't forgive so easily," Leo said.

"You're right, baby," I agreed.

I called Nina, and to my surprise, she answered right away.

"Hello?" she answered.

"Nina! Hey, girl, how are you feeling?" I asked her.

"I'm doing great, actually. I just left from seeing Destiny," Nina said, sounding upbeat.

"Aww, that's so cute. How is Destiny doing?" I asked, beaming with happiness.

Leo reached over and grabbed my hand, and I felt complete in that moment.

"Destiny is doing so good. She should be home in the next month or so," Nina said, sounding optimistic.

"I can't wait to see her. I bet she is a doll," I said.

"Lena, she is so perfect. I'm so glad she's mine. God really blessed me with this beautiful baby girl," Nina bragged.

"Nina, I just wanted to say that I'm sorr-,"

"No girl, don't. It's ok. One thing I learned from all this craziness is forgiveness, and that it was important for me to forgive, not only for others, but for myself," Nina said.

"Wow, Nina, you are truly amazing."

Chapter 39

Reno

"I really like her son. You need to marry that one," my mama said.

"How you know I want to do all that?" I joked.

"I see how you look at her. Plus, she is beautiful with a nice body," my mama added.

I watched Serenity as she played the game with RJ. RJ was beating her ass, and she was pretending to be sad. I honestly don't know how I got so lucky with Serenity, but I'm glad she came in my life when she did. Everything about her felt so right to me. It took everything in me not to go fuck up everything around me. Whenever I was around her, I would be calm and almost weak. My mom was now chilling in the massage chair in my game room, and I was leaning against the door watching Serenity's ass jiggle in her dress every time she moved. She was now standing up trying to beat RJ, but he was cold just like me.

Ding! Dong!

"I got it," I announced.

I went upstairs and left them downstairs. Once I made it to the living room, I pulled one of my pistols from my waist and answered the door.

"What's up?" I asked Drake.

"What's good? How you been holding up?" he asked me.

"Keeping shit G. You need something?" I asked him, not caring for this small talk bullshit.

"I need to run something by you," he said.

"Ok, bet," I said, stepping back and letting him in.

I know he saw the gun in my hand; I wanted him to see it. Drake may be neutral, now, but I don't fully trust this nigga. He's sneaky as fuck.

"Let's go to my office," I said.

He knew where it was, so I let him walk in front. Like I said, I didn't trust the nigga. Once we got in, I sat at my desk and started rolling a blunt.

"You gone hit this loud?" I asked him.

"Hell, yeah. I need this shit," Drake said.

"How the baby?" I asked him.

"She's cool, man. Thanks for asking," Drake said. "That, kind of, is a reason on why I'm here."

"What? You gon' tell me the baby mine or some shit?" I asked, jokingly.

I guess Drake didn't find the shit funny, because he got quiet and started going through his phone like a little bitch.

"Man, get out your feelings. You see the one I got on my arm. I'm not tripping on Nina anymore," I said, meaning the shit for real this time.

Drake slid his phone over to me, and I looked at it. I saw a pretty ass little girl that damn near looked like my twin sisters and me.

"Damn, I know you don't have another one," I joked.

"That's Natalia's baby," Drake said.

I stopped rolling and looked at the phone again. It was no denying that she looked just like me. Damn, she was beautiful as hell. A nigga really had a daughter out here that I hadn't even met.

"How you get this shit?" I asked him.

"Finish rolling that blunt. You'll need it," Drake said.

"Man, I can barely roll this shit. My hands shaking and shit. Fuck man; this bitch really got me missing out on my daughter's life and shit," I vented, hitting the desk.

Drake nodded in agreement and slid the weed and rolling papers in front of him.

"You right. She is foul for that one," Drake said.

I felt myself getting more and more mad by the second.

"Be easy, man," Drake said.

"Shit, I'm trying," I said, breaking out in a cold sweat.

All I could picture was wrapping my hands around Natalia's neck. I stayed calm enough to hit the blunt, and then, Drake started talking again.

"When I moved out to Atlanta, I linked up with my boy and later found out Natalia was his cousin. She was still pregnant then, but shit, with all this extra bullshit that happened, we lost touch. She reached out to me a few days ago and said she wanted me to talk to you, because she wanted you to be in your child's life," Drake explained.

"Where the fuck is she?" I asked.

"Hiding," Drake replied.

"Hiding? For what?" I asked, blowing out a smoke ring.

"Reno, you know damn well she's scared of you," Drake said.

"Shit, I can't tell. The bitch pulled a gun out on me last time I saw her," I told him.

"Reno, on some real shit, I'm not bringing her here if you still on that wild shit," Drake said.

"Call her ass right now," I demanded.

Drake hesitated for a minute, but he finally pulled out his phone and called her. Shit, he didn't have a choice. Otherwise, I would be out looking for her my damn self.

"Hello?" Natalia's voice said over the phone.

"Hey, you busy?" Drake asked her.

"Not super. I just laid Ramona down for a nap," she said.

"Natalia," I said.

She got quiet, and Drake shook his head. I motioned for him to put the phone on the desk, as I passed him the blunt.

"Judging by how quiet you got, you already know who the fuck this is. Natalia, is Ramona my daughter?" I asked her calmly.

"Yes," she said in a low voice.

"I want to see her," I told her.

"Reno, I-I don't feel like that's safe just yet. I mean, I do, but it's too soon," Natalia said.

"Natalia, miss me with that shit. I'm not worried about you. I have a real woman who I'm not about to lose behind no dumb shit. I just want to see the daughter you kept away from me," I said.

"You didn't even want the baby, Reno," Natalia tried to argue.

Women and their irrelevant ass arguments. No, I didn't want the baby, but a nigga was trying to do right by it now, so what was the issue? I would bet my last dollar Serenity wouldn't do me like this.

"I want to see her tomorrow," I told her.

"Only if my family is present, and Drake is, too," she demanded.

"Cool. What size clothes does she wear? What's her full name? Damn, Natalia this is fucked up. I don't know shit about my own little girl," I said, trying not to break.

Shit, I was going to need another blunt and a few drinks.

"I'm sorry, Reno. We will see you tomorrow, and I'll text all her information to you. Your number is the same, right?" she asked.

"Yeah."

I sat and smoked another blunt with Drake in silence and then he left to tend to Nina. He showed me a picture of their baby, and as much as I didn't want to admit it, she was beautiful as hell. I went to the bedroom and stood in the shower hoping the hot water would calm me down. When it didn't, I started kicking and punching the walls, trying to take the pain away.

216

"Reno? Reno, baby, calm down," Serenity said, coming into the bathroom.

I tried to calm down and not let her see me break, but I couldn't help it. All of this shit was too much. I wanted out of this fucked up ass life I was living. I could see her through the glass shower wall undressing. She finally stepped in with me, and I just took her in. This was the first time she's stood before me fully naked, and she was breath-taking.

"Come here, Reno," she said to me.

Shit, I was stuck. For the first time ever, I was a deer in headlights in front of a woman. She closed the space between us and wrapped her arms around me.

"It's ok to cry, baby. Don't ever deny yourself that right," she whispered to me.

"I can't do this shit," I cried.

I felt like my chest was about to explode at any minute.

"Yes you can, Reno. I'm right here with you," she told me.

She held my face in her hands, and I got lost in her eyes. You don't understand how much I meant it when I said that I needed this woman. She leaned up and kissed me, and suddenly, my tears went away. I felt a feeling I've never felt before, not even with Nina. It was deeper than me wanting to be inside of her.

"Serenity, I love you," I told her, breaking the kiss.

She stared into my eyes with tears in her eyes, and I felt my heartbeat in my ears. I needed to hear her say it back. Every second that passed felt like minutes as we stared at each other in silence.

"Reno, you can't hurt me," she whispered.

"Why would I do that to you? I love you," I told her.

"I-I," she started, but stopped.

"Say it," I demanded.

The tears started running down her face now, and I watched her finally break down in front of me. It was jaw dropping. This woman who seemed so in control was getting weak for me right in front of my eyes. The bathroom was steamy now, and I could hardly see, but I saw that shit. I pulled her in for another kiss, this time grabbing her ass and placing her right hand on my rock hard dick.

"Say it, baby," I whispered to her.

"I love you even more, Reno," she moaned, out of breath.

"Come here," I told her.

I washed her body while she stood there crying. Damn, was she really that scared to love a nigga like me? I was about to show her why I had the women crazy over me, only this time, I wanted to commit only to her. After I had finished showering, I picked her up like a baby and carried her wet body to the bedroom. I went to get a towel to dry her off and laughed a little bit.

"What happened to that strong woman I had earlier?" I joked.

"I'm scared, baby," she admitted.

"Shit, I'm scared, too. I can't be hurt, again, but I trust you with my life, Serenity," I told her, truthfully.

I laid her body on the bed and climbed on top of her.

"Can I have you?" I asked her.

"I'm already yours," she whispered.

Shit! I damn near busted one just from her saying that. I kissed my way down her body until I got to her hips. She already knew what time it was, because she started breathing hard and shaking. I wasted no time in wrapping my tongue around her clit and torturing her.

"Oh, Reno, you feel so good, baby," she whispered, grabbing the back of my head.

That shy shit was gone out the window this time. She started grinding on my face, and I went harder until she backed down. I didn't need her help.

"Do it for me, baby," I mumbled, with her clit still on my tongue.

"Ooooo, baby right there. Oh, right there," she started screaming.

I stayed right where she wanted me and spoke to that clit the way a real nigga should. It was less than a minute before her legs started shaking, and she was crying and screaming my name. I didn't stop until she was hitting me in the forehead and begging for me to stop. She looked so helpless that I almost felt sorry for her, but she still hadn't gotten the real deal yet.

"You ok, baby?" I asked her, kissing her lips softly.

"I love you so much," she said.

"I love you, too," I told her.

I positioned myself between her legs, and she got a little shook.

"I'll go slow," I told her.

I started working my way inside of her, and she instantly flinched.

"Shit, Reno, how big are you?" she moaned.

"It's a little big, baby, but I got you," I whispered in her ear.

I had to lean down on her and pin her down so she would stop running and take it. Once I got all the way in, I was stuck. Literally. I felt like if I made one small movement, I would get her pregnant.

"You better not ever fucking leave me," I moaned in her ear.

"I promise I won't," she told me.

I started stroking her slowly, and she made the sexiest moans in my ear. Damn, that pussy was good, and I'd had some good ones in my day. I was ready to give her my last name, all of my money, everything. This shit was dangerous, but shit, I'm Reno, and I don't give a fuck about danger.

****

"Thank you for being here," I told Serenity.

"I'm your woman; I'm supposed to be here for you," she told me.

"She gon' be jealous as shit when she see you," I told Serenity.

"I'm positive that she is beautiful. All of the exes you've shown me have been," Serenity said.

"Yeah, but not like you," I told her. "That looks like them now," I said watching a car pull up.

We were at Murray Lock and Dam on the Arkansas River. It was public, calm, and peaceful, as Serenity would call it. Serenity was about to make me shoot a few people because of the white jeans and pink crop top she wore that exposed the bottom half of her abs. She looked sexy, but shit, I didn't want nobody but me to see it.

Natalia was typical Natalia. She was wearing a dress with over half her chest spilling out and heels. She was a little thicker than I remembered, but she still looked good. My attention was on Ramona, holding her hand and walking beside her. Damn, she looked just like I pictured my daughter would look. She looked at me and started waving, and I already knew that, from that point on, she would be a daddy's girl.

"Damn, that's really my daughter," I said.

Once they reached us, I reached out for her, and she jumped in my arms like it was nothing.

"Ramona, this is your daddy, Reno," Natalia told her.

She was too busy playing with my necklaces to pay her any attention. Drake stood off to the side with his hands in his pockets.

"Hey, I'm Serenity," Serenity said, hugging Natalia.

"Hello. I'm Natalia," Natalia replied.

I let them have their moment and walked over to Drake.

"Aye, man, thanks for this. I appreciate it," I said, shaking his hand.

"No problem. You deserve to be a father," he said.

That struck a chord with me. Ramona was officially my first child by blood. I shrugged it off and tried not to let it show on my face.

"You're right," I simply said, walking off.

Chapter 40

Drake

"It was one of those nights when you and Reno were good, and I didn't have anyone to talk to. Drake was always a shoulder cry on, and one thing led to another, and well, you know," Xena said.

Nina sat stone-faced, while I was sweating bullets. Reno was just chilling and eating his food without a care in the world, and Serenity picked at a salad.

"It was never a love thing, baby," I added.

Nina just nodded and looked back at Xena, who held her head down in shame.

"I don't judge you. I actually don't judge anyone at this table. I just realized that people are who they are, and I have to accept that," Nina said.

"Baby, I-,"

"No, Drake. It's cool. Don't make any excuses. I was Reno's girl back then, so you were free to fuck who you wanted to," Nina said.

Everybody got quiet, as we struggled to find the right things to say. Finally, Reno broke the silence.

"So, what about RJ, because I'm the one who stepped up and took care of him all these years. I'm not walking away. That's my son, too," Reno said.

"Reno-," Serenity said, before he cut her off.

"Nah, baby, I'm serious right now. Everybody wants to act like I'm the bad guy here, but look at this shit. Yeah, I probably didn't treat Nina right, but nobody else around this motherfucking table is a saint either. Xena, you fucked over your girl to fuck me knowing we were together. Drake, you fucked me over when you sat back and watched me raise RJ knowing he was your son. Let's also not forget that you've been wanting my girl since day one. Nina, I know I was wrong for the shit I did, but damn, did you really have to fuck my homeboy? Let's face it, we all fucked up at this table," Reno said.

"Reno, nobody is saying that we aren't," Xena said.

"I'm just saying, before somebody tries to pull some bullshit this way," Reno replied, pointing to himself.

Reno was always jumping the gun. Don't get me wrong. He was right, but shit, he was always on defense when nobody was blaming him for anything.

"Well, I think we should both sit down and talk to RJ," I told Reno.

"Cool, but how is this co-parenting shit going to work, because I still want my time with him. I'm not just walking away from none of my kids," Reno said, handing Ramona another breadstick.

I was shocked as hell when I saw Reno walk in with Ramona. I didn't think Natalia would be so open to him having her alone so soon, but shit, Reno was a good father. I don't think I've seen him so much as whoop RJ before, and I could tell he would have Ramona spoiled. She was kicking her feet in the highchair and smiling at everybody that walked by.

"That's cool, man. I don't want to hurt RJ in none of this," I said.

Nina reached over and grabbed my hand. I loved that woman. She was supportive as fuck of me and willing to figure this shit out with me. I really didn't deserve her. She was too damn perfect for me. Really for any of us.

"If you want to get courts involved, that would be ok, but I really think we can figure this out by ourselves. I don't mind paying Xena the child support you've been paying," I told Reno.

"Well, that actually brings me to my next topic," Xena said. "I want to go back to school, and with me being a single mother, it's going to be hard. If you didn't mind, Reno, I could give you temporary full custody until I'm done and get myself situated with a job and all," Xena said.

"Shit, I don't care," Reno said shrugging.

"And Drake, I don't need the child support. I actually would just rather clear my conscious from this all," Xena said.

"So, what are you saying? You need a break from RJ, too?" Nina asked her.

"No, I mean, well, I don't know. I just feel kind of lost, and I don't know what kind of parent I could be to RJ right now," Xena replied, with tears running down her face.

Nina reached over and grabbed her hand.

"You should start by forgiving yourself first," she said.

"That's right, and then accept the things you cannot change," Serenity added.

****

Two Months Later

"Welcome Home!"

Nina, Destiny, and I walked back into my house in Atlanta and damn near had a heart attack. Everybody was there for the surprise party. I even peeped her mother, Leo and Lena, and even Tamara and Serenity in attendance. I felt like I had been gone for two years, but now I was back and more ready than ever to make this money and take care of my fiancé and daughter.

"Oh, let me see my grandbaby," my mother said, pushing me out of the way to get to Nina and Destiny.

I wasn't feeling this whole party thing, but Nina looked happy, so I let the shit slide. I really wanted to take her upstairs and make love to her for hours. She looked good as hell in the romper she was wearing.

"What's up, nigga?" Leo said, shaking my hand.

"Not shit. I see you got your lady with you and shit," I said.

"Yes, I'm here. Hey, Drake," Lena said, hugging me.

"Aye, Leo, let me holler at your man for a minute," I told her.

"That's cool. I need to go see Destiny, anyway," she said, handing Leo her drink.

We walked to the patio area I had outside of my kitchen and away from the loud ass women in the house.

"So, what's up? You still trying to hit this play with me for the next few years until we stack our bread right?" I asked him.

"You know I'm down, fam. You got Oscar back on your side?" Leo asked me.

"Hell, yeah, I been setting that shit up since we found Nina. He gone front us on the low until he get his pops to come around, but once he sees how fast we move that shit, that old man ain't gon' have no choice but to fuck with us," I told him.

"That's all you had to say; I'm ten toes down in this shit," Leo said.

"Already," I said, shaking his hand again.

We went back inside, and I thanked my moms for staying as long as she did. Leo's mother left a few months ago, but the way they were talking, I think they wanted to move to Atlanta, too. It didn't seem like the party would die down anytime soon, so I grabbed Destiny and took her upstairs. She needed a nap, and so did I.

"You need help changing her diaper?" Nina asked me.

"I might. I never changed a diaper before," I told her.

I could do it; I just wanted her alone with me. I stood back and watched her bond with Destiny while she changed her. Fuck, Nina was like a goddess. If you could see her, you would know why I was so stuck on her.

"What, baby?" she asked, as she bounced Destiny, who was still fussy after being changed.

I smirked at her, and she laughed while looking down. She already knew what was up. Destiny fell asleep fast, and Nina tried to tiptoe out, but I was on her like white on rice.

"Nah, bring that ass here, girl," I said, grabbing her by the waist.

"Drake, no, it's people downstairs," Nina laughed.

I turned her to face me and started kissing her.

"You think I give a fuck? You looking all good and shit in this romper, and I haven't had a taste in damn near three months," I stressed.

"Oh, so you want a taste?" Nina teased.

I didn't give her a reply. I just picked her up and carried her into the bathroom. I put her on the sink and started struggling with her romper.

"No, silly, you have to take it all the way off," she laughed.

She pushed me back and jumped off the sink. She untied the romper from behind her neck and dropped it to the floor. She was looking sexy as hell in only a black thong, and my dick couldn't wait any longer. I undressed, put her back on the sink, and plunged deep into her.

"Ah, fuck baby! Shit," she screamed, trying to run.

"Shhh," I said, silencing her cries with a kiss.

I pulled halfway out and started stroking her softer until she moaned and started dripping on the sink.

"Oh, baby, I missed you so much," Nina moaned.

"I missed you more," I moaned back.

She had me about to bust early, so I pulled out and yanked her body to the edge of the sink.

"Baby, what are you, ahhh yes!" she moaned, grabbing my head as I stuck my tongue deep inside of her.

I didn't care about the party downstairs. I didn't care about any of the past. All I cared about was the woman in front of me, and my baby in the other room.

Chapter 41

Nina

"Thank you so much for coming favorite cousin," Tamara said, as I sat down at the Cheesecake Factory in Lennox Square.

"You didn't have to convince me too much after you mentioned cheesecake," I joked. "Hello, Serenity, nice to see you again."

"Hello, Nina, it's nice to be seen," Serenity said, leaning over the table to hug me.

I really liked the calming vibe I got from Serenity. For as much as Reno has done to me, I was actually glad that he had someone like Serenity in his life. Knowing his past, I felt like he couldn't help some of his actions, but by no means was I giving him a pass.

"So, brace yourself, because what we are about to tell you might shock you," Tamara said.

"Spare me the dramatics, and tell me," I said, looking over the menu.

I browsed for a few minutes while waiting for them to continue, but the silence remained. Finally, I looked back up and saw them looking at each other. Serenity took a deep breath before deciding to speak first.

"I was sent to Reno by Tamara. Well, actually, let me back up here. The therapist that you and Reno used to see, is actually my mother. Tamara and I are actually old college roommates and good friends, and one day I saw her crying after class. We talked, and she told me all about her favorite cousin, who was stuck with an abusive man. The more she talked, the more I started to feel connected. It wasn't until I realized that my mother was a therapist to you two that we came up with a plan," Serenity said.

I sat with my mouth open and my mind racing. I had underestimated my cousin completely.

"I was sent to seduce Reno, so you could finally see the light and leave him for good," Serenity said.

I was at a loss for words. I vaguely remember Reno smiling at his phone during our last moments together as a couple and being jealous, but I couldn't be too mad. Had I not left him, I would have never found happiness with Drake.

"Cousin, I've always known Drake was the one for you," Tamara told me.

"So, this whole time you've been setting Reno up?" I asked Serenity.

"That was my initial plan," she said, before looking down.

I saw through her. She was in love with Reno. I would know, because I was once in love with him, too.

"But now that you're back, everything is back to normal, and we can put Reno behind us," Tamara said.

I saw the way Serenity shifted her eyes and did a sad smile. I took a sip of the water that was already on the table before speaking.

"You love him, don't you?" I asked Serenity.

Tamara raised an eyebrow and looked at Serenity like she was crazy. Serenity shook her head, but her eyes started to water. I knew that part all too well, too. That was the fear. The fear of being in love with a man who had so many issues and wanting to be with him to save him. On the outside looking in, Reno was picture perfect, but once you get inside, you see that he has horrible demons.

"It's ok to love him. You would think that I would hate him after all of this, but I don't," I said, feeling myself start to cry, too. "Reno isn't a monster. He's been hurt really badly in life, and he needs a strong person to help him. I met him when I was young, and I was looking for help myself. We both ended up being toxic to each other," I said.

"This wasn't supposed to happen, but the more I watched him, the more I started to understand him. I became so intrigued by him that I secretly started going through his file. This was all before I ever met him face to face, and once we did meet, I was almost star struck. I know the Creator works in mysterious ways, and for some reason, I feel like this was supposed to happen," Serenity said.

By now, even Tamara was crying. People around us were giving us weird looks, but we didn't care. They had no idea what we had gone through. I reached out and touched Serenity's hand, because she was crying the hardest.

"I've been around him for so long that I know him more than anybody. You're perfect for him, and you don't even know it," I told her.

"Oh, you ladies are going to make me cry, too. Let me hurry up and take the order before I ruin my makeup," our waitress said, walking up.

We all laughed and placed our orders. Once she left, I decided to change the topic to a lighter note.

"You know what's funny?" I asked them.

"What?" they both asked at the same time.

"How we all are connected. I'm dating Drake, Serenity is dating Reno, Lena is dating Leo, Drake's cousin, and Jace is dating Amber, who is also Drake's sister. That is so crazy," I laughed.

"Can I add a jaw dropper to the mix?" Tamara asked.

"Oh, gosh, what is it?" I asked.

"I think Tena is so sexy," Tamara said.

"Wait a minute! What? Tamara? You like women?" I yelled.

"Ayyee!" a group of ladies said behind us.

"Shhh, girl shut up," Tamara said.

"I knew it! I knew it!" I exclaimed. "No wonder why you never brought a boy around, and I don't know, Tena might make you crazy."

"Or I'll make her crazy. She's so cute with that long, curly hair and those dimples," Tamara blushed.

"Damn, you've really been checking her out, huh?" I laughed.

"I always knew it. You know I can read people, and plus, you turn down too many fine guys," Serenity said.

We laughed and ate, and by the time it was over. I felt like I had gained a new friend in Serenity. She was the exact same age as me, but she felt older and wiser. That could be because she had an amazing mother and father, who she spoke highly of. I wished I had those things coming up. I pulled her to the side before we left and debated on if I should ask her what I was about to ask her.

"What's wrong, Nina?" she asked me.

"I don't want you to take this wrong, but I really think I should sit down and talk with Reno. I learned some things about him, and I wanted to let him know that it's ok," I told her.

"I am actually all for that. I think you two should find solid ground, especially for RJ," she said.

"I don't have his number," I told her.

"He recently changed it. Here, I can give it to you," she said, taking my phone from my hands.

I secretly admired her. She was gorgeous, smart, and she seemed so secure. She wasn't even self-conscious at the thought of me; Reno's ex, conversing with him. Her energy was amazing, and it was as if she didn't even know it.

"Here you go! Thank you so much for meeting with me. I am in love with this city, so I'll be back soon," she smiled, hugging me again.

"Don't hesitate to give me a call," I told her.

On the drive back home, I debated on how I should confront Reno. I was relieved to see that Drake and Destiny were fast asleep on the couch when I walked in. I kissed them both on the forehead and went upstairs. We had a balcony right outside our bedroom, so I sat outside and decided to FaceTime Reno. I knew how he was about talking on the phone, but I figured FaceTime would be a bit better since I didn't feel safe with him face to face just yet. It rang three times before he finally answered. He was in his car nodded his head to a song by Big Krit.

"Wasn't expecting to hear from you," he said.

"I honestly wasn't expecting to give you a call, either," I admitted.

"Shit, so what's up?" he asked.

I could hear a crying voice in the back and watched him pull out a bottle of juice. He told RJ to give it to his sister, and I felt my heart shift. On the one hand, it was so adorable to see the infamous Reno out driving with his kids, but on the other hand, it hurt to know that he wouldn't let me keep my kids all those years ago.

"You good?" he asked me.

"Yeah. Hey, I can call you back when you're free," I offered to him.

"Nah, you good. I'm dropping them off with my mama," he said.

I could tell he was back at his house. I silently observed how gentle and loving he was with Ramona and patient with RJ. Don't get me wrong, Reno has always been a good father, but he was a little different now. I was happy that he seemed to find a little peace, because I sure as hell had found mine. Once he came back to the phone, he pulled a blunt from behind his ear and lit it up.

"So talk," he said.

I laughed a little at his ways. Reno would always be Reno. He looked at me funny as I stopped smiling and suddenly became serious.

"I know what happened to you. As a child," I told him.

"Fuck you mean, Nina?" he asked mugging me.

"Reno, the woman who kept us told me she was your aunt and that-"

"Nina, that bitch is a liar. Don't believe that shit," Reno said, blowing out smoke and shaking his head.

"But you don't even know what I'm talking about," I said.

He continued to shake his head and took a puff on the blunt again. As handsome as Reno was on the outside, he had some deep hurt on the inside. It was hard for me to not feel pity for him, regardless of how many times he put his hands on me. I guess a part of me would always be or feel connected to him.

"You never could leave shit alone. That shit was years ago, man, but what you want to me to say about it?" Reno finally asked.

"I just wanted you to know that I understand you completely now, Reno, and I don't judge you for the way you come off. I never knew a lot about your past," I told him.

"Look, I'm only telling you this shit, because I know you, and I know how you are when shit is on your mind. I ain't half as bad as I should be right now. My moms was cool at first, hell, she was damn near perfect. I guess being with Pops was too much, because next thing I know, she was strung the fuck out. I would come home from school with Drake, and she would be high as fuck running around or passed out on the couch. Then, one day, Pops kicked her out, and I saw her one more time after that, and she looked real bad. A few weeks later, they told me she was dead, and I had missed the funeral, but they took me to that fake ass grave I always went to. That bitch that was keeping y'all didn't come into the picture until a year after that. Yeah, she used to do little shit like make me suck on her titties and finger her and shit at first, but then she started doing extra, and well, you know what comes next," Reno admitted.

I wiped away tears as I held the phone.

"Reno, I'm so sorry. You didn't deserve that for your childhood," I cried.

"Neither, did you. It's cool, Nina, I know it's not a lot we can ignore, but real talk, I never meant to hurt you, man. I barely loved my own self, and sometimes, I still don't," Reno told me.

"Reno, you take care of yourself out there; especially, for those kids," I told him.

"I got you on that, but Nina, you take care, too. Oh, and you better get off the phone with me before Drake gets jealous back there," Reno laughed.

I saw him look behind me, and I turned to see Drake holding Destiny and watching me closely. I got a little nervous, but it all faded when I realized that Drake was more mild-mannered and wouldn't hit me.

"Thank you for hearing me out, Reno," I said, ending the call.

I walked up to Drake, and he stared me down with no expression. I was scared shitless, because he's never so hard on me.

"Baby, I-,"

"Why are you scared of me? You don't have to fear me, Nina. I heard everything," Drake said.

I breathed out a breath of relief and rested my head on his chest as I wrapped my arms around him.

"Did you get the closure you needed?" he asked me.

"Yes baby, I did," I told him.

"Good, because I need you to be ready to be my wife now," he said.

Chapter 42

Jace

"Who the hell are you?"

I held my tongue as I struggled not to curse the woman Amber called "Mama" out. I was standing at her doorstep holding a big ass bear and rose, and she was acting like I was a damn thug or something.

"Auntie, that's our friend, Jace," Ray, the cousin I saved from the fight that day, said.

Amber's mother looked me up and down and finally moved to the side so I could walk in. The inside of the house was a mess. Clothes were everywhere, old dishes were in the sink, on the table, and even on the couch. Ray tapped me and motioned for me to follow him to a back room.

"Well, I don't trust no city nigga, so leave the door open," Amber's mother yelled behind us.

She had me fucked up if she thought I was going to steal anything out of this dirty motherfucker. I didn't initially tell Amber I was coming, so I didn't know if she would be mad or happy to see me. I haven't talked to her in three days, and I knew she felt some type of way. Shit was crazy on my end, honestly. With my Pops being locked up, and not remembering me, I basically only had my siblings. Lena and Tena stayed at Reno's house at lot, so I was stuck at the house with Michelle and a paralyzed Jasper. I pretended not to pay them any attention, but it was hard not to notice how extra she was with him. I let Reno know, and he told me to sit tight because he had a plan.

"Ray, what the hell is she yelling about now and who was at the door?" Amber yelled.

I stopped in the doorway and watched her. Her room was spotless, which was impressive compared to the rest of the house. Everything was girly as hell, and either pink, or black. Her hair was pulled up in a messy bun, and she was in leggings and a big t-shirt with some oversized glasses on her face. She was sitting in front of a mirror watching a YouTube video and doing makeup. Ray smirked at me and played along.

"You know how Auntie is. Girl, you are killing this makeup," Ray said walking up to her.

"Thank you, cousin. So, what do you think I should do? I feel like I'm blowing his phone up, but I'm confused on what I did wrong, and why Jace isn't answering me," Amber asked him.

"You're not doing anything wrong," I said.

She gasped and turned around. "Jace! Oh, my gosh, what are you doing here?" she asked, standing up so quick she knocked her chair over.

"I came to apologize in person, and probably take you out to eat or something," I shrugged, pretending it was nothing.

She ran up to me and jumped in my arms. Damn, I missed the fuck out of her.

"Oh, no, am I hurting you, baby?" she asked me.

"Baby? Amber, I know good and damn well you don't have a boyfriend, and in my motherfucking house?" her mother said, walking in the room.

"Mama, please-,"

"Mama please nothing. Little boy you have to leave," she told me.

"Look, no disrespect, but your daughter is almost seventeen. Plus, I drove all the way here to take her out to eat. I mean, you can come, too, so you can see I'm not a bad guy," I said.

"Oh, can I come, too?" Ray jumped in.

I peeped what he was doing and nodded. He was cool with me for real.

"Well, what you spending?" she asked.

"I can spend whatever I need to," I said, knowing her type.

"As long as I pick the place, and we can get extras for tomorrow. My stamps ran out for the month, and I don't have no extra income," she said.

"I can take you shopping for groceries, too," I threw in.

"Jace, you don't have to do that," Amber said.

"Girl, hush. If your boyfriend wants to spend money on us, then let him," she said.

I peeped that she acknowledged me as her boyfriend, and I felt like I won the battle.

"Let me go get presentable," her mother said, walking off.

"Jace, I'm so sorry about her," Amber said.

"She's straight, baby. Hey, good looking out, Ray," I said.

"I got your back. Just make sure I get to plan the wedding, because I can decorate my ass off. I did her room," he said.

"Aw, for real? That's what's up," I nodded, as I looked around again.

"Shut up, silly; we aren't even engaged," Amber laughed.

"Not yet," I said, pulling her close to me and kissing her. "You really thought a nigga was mad at you?"

She looked sad before answering.

"I did. I didn't know why you were ignoring me," she pouted.

"I won't ever ignore you again. A nigga was just in some deep shit. I mean, I got shot and everything," I told her, nonchalantly.

I really said that shit like I get shot on the regular. I felt like a real thug for a minute.

"You got shot?" Ray asked me in shock.

"Yeah, right in the back," I said.

"Oh, my goodness! Jace, are you in a gang or something?" he asked.

"No, Ray, my baby isn't in a gang," Amber informed him.

"Nah, I don't do that banging in Little Rock shit; it's just life man," I said, running my hand down Amber's cheek.

Amber had to change clothes, too, so I decided to sit in my car instead of on the clothes-filled couch. I couldn't wait until Amber was out of high school. I would have my money all the way right then, and I could take her out of this place. She was too pretty for the way she lived, and shit, I was getting tired of fighting hoes off left and right. I needed her to represent in the city for me. They all walked out, but my eyes were on Amber. She was so fucking sexy in her Polo outfit with the matching hat I got for her a while ago. I knew she based that shit off of what I had on.

"You killing that outfit, baby," I told her, grabbing her hand.

"You really love my mean ass daughter, don't you?" her mother asked, climbing in the backseat.

She actually looked decent as hell when she cleaned up.

"I never thought I would, but I do," I replied, looking in Amber's questioning eyes.

"Awww, baby, I love you, too," Amber replied.

"My stomach sure is growling," Ray said.

"Boy, hush," Amber's mother said.

We ended up going to a little shack that had the best barbecue I've ever had. That shit was so good I got extras to take home with me. I saw the way people looked at me when I pulled out my stack of money to pay, but I know they saw the pistol resting on my hip, too. Reno was always on me about flexing like that, but I felt like it was more player to have cash than a card.

"Jace, let me ask you something," Amber said.

"Go ahead," I said.

"Is it true that your whole family sells drugs?" she asked me.

I looked around before I answered her. I knew she would ask this sooner or later, but I was about to kick some game to her and have her looking at shit in a different way.

"What's the difference between the men in the pharmacy selling pills than the one on the corner selling pills? The only difference is one went to school to do the shit and one didn't. The people in the pharmacy are giving people shit they most likely don't want or need, but the shit in the streets is giving by request. Nobody is forcing them to buy the shit, and understand me when I say they will buy, whether it be from their own people or the white people, so to answer your question, yes most of my family does," I told her.

She looked at me for a long time with no words. I almost thought she was judging a nigga, but if she was, what could I do about it? At least I kept that shit all the way real.

"Do you sell them Jace?" she asked me.

"Nah, I never have. My people have so much money that I don't have to do the shit to get money. To be completely honest, I don't aspire to do the shit, either. I actually want to go to college and study Business," I told her.

"Business? Wow, I never knew you were into that," she smiled.

"I'm into a lot of shit, baby. I want to open up clothing stores and hire people to design shit. This Polo and shit is cool, but I want to wear some fly shit and be able to take a picture with the designer," I explained.

"I'm the first designer. I draw and everything," Ray blurted.

Dude was funny as hell. I already knew he was ear hustling the whole time.

"I'm serious; you do know most fashion designers are gayer than me, right?" Ray said.

"That shit might be legit," I told him. "Come sit in the car with me," I whispered to Amber.

We got up, and I told them where we were going while dropping a hundred on the table. I figured they would either order more food or leave a hell of a tip. Once we got in the car, I kissed her for what felt like hours. Shit, she was like heaven to a nigga like me.

"When you graduate, I want you to move in with me. I'll have all my shit together by then," I told her.

"Jace, I would love to live with you, but you don't think that's moving too fast?" she asked me.

"Nah, I don't," I told her, seriously.

"I've just always heard that shacking up before marriage was a bad idea," Amber said.

"Fuck what everybody else is talking about. If you don't leave, I won't leave. Hell, if we get into it, I'll sleep in the other room before I leave. I don't want to be reckless out here. I need you to slow me down and take up my extra time," I told her.

I may be young, and I admit I don't know it all, but I knew what I felt was real.

"Ok, but only if there are two separate rooms in case we need space," Amber said.

"I can do that," I told her.

"Jace, you're serious about all of this?" she asked me, turning her body to face me.

"Hell, yeah, I'm serious about all of this," I told her. "Why you keep doubting a nigga's feelings for you?"

"You know, with how we met and everything. Then, I heard that Reno and Drake were into it, and Reno is your brother, and Drake is my brother, and-,"

"Amber, you worried about the wrong things, baby. I was honest when I told you what my first plan was, but Amber, you stole a nigga's heart from the jump, and you don't even realize it. My brother was ready to beat my ass for fucking up the original plan, but if that never

240

happened, I never would've met you. Don't worry about Reno and Drake, either, because they hashed that shit out and are cool again from what I see," I told her.

She was blushing and shit, so I reached over to kiss her, just so she could know it was real.

Chapter 43

Lena

"I say we should sell it," I said.

Everyone turned their heads and looked at me crazily for a minute.

"Reno, you already have a house. It's too much house for me, and I know it's too big for Tena and Jace, too," I said.

"We are not selling my husband's house," Michelle said, angrily.

"Well, he did leave it to us in the event that he died or went to jail," I replied, smirking.

"This is some sort of misunderstanding, sir. That will was written by my husband a long time ago, so he may have forgotten to change it. How can there be nothing at all left to me?" Michelle asked, on the brink of tears.

"I'm sorry, ma'am, but when I was requested to read the will, this is the only one he had made out," Mr. Peoples, our family lawyer explained.

"Well, we can settle this. We can both go visit him and get his opinion on this," she said.

"He doesn't even remember who the fuck you are," Reno said, shaking his head.

"Oh, and you take delight because he remembers you? You kids are spoiled, and even and I hate the way he has you all. Coming and going as you please, spending stupid amounts of money, and driving his cars. I bet you all didn't tell him how we really have this money," she cried.

"There is no *we* in this shit. *You* don't have shit!" Tena yelled, slamming her fist on the table.

"Mr. People's, please," Michelle cried to him.

"I'm not sure if we can do that, but I will check," he shrugged.

"And what if we dispute? My father is already having a hard enough time as it is adjusting to his memory loss. If he wanted her to have anything, he would have stated so. I don't want her going in there and disrupting him about money," I said, pretending to be on the verge of tears.

I peeped Reno smirk at my display and knew my brother caught onto my game. As far as I was concerned, my father could die and go to Hell. I know that sounded harsh, but once it came to light on everything that he has done, I realized how evil he truly was. I honestly wanted nothing to do with this house or anything else he owned.

"I cannot be in this room with you evil souls," Michelle vented, standing up dramatically and fanning herself. "All of you are just like him. Benard wasn't the best husband to me, but I was an excellent wife, and this is the thanks I get? No good stepchildren, and not a dime to my name? I traded my life to marry him, and he can't even give me thanks. This is nothing but the devil," she cried, hysterically.

Mr. People's looked irritated, but he politely stood up to console her. I sat back and watched the show emotionless. Michelle was a trophy wife, and she knew it. She's acting like she came in this relationship with money and is walking away broke. I know for a fact that Daddy had given her thousands of dollars at a time to go shopping, so if she didn't save any of that, then that was completely her fault. Once she was out of the room, Jace spoke up first.

"Since I'm eighteen, now, I can technically live by myself now, right?" Jace asked.

"Yeah, but you sure you want to do that? Can you handle it?" I asked him.

"Hell, yeah. I probably can't sign the lease and shit, but I can handle the bills. I got like fifteen stacks saved up in my personal account. Plus, if we sell this house, and I get my cut, that'll be even more. I can take the Camaro and just drive that instead of buying something new, and I can go to college in the meantime," Jace said.

"Damn, bro, you really been sitting over there plotting, haven't you?" Tena asked.

"Yeah, sis, I've been plotting for years. I knew that, once I got the chance, I was going to leave this house," Jace explained.

"Bro, I got a spot out in Chenal that I pay rent on. I used to have it just in case I had a bitch on the side. The shit is fully furnished and everything," Reno said.

"Damn, Reno, you a real deal pimp out here, but nah, no thanks, bro. I want my own place and something I can call mine," Jace replied.

We shot out ideas on how to flip the money and stay paid, and by the time we left, I finally felt like a new woman. Jace had a dream of opening a clothing store, Reno wanted to invest in giving Serenity a spot to do yoga with clients, Tena wanted to hustle, which I didn't understand, and I wanted to follow Jace and open an online boutique. If everything went right, we would never have to punch a clock at a corporation for pennies on the dollar. At least Daddy set us up to not be broke. I walked to my car and called Leo.

"What's up, baby? What you got going?" he answered after the second ring.

"I just left the reading of the Will at Daddy's place," I told him.

"Who all was there?" he asked.

"All of us except for Jasper," I told him.

"You near Reno?" Leo asked me.

"Yeah, he's right here, why?" I asked him.

"Change of plans, let me holler at him real quick," Leo said.

Reno was already watching me since I was the only one to take a private call at my car, so I waved him over. Of course the entire clan came in tow. I rolled my eyes and shook my head. We all were nosey as hell.

"Leo wants to talk to you," I told him.

Reno took the phone, and I shrugged at Tena and Jace, who were looking at me with questioning eyes. I got inside of my car and rested my head on the seat. I finally felt at peace with my life, which was crazy as hell. It was almost as if my father's presence produced a negative energy, because in his absence, I felt like I could do any and everything. Now, I just needed my own space, and I was tempted to take Reno up on that offer to take his apartment he had hidden.

"My twin is finally growing some balls," Tena said, climbing in the passenger seat.

"Shut up, silly," I laughed.

"I'm proud of you. At first, I was confused on what to do with this house, but your idea of selling it was genius. We could all eat off the money for a lifetime if we don't go overboard," Tena said.

Before I could tell her she was right, Reno tapped on my window. I rolled the window down, and he looked at me like I was crazy.

"You better get your ass out. Don't be rolling the window down like I'm one of your hoes or something," he snapped.

I shook my head and got out. He gave me a hug, which shocked the hell out of me.

"I love you, little sis. You be safe out here and shit and stick with Leo. He got your best interest at heart," Reno said.

"I don't know what Serenity has done to my big brother, but I like it," I laughed, hugging my big brother.

Maybe there was some hope for him after all. Reno could really be a monster sometimes, but then turn around and do some nice shit. His ass was still dangerous, though. That's why I was so on the fence about him being with Nina. When he had Nina, he was bad, but when he didn't, he was worse. Something about this new woman just felt right this time. I still don't understand what she saw in Reno other than his looks. Reno wasn't dumb or anything, but at times, he could lack manners and maturity, and Serenity seemed so high-class. I guess the saying was true, "Good girls have to get down with the gangsters." Look at how crazy I was over Leo.

"Your man is still on the line," Reno said, pushing my emotional ass off of him.

"Hey, baby," I said to Leo.

"What are you about to get into, baby?" Leo asked me.

"I have no plans," I told him.

"Good, because I have a few for you. Meet me at the address I'm about to send you," he told me.

I hung up and turned to Tena, who was smiling in her phone.

"What the hell are you smiling so hard at?" I asked her.

"So, apparently, I have a secret admirer," she said.

"Oh, yeah? Who?" I asked.

"Shit, I wish I knew. She just told me we've been in each other's presence for years," Tena said.

"What if she's ugly?" I laughed.

"Nah, she's damn sure not ugly, I think. She sent me a body picture with the face blurred out," Tena said.

"Let me see," I said, getting happy for my sister.

As soon as I saw the picture, the light clicked on. I would know that perfect body anywhere, because I remember being envious of her.

"Tena, that's Tamara, Nina's cousin," I said.

"Hold up," she said, looking at the picture again. "Shy Tamara, who always plays the background?"

"Unless she has a twin, I would know her body anywhere," I said. "Ask her how she got your number."

Tena started texting her, and I started to text Nina.

Me: *I'm onto you and Tamara (insider)*

Nina: *Shhhh, big mouth. Don't tell Tena.*

Me: *Too late. Oh, my gosh, this is so cute.*

Nina: *I know! I'm low-key excited.*

"She said she got it from a close friend of mine," Tena laughed.

"What did I tell you? You two are going to be so fucking bomb together. Please ask her on a date, Tena," I begged.

"Alright, calm down, sis. I'll ask her out tonight," Tena grinned.

"Good, now get out so I can go meet my man," I said, lightly shoving her.

"Damn, the dick not going nowhere," Tena joked.

"You perverted freak," I laughed, flipping her off.

I zoomed away from my father's house and headed to the address Leo gave me. I pulled up to a modest home in southwest Little Rock and texted him that I was outside. Before I could press send, he was knocking on my driver's side window.

"Oh, my gosh, baby, you scared the shit out of me," I jumped.

"Get your scary ass out and come here," he said.

I got out of the car and hugged him as if I hadn't just seen him earlier this morning. I saw a pretty woman walk onto the porch and smile at us. Leo finally let me go and grabbed my hand. I assumed she was his mother, because the resemblance was almost uncanny.

"Mama, this is my fiancé, Lena," Leo said, putting his arm around me.

"Nice to meet you. Wow, Leo, she is more beautiful than you told me," she said, pulling me in for a hug.

I fell into her arms, and instantly, felt at home. This was it! This was everything I've ever dreamed of. I knew at this moment that she was meant to be my mother-in-law, and I cried happy tears.

Chapter 44

Leo

I blew smoke out of my mouth as I watched Lena sleep. I had just finished fucking her straight to sleep, and her hair was sticking to her face. The white hotel sheets made her look like an angel. In a few short months, she would officially be mine. Fuck all that waiting for a big wedding and having a long ass engagement. I was going to throw some money at the women in my family to make magic happen, ASAP, and walk her ass down the aisle so niggas would know that was all me. My phone vibrated in my hand, and I tore my eyes away from her.

Drake: *You ready, nigga?*

Me: *Yeah, give me 15.*

Drake: *Bet, I'm up the street. I'll be downstairs.*

Drake flew back in town just for this mission. After we had finished this, he was going to hold shit down in Atlanta, and I was going to plug in out here Arkansas for a minute until I convinced Lena to pack her bags and head to Atlanta. In my opinion, it was more money to be made out here in the natural state, because half the time, it wasn't shit to do but get high. I took a quick shower and dressed down in all black. I kissed Lena on the back of the neck while I put my guns on my hip. She moaned and stirred a little, but she was still knocked out. I had to come back to her, because I was going to wake her ass up and put her right back to sleep. I left and got in the backseat of the throwaway car.

"What's up, fam," I said, shaking Drake's hand.

"Ready to get this shit over with," he said.

"What up, Reno?" I nodded towards the driver's seat.

"Not shit, chilling. You want a hit?" he asked, extending his blunt towards me.

"I'm good. I just killed one not long ago," I said.

We rode in silence until we made it to a neighborhood on the outskirts of Little Rock. The houses were nice as hell, and I could tell they weren't too old.

"This is where Jasper copped a crib. He got this shit recently, and I know it's most likely with stolen money, because my pops never paid that nigga much," Reno explained. "His shit is right up the street."

With that being said, we all exited the throwaway car. I noticed Reno drop his I.D. and shook my head. How the fuck is this nigga slipping like this?

"Aye, Reno, you dropped something," I said.

"No, I didn't," he said.

"Nigga, I just watched you," I said.

Reno pulled the black ski mask over his face and walked up to me.

"I said no the fuck I didn't, now walk and quit making a scene. I'll explain later," he said.

I was two seconds away from slapping this nigga to the ground, but Drake motioned for me to leave it alone. I pushed past him and headed towards the target house. Reno ended up walking ahead of us and led us to the back of the house. He stopped us and pulled out a gun.

"I been watching this bitch Michelle for a minute, and I did my research on her. She used to fuck with this typical cat, you know, college degree having church boy that falls in love with the pussy. The thing is, he didn't have enough legal money to keep Michelle around, so she dropped his ass for my pops. They say he never really got over her, and she still gives him the pussy from time to time. That was his I.D. I dropped back there on the ground and this…," Reno smiled, "… is his gun. I snuck into his house and got this shit while his ass was sleep. I hate to set up an innocent person but he fucked with the wrong bitch."

With that being said, Reno started working on getting a window opened. I just shook my head at this crazy nigga. He was either a genius or real deal, clinically crazy. It was like he didn't have a conscious sometimes. I didn't trip too much on it, because if it ever came down to it, I knew I could take him.

"Ok, I'll lead, and y'all watch my back," Reno said, sliding the window up.

We climbed inside, and I hoped like hell none of the neighbors were being nosey. We were able to get in undetected since it sounded like Jasper and Michelle were arguing. We tip-toed towards the sounds of them arguing, and Reno stopped us to listen.

"You have to get close to Jace. Reno is too wild, and the twins are too close to him, but Jace is still young. Put that pussy on him and find out as much as you can about his money. They all have stashes, because I used to ride with Boss to deposit the money every other week," Jasper said.

"Fucking him and turning him out isn't the problem. It's getting those siblings of his out of the way. Damn it, Jasper, how could you only have $30,000? Hell, I know bitches with a 9 to 5 making more than that in a year," Michelle said.

"Damn, Michelle, you just fucking anybody for money now, huh?" Reno laughed, coming from behind the wall with his gun cocked and aimed.

"What the hell?" Jasper exclaimed.

"Oh, my god! Reno, please don't shoot me. Let me explain," Michelle begged.

"Explain what? You know what, I don't got all day for this shit," Reno said.

The next thing I knew, he pulled the trigger and shot Michelle right in the throat. She clutched at her neck and gargled blood as she dropped to her knees. The shit was kind of impressive.

"Reno! What have you done? You are no better than your father. Your soul will be damned to hell just like his," Jasper said.

"Yeah, but yours is going first," Reno said.

This nigga pulled a trash bag out of his back pocket and tied it around Japer's head. I thought he was going to suffocate him, but he stepped back and shot Jasper in the head. Just as quickly as we came in, we left. Drake and I didn't even have to shoot shit. On the ride back to the city, curiosity got the best of me, and I had to ask.

"Reno, what was up with the trash bag?" I asked.

"Man, I've been knowing Jasper since I was a kid. I couldn't look him in his eyes and do him. That shit would've fucked with me," Reno said.

"That's real," I nodded.

I guess he wasn't as cold-hearted as he seemed. I made it back to the hotel, and luckily, Lena was still asleep. I took a quick shower and climbed into bed with her. I watched her sleeping and vowed to create heaven on earth around her. When a nigga got in from doing some devilish shit, he needed an angel to greet him. Lena was that angel for me. I pulled her onto my chest, and she woke up a little.

"Baby," she whined.

"You perfect, Lena, you know that?" I asked her.

"Awww, baby, you're the perfect one," she smiled at me.

"Nah, a nigga is flawed as hell," I countered.

She climbed on top of me and kissed me softly.

"I don't give a fuck about your flaws. You're perfect for me, and that's all that matter," she said.

Chapter 45

Reno

"She's the therapist's daughter? Wow, I'm proud of you being brave enough to go see a therapist. I tried so hard to get you help when you were younger," my moms said.

"Yeah, crazy part is, Nina is the one who made me go," I told her.

"I can see that. Nina is really a great soul, but when I watch you and Serenity interact, it's almost like I'm watching a movie. You two seem made for each other," she said smiling.

"I'm not gone lie; I'm scared as fuck. I thought I was in love with Nina back in the day, but how I feel for Serenity is something deeper. I can't even control myself around her," I said.

"That's love, baby. Aww, my son is in love, and I'm around to witness it," she smiled.

The conversation was getting too mushy and shit, so I grabbed the plates and took them to the sink.

"So where are my grandbabies?" she asked me.

"RJ is spending time with Drake, and Ramona is with her moms. I'm trying to work out a deal with her to get her more than just a few days. I already missed so much," I said.

"So, I have to ask. Is Drake RJ's god dad? Is he helping you parent him?" she asked me.

I thought about telling her the truth but quickly thought against it. I already had my mind made up that I would take care of him as my son no matter what.

"Yeah, he's his god dad," I simply said.

She gave me a look as if she knew better, but she didn't say anything else.

"So, what's this surprise you have for me?" I asked her.

"Oh, yes, let me show you," she said, going into her designer bag.

I looked her over and took her in. She had on brand new clothes, and she drove a new car to my place that I assumed she was borrowing at first. I knew when someone had money; I just wondered where she was getting hers from.

"Take a look at this," she said.

I read over the paperwork and knotted up my eyebrows. *What the fuck?*

"You're reading it right. Your father has kept an account for me all these years. I'm assuming it was before he took me away, and he may have forgotten about it. It's been drawing interest all these years. The first thing I did when I got access is get my car and secure a deposit on a nice townhouse in North Little Rock. I don't think I'm ready for my own house just yet, and plus, they wouldn't approve me since I have no credit history," she explained.

I sat back and thought on it for a minute. What kind of shit was Pops on? He claimed she was dead but kept money aside for her.

"Mama, you know you can stay here," I offered.

"Oh, no! I need my own space, and plus, I can watch the kids whenever you and Serenity need alone time. Well, I have a meeting to attend, so I'm about to head on out," she said.

"A meeting where?" I asked, being nosey.

"Well, I got asked to speak to women and young girls going through abuse," she smiled.

"Oh," I said.

What else was a nigga supposed to say? I felt like shit knowing I've beat a few bitches up in my day.

"Reno, remember this, until you forgive yourself, you can never truly move on," she said.

I hugged her and gave her a kiss on the cheek and then sat for a minute thinking on what she'd just said. I didn't like being alone, because my mind got to racing a lot.

Serenity left earlier and headed to her apartment to get more clothes since she had been staying with me so much, so I decided to go help her. I grabbed my keys, put on my J's, and headed out the door. I rode in silence like I normally did until I got a call from Lena.

"What's up, sis?" I said.

"Hey, Reno, are you busy?" she asked me.

"A little, why?" I asked.

"I have something to give to you," she said.

"Something like what?" I asked.

"I would rather show you in person," she said.

"Alright, well come to the house tonight," I told her.

"Will do," she said.

Once she hung up, I decided to play some Big Krit to drown out the silence. I started getting nervous, the closer I got to her apartment. She did shit like that to me for some reason. It was crazy but refreshing at the same damn time. I drove by slowly and randomly looked at two women hugging in the parking lot. It wasn't long before I noticed that Serenity was one of them. *What the fuck?* I immediately felt rage when I watched a familiar man walk up and hug Serenity as well before handing her an envelope. I would bet my life that it contained money.

"That fucking bitch!" I whispered, before busting a left and driving off.

***

I was sitting in the dark throwing back shots when she walked in. She didn't see me, but I sure saw her. She almost looked angelic in the white dress with her hair pulled back. Almost.

"Baby!" she called out.

"What's up," I said, getting up from the couch, stumbling a bit.

"Baby, why are you sitting here in the dark?" she asked me, turning on a light.

"Come here," I said to her.

"Reno? Are you ok?" she asked me, looking afraid.

A part of me wanted to hold her close, and that shit pissed me off. She had me weak as fuck. I walked up on her and grabbed her purse out of her hands. The same purse I got her the other day with a gang of other shit.

"Reno, talk to me! What's going on?" she asked.

I pulled the envelope out and threw the purse to the side. I opened and saw all the money and tossed it at her before yanking her towards me by her hair.

"Reno, please stop," she screamed.

"Shut up! I haven't even hit you," I gritted. "How the fuck do you really know Tamara and Drake?"

"Reno, please-,"

"Reno, please, nothing. Bitch, I saw you hugging them and shit. So, what's going on? Y'all plotting on me? I knew that nigga wasn't fucking loyal," I gritted, throwing her away from me.

She fell on the floor and broke into a deep sob. I wanted to punch her, kick her, hell do something, because she had a nigga in his feelings, and I didn't like this shit.

"You better get to talking before I stop holding back and fuck you up," I said.

She wiped her face and sat up on the floor. She looked up at me with fear-filled eyes and started crying even more.

"Reno, you have to believe me when I say I love you. Please, baby, stop looking so evil at me," she cried.

"Bitch! Explain and cut the act," I gritted.

"I-I went to college with Tamara. She always told me about Nina and you, and I didn't pay it any attention until she told me about the abuse. It just so happened that my mother was your therapist, so I thought it was a sign for me to step in. The plan was for me to sidetrack you long enough for Nina to escape, but she left before we thought she would. Then, you kidnapped her and the plan changed," she said.

"So, this whole time, you've been gaming me? All of this shit was a game?" I asked in disbelief.

"No, Reno, you have to listen to me. My feelings for you are real. It wasn't in the plans for me to fall in love with you; it just happened. Baby, please come here," she said, standing up to hug me.

I pushed her away, a little harder than I intended to and she went flying into the entertainment center. I didn't know if she was hurt or not, but I sure hoped she was. Then, maybe she could feel how I felt right now.

Ding! Dong! Ding! Dong!

I forgot I told Lena to come by, and I was sure it was her.

"Go upstairs and stay there," I told her.

She got up on shaky legs and walked slowly to the stairs. I waited until she was halfway up to let Lena in.

"Damn, bro, it's about time. Why you looking all evil and shit?" Lena asked.

"A nigga drunk," I shrugged.

"Ugh, I don't see how Serenity deals, but anyways, before I give you what I came to bring, I have to tell you something," she said.

"What?" I asked.

"I went to see Dad. I just wanted to see if he remembered me, but he didn't. I guess it really is true," she said.

"Lena, what the fuck you want to see his ass for? I don't believe that amnesia shit for one minute; he just wants to get off for the shit he did," I told her.

257

"But, Reno, for as bad as he is, I still love him," Lena cried.

"Sis, I'm not trying to make you cold-hearted towards him, but just don't let your happiness be with him. Whether he accepts you or he doesn't, don't let it have you all fucked up in the head," I said.

"Wow, Reno, that was deep. Serenity taught you that, didn't she?" Lena asked me.

Just the mention of her name put me in a rage again. I think Lena saw it, because she switched topics.

"Before I left, he told me to this to give to you," Lena said, handing me an envelope.

"Damn, did you read it already," I asked her, looking at the opened part.

"No, a guard did that to make sure no contraband or anything illegal was inside," Lena said.

Knowing her, she probably did read some of it. Women were nosey as hell sometimes.

"Let me get out of here before Leo starts wondering where I went. He doesn't even know I went to see Dad. He's against it right now," Lena said.

"He should be. No telling where that nigga's head is at," I told her.

I hugged Lena and locked the door behind her. I didn't want to read the letter, but what's the worse it could do. I turned a lamp on and opened the letter.

Reno.

I don't know if you're reading this or not, but I hope like hell you are. I really don't know what to say here, because I don't remember all that I've done, but from what they are telling me, I've done a lot of fucked up things to you. I really don't know how to apologize, and I don't want to sound like a broken record, so I won't do it. I know you don't want to see or speak to me, anymore, and I won't pressure you to, anymore. Have a nice life son. I've always loved you!

That was it? That's all the motherfucker could say was, *have a nice life son?* I balled the letter up and threw it. That wasn't enough, so I kicked over the coffee table. He really just gave up on me like that? Like, I was nothing at all. His firstborn son, who he gave a fucked up mental illness and a fucked up childhood didn't even get an apology? I kicked the sofa and punched the lamp, knocking it to the floor and shattering it.

"Reno!"

I ignored Serenity calling for me and picked up a sculpture Nina picked out years ago and threw that shit at the wall.

"Reno, stop it! Stop it!" Serenity cried.

She ran up to me and wrapped her arms around me.

"Serenity, get off of me before I hurt you, too," I yelled.

"No! I love you, and I'm not letting you go," Serenity said.

Fuck! It felt like all of the strength I had left my body when she said those words. A nigga did some shit he's never done before. I broke the fuck down.

"Reno, it's ok; I'm here for you," Serenity's soft voice said in my ear.

"I can't do this shit man," I cried.

I felt rejected all over again.

"Don't nobody give a fuck about me. Motherfuckers are always giving up on me," I cried out.

"I care about you, Reno. You know what, forget what anybody else thinks. They don't matter, because I'm here now. The creator put you in my path for a reason," Serenity said, holding my face in her hands.

I moved out of her embrace and took a step back.

"What you want from me? Money? Sex? What you want, cause everybody always wants something," I asked.

"I only want you, Reno. Why can't you see that?" she asked, looking deep into my eyes.

I heard what she was telling me, but my head was telling me she couldn't be trusted. She's a woman and women do sneaky shit all the time.

"Reno, look at me," she said, walking back up on me.

I pushed her away, and she shook her head. I could tell she was giving up. She turned and walked towards the front door. She stopped and looked at me one last time as if she expected me to stop her. After a minute, she finally walked out the door. What the fuck was I supposed to do? I loved her, but I didn't feel good enough for her.

"Serenity, wait!" I called behind her.

She turned around with her dress flowing in the wind. If there was a such thing as Earth Angels, then she was proof of it. She just stood there, forcing me to walk to her.

"I don't want you to leave, Serenity. I don't, but eventually, you will. Look at me! Look at a nigga real good. I'm fucked up in the head, and I know it! One day, it's going to get too hard, and you'll walk away, too. This shit is like living in hell, because I can't stop the shit. That's probably why my pops lost his mind for real and just forgot everything. I'm too much for you," I told her.

"You're just right for me, Reno. I've been living my whole life hating the easy shit. I never wanted the easy guy who gives me the easy love. That doesn't stimulate me. I'm iron, and I need iron to sharpen me. I need you Reno, I need your love," she said.

"What if my love is too much? Then, what? You gone leave me and shit?" I asked, walking up to her with my arms out. "I love too damn hard, and it's too much for you."

"Well, then, I'm willing to drown in your love," she said.

We stared at each other for a long time. A light flashed across the sky, and soon after, there was thunder. *What the fuck? Did she have magical powers or something?*

"Come here," she said.

I got in her personal space, and it started raining.

"Let me love you, Reno. Let me drown in your love," she said, making my heart heavy.

I pulled her to me and kissed her. Maybe this shit was supposed to happen. Maybe she was the cure to my madness.

Chapter 46

Nina

Two Months Later…

"So how do I have two daddies?" RJ asked.

"You got lucky. Son," Drake said.

Reno and Drake made eye contact, and I felt uneasy for a minute. It was the first time Drake had ever called RJ son before. I switched Destiny from my right hip to my left hip.

"That's cool. None of my other friends have two daddies," RJ said, breaking the tension.

"RJ, why don't you come bring your bags upstairs, so I can show you your room while you're here," I told him.

"Ok. Nina, why do you live with Daddy Drake now?" RJ asked me.

"Boy, you sure do ask a lot of questions now," I joked.

I walked RJ to his bedroom we had made for him, and he looked wide-eyed at his favorite things being around.

"Nina, you and my daddy Reno don't like each other no more?" RJ asked me.

"Of course, we do, I just like Drake more," I smiled.

"Oh, ok. I must be rich; I have two houses," RJ said.

"You are rich," Reno's voice said behind me.

I turned and saw him walking in and admiring the room.

"Damn, you remember that he liked all of this?" Reno asked me.

"I did," I smiled, looking him over.

I don't know what it was, but he looked and seemed different. It was almost like he was a different person from the Reno I once dated.

"What?" he asked me.

"You seem so happy. I'm proud of you," I said.

Reno was never really the mushy type so he shrugged it off with a half-smile.

"Aye, take Mama number down, so she can stop bugging me about you," he said.

"Oh, yes, I have to let her see Destiny soon. Let me grab my phone. Here, do you want to hold her?" I asked him.

He took Destiny, and she fussed a little before calming down. Reno always did have a way with kids. I went to my bedroom and grabbed my phone off the charger. I bypassed the bathroom and caught a glimpse of myself in the mirror. I stopped and stared at myself before walking closer to it. For the first time in a long time, I truly loved the woman I saw in the mirror.

I made my way back to RJ's room, but as I rounded the hallway, I heard Reno and Drake talking.

"Mama doesn't even know we've ever beefed before. I just told her we still cool cause you know how she is," Reno said.

"All that shit that happened between us, I'm willing to drop it if you are. At least for RJ," Drake said.

"Shit, it's a part of the game. A nigga can take his L and live. At least, we ain't dead behind this shit," Reno said.

They shook hands, and I made my presence known.

"Ok, I'm back," I said, taking Destiny back from Reno.

I handed him my phone to enter the number, and Drake took a fussy Destiny from me.

"I think it's time for her another bottle," I told him. "I warmed one up for her already."

"Bet, I'll go get it," Drake said.

Once he left, I caught Reno staring at me this time.

"What?" I asked him, growing shy.

"You seem happier, too. Look at you, somebody's mama and shit," Reno laughed.

"Yeah, who would've thought? I used to be scared to hold RJ," I laughed with him.

"It's a good look on you, though. Well, I'm about to get back on this road to Arkansas. Stay up, Nina," Reno told me.

He surprised me when he pulled me in for a hug and kissed me on the forehead. As quickly as he hugged me, he let me go and hugged RJ goodbye. I walked him downstairs, and Drake walked him the rest of the way out the front door while I waited at the staircase.

"Nina, can you cook spaghetti and meatballs?" RJ asked me, coming downstairs.

"I knew you would ask for that. I already made it," I smiled at him.

"Yay!" he cheered, hugging me.

Drake came over and hugged me, trapping RJ in between us, but he didn't seem to mind.

"I love you, baby," he told me.

"I love you more," I told him.

I loved him more, and I meant it.

THE END

CPSIA information can be obtained
at www.ICGtesting.com
Printed in the USA
LVHW050800090719
623539LV00004B/354/P